AUGUST 1st

A Novel

Beverly Roberson Lofton

Professional Publishing House   California

Published and Distributed by:
Professional Publishing House
1425 W. Manchester Ave., Suite B
Los Angeles, California 90047
 (323) 750-3592
Drrosie@aol.com
www.professionalpublishinghouse.com

Cover design: Richard Ike
First printing December 2011
978-0-9834444-8-0
10987654321

This book is a work of fiction. Names, characters, places, and incidents are products of the author's imagination or are used fictitiously. Any resemblance to actual events or locales or persons, living or dead, is entirely coincidental

To contact the author e-mail: blofton357@yahoo.com

DEDICATION

To my first teachers, my parents, Harold and Glodene Roberson
To the love of my life, La Salle Lofton, Sr., my husband who has given me
a life with never a dull moment
To all those who encouraged me to keep writing, my gratitude to you
cannot be measured

ACKNOWLEDGMENTS

Thank you to all who encouraged me to pursue writing, especially my lunch buddy TMS, and my sisters, DKR and PJK. Thanks to Coach Lynch for his insight regarding police procedures. Thank you, Dr. Rosie Milligan of Professional Publishing House for your input and foresight in moving this project from a 3-ring binder to a published novel. Thanks to A REAL Saturday Afternoon Book Club for your support (EH, ZA, PW, BR). Thank you to my husband who listened to my ideas while fixing the most amazing meals. Honey, you are the best cook in the world. To my kids and grandkids: Nana loves you. And most of all, to God be the glory for giving me gifts and talents. I truly appreciate all that You have done for me. Thank you, Lord.

BIOGRAPHY

Beverly Roberson Lofton was born in Ann Arbor, Michigan, grew up in San Diego, California and attended the University of Southern California in Los Angeles, where she earned her B.S. in Business Administration and later an M.B.A. from Cal State University Dominquez Hills. Beverly is happily married and currently lives in Los Angeles, CA. This is her first novel.

rologue

Late July 2010

*R*ev. Harvey McMillan looked at his calendar. "The first of August?" First Sundays at the Church of Christ of Los Angeles were always full of activities, including Holy Communion, and they usually ran longer than usual.

"Yes, my brother," Jeremiah Stewart replied. He was the senior pastor of Ebenezer Baptist Church. "I really feel a burden to pray for our city, for our city leaders and especially for our police force. We need to join together in this. Between Ebenezer Baptist and Church of Christ we'll put millions of the enemy to flight."

"Absolutely," Harvey said. "How did the last hearing go?"

"It was a closed door meeting, and as usual, nothing much was said to the public, but the same police officer was brought up on brutality charges for the second time. The last time, he was given a paid leave, and then he was moved to another precinct. If the department doesn't discipline him this time, I have it on good faith; the inner city is going to ignite."

Harvey closed his eyes against the forlorn hopelessness that dropped into his spirit and allowed him to feel and understand Jeremiah's urgency for corporate prayer. He tried unsuccessfully to suppress the images of his beloved city on fire again—the people expressing their frustrations with a broken system as they rioted and destroyed their own neighborhoods.

"Oh yes. We have to pray. At ten o'clock tomorrow morning on August 1st, I'll make the announcement, and at 10:05 am our churches will link in the spirit."

"Thank you my friend," Jeremiah said. "Bless you and say hello to your wife."

"You do the same," Harvey said. He dropped to his knees and began to intercede in the spirit.

Chapter 1

"Why am I here? What did I do?" Nichelle demanded. She didn't have a job to go to, but that didn't mean she had time to waste at the police station.

Wade Dennis was tired. Retirement was ten years away, but twenty-five years of interviewing clients, like the one standing in front of him, had worn him down. His eyes were drawn to the framed photograph on his desk and the fresh face of his son, a recent college graduate. Looking into Keith's blue-green eyes was like looking into a mirror of his own past. He began to think, *had he ever been that excited about life?*

Nichelle cleared her throat. "Excuse me. Hel-lo. Are you listening to me?" It was warm outside, but her cut-off short shorts and thin tank top looked out of place in the air-conditioned room.

Wade rubbed his eyes then looked back at her. "I'm sorry Miss Evers. You're free to go." When she didn't respond he looked up, then he wished he hadn't.

"Oh, hell no," Nichelle said, hands on her hips and moving her neck from side to side. "You not gonna drag me down here for the hell of it and then say go. It cost money to ride the bus back home."

Wade debated on telling her the truth…that she was picked up because a rookie cop mistook her for a prostitute, but he could see it turning into the birth of a lawsuit or a visit by the NAACP or that Sharpton guy. He fished his hand inside his desk drawer and grabbed a handful of change from his jar of quarters.

"This should cover your bus fare Miss Evers. We're sorry to have inconvenienced you."

Nichelle smiled the smile of a person who liked money—especially easy money. She hadn't pegged Wade Dennis as a man who would pay her to leave his office, and she was sorry it was too late to change her need from bus to cab fare. She wondered, *How much would he have paid if she'd read him right from the jump?*

Nichelle pocketed the money and left Wade's office but not before estimating the amount in hand to be enough for a snack from the Mc Donald's dollar menu, some new flip flops from the 99 cent store, and maybe enough left to buy another lottery ticket. Forget the bus. She was close enough to walk or hitch a ride home.

At three o'clock in the afternoon, Wade closed and locked his file cabinet. He hadn't eaten since that morning. Mr. Sanchez' lunch truck was usually parked across the street near the car wash and there were several eateries within walking distance of the MLK precinct. Once outside, Wade donned his sunglasses and proceeded to walk east on Martin Luther King, Jr. Boulevard toward the Café Culver.

Café Culver specialized in burgers, fries, and ice cream. Wade ordered the $4.99 deluxe hamburger special and found a vacant table near the television. The other four tables were occupied by groups of teenagers on summer break from school, who were talking loud and would no doubt leave their trash on the floor or the tables.

The teens pretended to ignore Wade, but he knew better. Someone must have seen him come from the direction of the police station because the noise level decreased by half and individuals began sneaking glances at him. Eventually, the youth left the Café and only sounds from the television filled the room.

Wade watched the news and began eating his burger and mountain of fries.

"Come here often?" Nichelle asked.

Wade was sitting near a large picture window, but he still didn't like the fact someone snuck up on him. "Sometimes," he replied.

Nichelle was twenty-three years old, but she stood next to his table like a child waiting for the adult to acknowledge her.

Wade looked away from the television. "Did you want something or are you planning to stand there and watch me eat?"

"Can I order what I want?" Nichelle said.

"That's not what I meant, Miss Evers." It was hard not to notice her thin brown legs and knobby knees as she turned and walked away.

Nichelle plopped down into the white plastic chair at the next table. She looked at the menu, then pulled a handful of quarters out of her pocket and spread them out on the table. She slowly counted the money until Wade said he would buy her a hamburger and a drink, but she had to help him eat his French fries. Nichelle hurried up to the counter and placed the order, and then she pulled out the chair across from Wade. She frowned.

"I don't know why you're watching the news when Wendy Williams is on."

"Who?"

"You never heard of Wendy Williams?" Nichelle held a bottle of ketchup over the remaining fries with one hand while pounding the bottom of the bottle with the palm of the other.

Wade wiped his mouth with a paper napkin and tossed it into the trash.

"Two points," Nichelle said. "That's what we say when anyone makes a basket."

Wade stood up, "Enjoy your lunch."

"Where are you going?" Nichelle asked.

"Back to work." He walked to the counter and gave the cashier a five dollar bill before exiting the eatery.

Nichelle eyed the cashier. If she stuck to her original plan, she could tell the cashier she didn't want the food and to give her the five dollars, but the cashier scowled back at Nichelle as if daring her to ask for the money.

She sighed, "Can you make it to-go?"

The cashier nodded and said something in another language to the cook.

"Can you change the TV to channel 13?" Nichelle asked as she snacked from a paper plate of French fries doused in ketchup. When her food was ready, she tossed away the cold fries and took the bag. No need to stay any longer because the Wendy Williams episode was a re-run.

Chapter 2

Wade debated on picking up the call that was ringing on his direct line. It was past six o'clock, and technically, his workday ended an hour ago and he was on his own time. When the phone continued to ring, Beth, one of the pool secretaries, stuck her head inside his door.

"It's Keith." She said and hurried away to catch the slow moving elevator. The door was held open for her by another secretary in spite of the grumbling from a few of the other passengers anxious to get home.

The only highlight to what had been a grueling day would be speaking to his son, so Wade scrambled to pick up the phone.

"Hello, Keith."

"Hi, Dad. I'm glad I caught you before you left work. I wanted you to be the first to know. I got a job today with Becker & Snowden."

"Great, son. Congratulations. You didn't waste any time," Wade said. Keith completed his Bachelor of Arts in English from the University of Oregon in 2008 and went straight to grad school. Two years later he graduated with a Masters Degree in Conflict and Dispute Resolution and now had a job with a reputable company. Wade couldn't have been more proud. His son was a success. Keith steadfastly focused on finishing school and now his efforts to become gainfully employed were rewarded.

"I was trying to hold out for the best offer," Keith said and went into detail on how the job offer came about. Becker & Snowden, was a professional law corporation established in 1980. The firm's primary focus was representing school districts in the states of Washington, Oregon, California and Hawaii and providing legal counsel to municipalities. Their areas of expertise included governance, labor and employee relations, personnel management, student issues, and litigation.

Keith framed his acceptance letter from Stanford's Law School and it hung on the wall between his dresser and headboard, so he could see it every day. It was his dream come true and the result of years of hard work. His ultimate career goal, after passing the Bar Exam, was to be an attorney specializing in student issues and litigation. Keith was offered and accepted the position of Assistant Branch Attendant in the law library of Becker & Snowden. He would work full-time for the rest of the summer. In September, Keith was entering the Jurist Doctorate program specializing in public interest law. He was scheduled to work part-time at Becker & Snowden while completing the three-year law school program in preparation to take the California State Bar Exam in 2014.

Wade told him again how proud he was then gave Keith the advice he wished someone had told him after college when he started his career. "Listen to your father and move up when you get an opportunity. Don't get too comfortable because if you stay in one place too long, the powers that be can't see past you doing anything else. You get stuck; pigeon-holed into doing the same thing year after year."

"I thought you liked your job?" Keith said. "I remember the fun we had at the company picnics and everyone seemed so friendly at the take-your-kid-to-work days."

Wade sighed, "That was a long time ago Key. This was a great place to work before all my close friends and colleagues moved on or retired. I should have done the same, but when your mother took sick, the job was the only stable thing in my life. After she died, I didn't have the same drive to promote. I focused my whole life on getting you through school."

"You were a good father, Dad. I couldn't have done any of it without you."

"You were all I had," Wade said. He cleared his throat after his voice cracked.

"About that…how come you never dated or had a girlfriend when I was a kid?"

"I dated some, but I never felt right bringing another woman into our house. It still felt like your mother's home."

"Oh Dad…"

"I know. It's crazy, but sometimes I still feel like she's going to walk in the front door and tell me to get my feet off the furniture."

"What about Miss Steph?"

"The housekeeper?"

"She's a nice lady. I always thought she was pretty too."

"I never looked at Miss Stephanie like that."

"Maybe you should?"

Wade chuckled. Stephanie Townsend was five years his senior and a compulsive cleaner. He couldn't ever imagine her out of her housedress, apron, and rubber gloves.

"When are you coming home for a visit?"

"Eight minutes and thirty-two seconds."

"Huh?"

Keith laughed, "I knew you were going to ask me that question. It was just a matter of time."

"Okay big time lawyer. What's your answer?"

"From your lips to God's ears," Keith said in response to the "big lawyer" comment. "I still have to pass the bar first, but I was thinking of coming home the weekend of August 15th after I get settled into my new apartment."

"Do you need any help moving?"

"No. I tutored most of the Oregon Ducks' football players. They owe me."

"Tell me about the new place."

"It's great, perfect for me. It's in a nice part of Palo Alto, about fifteen minutes away from where I'll be working and a half hour from the university. The apartment is one-bedroom, one-bathroom, located upstairs over a two-car garage. I have access to one of the parking spaces, so one day when I get a car, hint-hint, I'll have off-street parking. I'm renting from a lady with two kids who live in the front house."

Keith continued the conversation. Wade listened, but his real focus was on the weekend of August 15[th.] He could picture Keith back home, filling the empty rooms with life and purpose. It would be unbearably painful when his son returned to Oregon after his visit, but Wade pushed those thoughts out of his mind and enjoyed the thrill of Keith coming home. He would surprise him with tickets to a pre-season football game.

Wade was in parental bliss with his back to the door and his feet up on his desk. He assumed the noise he heard outside his office was the cleaning crew bumping around until the unmistakable click of a gun brought his attention back to the present. He never saw who held the gun, but after the weapon was discharged, he lay on the floor hovering between life and death while his life-blood slowly left his body.

$\mathcal{C}$hapter 3

$\mathcal{N}$ichelle was applying lipstick when the commercial for the lottery came on the television. She stopped and turned around to watch all of the happy winners and was gratified to know her tickets for the week were safely tucked away between her mattress and box spring. She would find out tomorrow if she would be joining these happy winners.

The first thing she would buy with her millions was breast implants. It wasn't right that her younger sister, Heavenly, got more than her fair share naturally. Heavenly was also thirty pounds overweight which added to the enormity of her breasts and took attention away from her less than flat stomach and thick legs. When Nichelle stood next to her sister and they faced forward, they looked like the number eighteen; Nichelle being the 'one' and her curvaceous sister, the 'eight'. To avoid the inevitable physical comparison, Nichelle didn't hang out with Heavenly, if she could help it. It wasn't difficult to avoid her sister because Heavenly, worked in a downtown high-rise as a receptionist.

Nichelle didn't like having to work, so she avoided it whenever possible. Friday night was a good night to meet someone who would buy her dinner after hearing her sob story and her need for a loan. A loan that she would later swear was a gift. Officially, Nichelle was a live-in caretaker for Glenda Carlson, a woman who for the last two months was living in Las Vegas with her boyfriend. Glenda sent Nichelle enough money to pay the gardener, buy food, and keep her mouth shut if the social worker called.

Nichelle usually confined herself to her own bedroom, so she wouldn't have to clean up any of the other rooms, but tonight she was going out and needed a new outfit to wear. She ventured inside Glenda's master bedroom closet. Most of the clothes were size twelve or fourteen, but Glenda once mentioned she had lost weight a few years ago and bought a bunch of clothes she never got to wear because within a year, she put the weight right back on.

Nichelle hit pay dirt when she found a box in the back of the closet. There were several outfits in sizes six and eight with the price tags still attached. She picked out a dark red one-piece with giant detachable shoulder pads. Borrowing a bra from Glenda's dresser drawer, she filled it with the shoulder pads and slipped into the garment.

"Damn, I look good." Nichelle complemented herself admiring her new curves. She brushed her hair up into a high ponytail, secured it with a thick rubber band, and blended her own hair with the twelve-inch silky straight hair piece. She stuffed Glenda's size nine black pumps with tissue, so they would stay on her size seven-and-a-half foot. The bus stop was a block from Glenda's house, and in less than thirty-minutes, it would drop her off in front of Club Night Train. It was a little early, but Club Night Train was the hottest local night-spot in the area, so it would be packed by midnight.

Nichelle locked the deadbolt and carefully made her way down the walkway to the sidewalk, taking her time in her borrowed and too-big shoes. She didn't notice the unmarked police car or the two white guys who immediately exited their car and met her on the sidewalk.

"Do you live here?" The first one asked.

"Yes. Am I being punked?" Nichelle asked looking around. It was very unusual to be questioned by the police twice in one day.

"I'm Detective Tony Sloan. May I see some identification?"

"What is it with you guys today? Is it harass Nichelle day today?" Nichelle said under her breath while looking through her purse for her California driver's license.

Detective Sloan studied the picture.

"This picture doesn't look like you."

"I just had my hair dyed red with the cascading curls," she explained.

"The address on this driver's license is not here, it's in East Los Angeles," Officer Sloan said and gave the card to his partner.

"This is where I work. I'm a live-in care taker for Miss Glenda Carlson for the last six months."

"Is Miss Carlson home?"

"No, but I can give you her cell number and she can verify I live here," Nichelle said.

The officer wrote down the telephone number and handed it to his partner then said, "A police officer was shot. I'm asking you to come with us, to the station, and make a statement." "For what? I've already been at the station today and I was told I could go."

"What were you doing at the station today?" Sloan asked.

"Don't you keep records? First of all, I need to know from you what this is all about. I just missed my bus and need cab fare." Nichelle said pointing to the city bus that passed them, leaving a cloud of exhaust. When she pointed toward the bus her hand grazed the cheek of Detective Sloan. The second officer placed a handcuff on her wrist while grabbing her other arm and cuffing it behind her. He began reciting the Miranda rights.

"You have the right to remain silent..."

Nichelle wanted to show-out, but she decided to cooperate since she knew they very well may have caught up with her for some illegal activity she had done in the past. No sense in tipping her hand and saying too much, besides when the time was right, she would drop the name of the cop who gave her the quarters. He must have a soft spot for poor, skinny Black girls, but if things got too heavy, her one phone call would be to Heavenly. They may not be close as sisters, but now would be time to pull the family card.

$\mathscr{C}$hapter 4

$\mathscr{K}$eith Dennis looked out of the window of the airplane determined to hold it together. He assumed the call dropped when one moment he was talking to his father and the next he heard strange noises then dead silence. Keith wanted it to be a sick joke when later that night the police officer referred to him as 'the next of kin.' Those words made the bottom of his world drop from beneath him. The only thing he could comprehend after the officer told him Wade Dennis had been shot was that he should come right away. It was an unacceptable reality he might have heard the murder of his own father.

Keith used his emergency Visa credit card with the five thousand dollar credit limit to get to Los Angeles. The cost of the ticket was the least of his concerns, so before nightfall, he was on a non-stop flight from Eugene to LAX-Los Angeles International Airport. When his plane landed, the midnight sky matched his mood. Keith took a taxicab to

Cedar Sinai Hospital. On the way, he made himself envision his father sitting up in bed and teasing him for taking the so-called emergency so seriously. The cab driver grumbled when the fare came just shy of thirty dollars and Keith handed him a twenty dollar bill and two fives. In his hurry, it was all the cash he brought with him.

The hospital lights were bright, reflecting light off the white floors and white walls. Keith hated the sterile smells assaulting his sinuses. After speaking with the hospital receptionist, he was handed a name-tag and followed a junior volunteer to the 3rd floor Intensive Care Unit.

In contrast to the brightness of the first floor, the third floor lighting was subdued. The ICU receptionist checked him in and asked him to wait while she called the doctor. She pointed to the coffee and tea cart in the corner and told him to help himself. Keith declined and sat down to wait. He picked up a two year-old Better Homes and Gardens magazine and studied the cover. His mother subscribed to this magazine. Memories of watching her get weaker and weaker then die in this very hospital brought unbidden tears to his eyes that he quickly wiped away. He thought, *No! It's not going to happen to me again. I refuse.* If he had to stand face-to-face with God to spare his father, so be it.

It had been a long time since Keith talked to God. It used to nag at him when he got up or went to bed without praying, but over time, it became less important as he focused on staying true to his self-imposed schedule. Since God knew everything already, talking to Him about everyday life was just a formality. Keith must have been doing something right because everything was going just as planned…until today.

Keith looked around the room at the other family groups sitting together. It looked like they had been there a long time because they were lounging in the chairs, and the trash can was full of fast food containers. A few of them were napping while others mindlessly watched a CNN news program projected from a flat screen television mounted to the wall.

Keith bowed his head. The words that used to flow from his heart when he prayed refused to come; instead, he felt like the *Wizard of Oz's*

Tin Man, rusty after the rain, when it came to praying. Minutes later when the one of the double glass doors opened, every one focused on the doctor, dressed in green scrubs, who stepped inside the waiting room.

He looked around the room. "Keith Dennis?"

Keith stood, grateful his wait was brief, but on the other hand, he braced himself for the possibility of hearing the worse news of his life, a second time. He didn't feel so confident anymore and wished he hadn't been so defiant with God, the only one who could really help him. *Please God. I'm sorry. Have Mercy.* The doctor escorted him into the corridor.

"I'm Doctor Keppel, Mr. Dennis." They shook hands. "Your father is on life support. We're keeping him in a coma to keep him stable because he lost a lot of blood and may have had a stroke. We gave him one blood transfusion and will monitor him and see if he needs another one."

"Does anyone know who did it? How did this happen at the police station?"

"There aren't any known witnesses, but the paramedics reported your father was in his office, seated, talking on the telephone and probably turned just in time for the bullet to go through his shoulder rather than his heart."

Keith wanted to faint, to shout or cry out, but instead, he ran his hand over his face trying to absorb the information. Someone shot and tried to kill his father? Who would want him dead?

"Let's sit down." Doctor Keppel said and led Keith to an area with backless benches covered in imitation leather. "I'm going to let the police detectives know you're here."

While waiting for the detectives, Keith's cell phone vibrated in his pocket.

"Hello?"

"Hi honey. How is your father?"

It was Trish Glover, his girlfriend of six months and soon-to-be-roommate, a minor detail he left out when he told his father about his new apartment. Keith relayed everything that happened since she dropped him off at the Eugene airport. He abruptly ended the call when two detectives entered the area.

"Keith Dennis?"

"Yes, sir."

"I'm Detective Grey Marshall, and this is Detective Mark Lindo. We are sorry to meet you under these circumstances, but I've worked with your father for years and don't know anyone who would purposely have it out for him."

Mark Lindo winced at the tone and manner of his partner. They were talking to a young man with fear written all over his face because he recognized the severity of the situation. Mark was a father of two and grandfather of seven and could see his son in Keith's shoes, trying to be brave but ready to crumble. Mark Lindo pulled rank and took over the conversation. "Son, are you here by yourself? Do you have any other family in the area?"

"It's just me. I have an uncle, but he lives in Arizona. He's coming tomorrow. I'm an only child and my mother passed away when I was a kid. I've been away in school in Oregon." Keith said his words spilling out randomly.

"That's right," Detective Lindo said softly. He placed his hand on Keith's shoulder. "Wade told me you just graduated. He's very proud of you."

Keith visibly relaxed and focused on talking to Detective Lindo while the other detective tapped his pen on the pad he was holding. This small talk wasn't going to get them the information they needed.

"I was talking to my Dad when it happened," Keith said. "I called him as soon as I got home. I remember the six-o'clock news was just coming on and I muted the sound and called the house. The answering machine came on, so I left a message for my Dad to call me, then I remembered he's been working late this past month, so I called his office number."

Detective Marshall stood by taking copious notes while his partner sat across from Keith and listened. Both detectives asked a few questions while Keith spoke until he wound down, seeming to run out of words. In spite of the circumstances, the young man's answers were very thorough and the detectives completed their questioning in less than twenty minutes.

"After you visit with your father, we'll take you home," Detective Lindo said.

Keith was allowed to see Wade for a few minutes. After the nurse left the room, Keith looked at the monitors and tubes running everywhere. Then he carefully placed a kiss on his father's forehead and whispered in his ear that he loved him and to get well. In a way, it was a relief to see Wade still breathing, even though he wasn't conscious and was being kept alive by machines. The nurse gave Keith a large plastic bag containing his father's wallet, watch and ring. He accepted the bag and stood looking with forlorn at his father's possessions.

"I'm hungry. Let's stop at Jack's," Detective Lindo said. He wasn't really hungry, but he wanted to make sure Keith had something to eat, and this *Jack-in-the* Box was one of the local eateries open twenty-four hours.

Loaded down with a Chinese chicken salad and a Jumbo Jack combo, Keith thanked the officers who escorted him inside his father's house and made sure everything was secure before returning to their car. Detective Marshall was glad the pampering was over and now they could get back to solving the case. He and the LAPD took it personally whenever one of their own was victimized and Marshall, for one, wouldn't rest until the perpetrator was caught.

Chapter 5

Nichelle posed for her mug shot like she was auditioning for *America's Next Top Model.* She smiled with her eyes, confident that she looked good. Her only regret was that the picture wasn't head to toe.

The woman dressed in blue who was taking her picture wasn't amused. "Look straight forward Miss America," She bellowed.

Nichelle looked straight, but she gave fierce eye-contact like Tyra Banks instructed the wannabe models on her show. Nichelle was fingerprinted and taken to a holding room with ash colored walls. The only items in the room were a metal table and four chairs. Nichelle estimated the time to be around nine-thirty at night. If the po-po could get their act together, there was still a possibility she might make it to the club tonight. She couldn't help but think, *Damn. They just wastin' my time today.*

Two white men wearing off-white button-down shirts, ties, slacks, and round-toed shoes entered the holding room. They both held manila folders and faced her with somber expressions.

"Nichelle Monique Evers?"

Nichelle looked around the ten-by-ten-foot room then back at the two men. "I guess that would be me."

"I'm Detective Lindo. This is Detective Marshall. Miss Evers, were you read your rights?"

"Yes."

"Did you understand them?"

Nichelle watched a lot of television including *Cops* and wondered what idiot didn't know the meaning of those rights. "Yes. I understand them, but what I don't understand is why I'm here again. I accidentally touched that policeman in the face when I was pointing to the bus."

"There's been an attempted murder..."

Nichelle suddenly leaned forward, "Is it Heavenly?"

Both men wrote the name down and Marshall asked, "Who is Heavenly?"

"Oh my God! Is she...dead? Is my sister dead?" Nichelle asked. Who could she call now?

"Why would someone want to murder your sister?"

"Jealousy," Nichelle answered. "Is it Glenda? Cause I don't trust her so-called boyfriend."

"What's Glenda's last name, and why would you think she might be victimized?"

"Don't you people talk to each other? Glenda Carlson is the lady I stay with and help out. She's been dating this guy, Muscles, who I just don't like. He's too young for her, just taking and spending her money," Nichelle said.

Detective Lindo decided to try another approach. "What time was it when you were last here?"

Nichelle sat for a moment wondering why they were asking her questions they must know the answer to. Her thoughts suddenly went to the possibility they were trying to set a trap and mix her up, so she'd say something they could use against her in a court of law.

"I was brought here at about 2:30. I didn't stay long. Wade told me to go."

Both men stopped writing and focused intensely on Nichelle.

"Officer Wade Dennis?"

"Yes. He gave me some of his quarters, and I left. I didn't see him again until he bought me lunch at Café Culver down the street."

"Officer Wade Dennis gave you money before you left his office, and then met up with you for lunch?"

"It wasn't a date or anything. He's not my type," Nichelle said. When the two men didn't say anything, Nichelle continued, "I saw him in the Café Culver window and he offered to buy me a burger and share his fries."

"How well do you know Officer Dennis?"

"I didn't really know him. We just met today."

"How much money did he give you?"

"Three dollars and twenty-five cents. It was thirteen quarters from his personal stash," Nichelle said proudly that she could remember the exact amount. She didn't notice how tense the officers were becoming and the change in their mood until the door to the tiny room opened.

This time, a dark-skinned Black man dressed in a gray suit entered the room. Nichelle studied his face to see if she knew him or any of his people because he looked to be around her age and somewhat familiar. The way the other two men moved aside must mean the brother outranked them.

"Good evening, Miss Evers. I'm Detective Phillip Covers."

Nichelle racked her brain while he was talking because she was trying to remember why his name sounded familiar. Then it hit her like a ton of bricks. Philly Covers was Miss Bessie Mae Baker's boy. She remembered sitting at the kitchen table doing her homework, but half listening to her mother and some of the older women talking in the living room about the latest scandal.

Philly's father, DeSean Covers, moved away from the neighborhood with his son after Miss Baker's new baby girl came out light-skinned with freckles and nappy red hair, just like Mr. Baldwin, the neighborhood grocer.

According to them, Bessie Mae didn't have a bit of sense for getting a baby with Tyrone Baldwin when she had exclusive use of deep-dark chocolate DeSean Covers at home. DeSean worked construction and brought Bessie Mae his paycheck every other week. All he wanted was her to cook, clean, and give him dessert a couple of times a week. Eleven year-old Nichelle didn't know what was so special about the dessert, but she listened hard whenever the women spoke certain words in a whisper and then laughed.

"Do I have to stay here? These two are talking about a might-be murder and asking me all kinds of questions they should already have the answer to…"

"Have you eaten yet?" Phillip asked.

Nichelle sat up straight. Now we're talking. If she'd met Phillip Covers in the club tonight she would have let him buy her a drink and see where she could lead the conversation. Philly wasn't as tall, dark, or handsome as she remembered his father DeSean, but he was good-looking in a nerdy sort of way.

"No. I haven't. I was on my way to dinner when these two Barney's pulled up to the curb and brought me here," Nichelle said.

Phillip nodded toward the men and they left the room.

"I can't promise you restaurant quality food, but it's edible. The good news for you is that Detective Sloan is not pressing any charges. He confirmed that you accidentally touched his face when you were pointing to the bus. Now, what I need from you is to tell me everything you did today. From the time you left your house this morning until I walked in that door," Phillip Covers said pointing at the door, but he was looking at Nichelle.

"Then will you tell me who got popped?" She asked.

Phillip sighed. God help her attorney. She'd be a nightmare on the witness stand. "Yes. I'll answer all of your questions."

Nichelle told Phillip Covers all of the details of her day including her purchase of a lottery ticket, but not what she planned to do with her winnings. She liked pretending this body was hers. Detective Marshall returned with a Styrofoam dinner plate holding a ham and cheese sandwich, snack-size bag of Fritos and a boxed fruit punch drink. Nichelle consumed everything, but the two slices of soggy white bread.

"Is there anything else you want to know?" Nichelle asked still hoping it wasn't too late to make it to the club. Maybe the police would give her a ride in one of their unmarked cars.

"You've been very thorough and cooperative, Miss Evers."

"You can call me Nichelle, Philly."

Phillip Covers didn't respond.

"Can I have a piece of paper to write on?"

Phillip tore off a blank sheet of paper from his legal pad and placed it on the table along with a pen. Nichelle wrote a few words and pushed the paper across to him.

Phillip read the note and folded it in half and put it inside his jacket pocket.

"I'm recommending you be released on your own recognizance. Do not leave the city without letting me know first," Phillip said and handed Nichelle his business card. "Do you understand me?"

"Yes," Nichelle said. "Stay in L.A., but right now I need cab fare or a ride to King and Van Ness. I would have caught the bus, but not this late. What time is it anyway?"

Phillip looked at his watch. "It's 10:15. I'll see if transportation can be provided." He stood up.

"Wait a minute, what happened today?" Nichelle asked.

"Police Officer Wade Dennis was shot in his office. He's on life support."

The detective thought Nichelle's shocked expression was empathy for Officer Dennis, but Nichelle remembered a person she saw hurrying out of the back door of the police station parking lot when she was walking past the building on her way home. It was strange for anyone to be wearing a long trench coat in the middle of a warm summer afternoon, even though the sun was on its way down, but it was the person's look of desperation, like they just shoplifted something for the first time, that she couldn't forget.

"Don't you have cameras around here?" Nichelle asked rubbing her hands on the top of her thighs.

"We're in process of a complete investigation. All evidence will be reviewed," Phillip said. "Come on out to the front desk and pick up your personal items."

Since Nichelle borrowed one of Glenda's small purses, she was grateful it only held her lipstick, keys and a few dollars and not the two joints and half-pint she usually carried on her when she went out clubbing. She picked up her purse from the front desk, and she was escorted to a side door where an unmarked police car was waiting.

Chapter 6

Keith turned the thermostat down after the police officers left. How his father could live in seventy-five degree heat day and night was a mystery to him especially after living in the cool climate of Eugene, Oregon for the last six years. Keith flipped the switch at the front door and the dim light illuminated the porch. He re-checked the front door locks and set the security alarm. In his hurry to get to Los Angeles, he hadn't thought to bring his cell phone charger, and since a call from the hospital might come at any time, he couldn't turn his phone off to save power. Keith went into the kitchen where his father kept a charging station. None of the chargers fit his cell phone.

"Tomorrow I'll go by Verizon and pick up a new charger," Keith said. It was comforting to hear some kind of noise in the empty house, even if it was just the sound of his own voice. He picked up the TV remote control on the kitchen counter and turned on the television. The ESPN news announcer spoke about baseball scores as if they were the most exciting information ever reported.

Keith settled into one of two kitchen chairs at the bistro table and opened the fast food bag. This three-bedroom ranch style house was the home where he grew up. As he began eating the hamburger, he reflected on the fact that their home had more televisions than chairs. Each bedroom—the den, the kitchen, the living room and even the garage— housed a television from the last five decades. The oldest was a twelve-inch black and white portable TV from the 1970s. Wade took it with him on fishing trips or turned it on when he wanted to tinker around in the garage and listen to a sporting event like golf or tennis.

The guest room was filled with 1980s furniture including Wade and Julie's first new bedroom set; a full size bed with an oak headboard and tall dresser. The nineteen-inch color television sat on one of the matching night stands and blended perfectly with the rest of the decor.

After Julie died, Wade painted over the flowered wallpaper in the master bedroom, but he couldn't bring himself to get rid of the black lacquer bedroom set they picked out together using their 1985 income tax refund. The furniture filling this room included a king-size bed, dresser and mirror, two night stands and an armoire that housed a twenty-five inch television. The flouncy pastel curtains Julie put up were replaced with black mini-blinds. The bed was covered with a black, tan, and white patterned bed-in-a bag comforter set purchased from *Anna's Linens*. If Julie were living, she would have bought the matching towel set for the bathroom, but Wade knew they had plenty of towels his wife squirreled away in case company came to visit. Wade was determined to use every one of them, a silent protest to the universe for taking his wife away before she could enjoy the use of her best towels.

The final bedroom was Keith's room. It was sparsely furnished, so he could use the empty floor space to exercise, completing his nightly routine of sit-ups and push-ups. He lifted weights on the incline weight bench in the corner. The biggest piece of furniture in his room was his grandfather's burgundy roll-top desk and antique chair where Keith spent hours doing homework. Across from the desk was a denim-covered futon bed centered under rows of shelves filled with athletic trophies, ribbons, and metals awarded for various sports from T-ball to high school track. The twenty-inch color television, a birthday present in 1990, sat in front of the only window. It came with built-in VCR and DVD players, which was cutting edge technology at the time.

In the year 2000, Wade's brother, Chris, bought himself a fifty-inch flat screen at an outlet store that he proudly mounted to his living room wall. A month later, Chris won a fifty-six inch big screen television in a Thanksgiving raffle that he gave to Wade for Christmas. After Julie died and before Wade received the big screen, the den was used mostly for storage, so having a place to put the new television was a good excuse to get rid of unneeded clutter. After the room was emptied out, Wade and Chris painted the walls a color in the tan family. They moved the dark brown overstuffed living room couch, love seat and some of the other furniture into the den. Then Chris showed Wade how to shop on the Internet for gently-used furniture.

Keith wasn't exactly sure where the kitchen television came from. He went away to school in 2004, and on one of his more recent visits home, there was a new twenty-inch flat screen television mounted under one of the upper cabinets in the kitchen. No doubt, Uncle Chris had hooked up all of the televisions to the single cable line in the den because all of the TVs showed the same premium channels and his father was never electronically savvy. For reasons Keith would probably never know, his father--a reasonably honest man, looked the other way when Uncle Chris was "hooking him up."

Keith called Uncle Chris with the bad news while waiting to board his flight. Chris immediately scheduled a flight from Arizona that would arrive at LAX in the morning.

It was almost two o'clock a.m. when Keith went to bed. Bad dreams kept him from sleeping soundly during the night, so at six a.m., Keith concluded there was no way he was going to get any real rest. He forced himself to get up and went into the kitchen to make a cup of instant coffee. After finishing the coffee, he rinsed out his cup and spoon and placed them inside the dishwasher. Keith showered, making sure his cell phone and the land-line receiver were in the bathroom just in case the hospital called.

After shaving, he put on a grey velour sweat suit he found hanging in his closet and was proud that it still fit. Keith hadn't been on any sports teams in years, but he still gravitated toward the "jocks" at the university and worked out regularly with them. At 8:00 that morning, he decided to make a quick call to Trish before going to the airport.

"Hello."

Keith could hardly believe a man answered her cell phone. "Is Trish there?" He looked at the clock again. Trish was a late sleeper, especially on the weekends.

"Hold on."

"Hello?" Trish said.

"It's me. Who answered your phone?"

"Oh, that's just Doug, my neighbor. I was fixing breakfast and told him to answer the telephone because I thought it might be you and I didn't want to miss your call. How's your Dad?"

"I don't know yet because I'm waiting for Uncle Chris to call me from the airport; then we're going to the hospital."

"How are you holding up?"

"I'd be a lot better if a man hadn't answered my girlfriend's telephone. Have I met Doug?"

"I don't think you two have ever met," Trish answered.

"I'll call you later," Keith said when he heard the house phone ringing. It was too much information to digest right now. He needed to focus on his father.

Keith was glad to hear that his uncle's plane had just touched down at LAX. He found his father's car keys in the mailbox and looked out of the side window of the living room at his father's car. It was parked in the driveway courtesy of the policemen who dropped him off at home last night. Keith locked up the house and went outside to the driveway. His father's 1994 Toyota Camry was in pristine condition and gleamed in the morning sun. Keith learned to drive on this 6V automatic and it brought back pleasant memories to be behind the wheel again.

The Saturday morning traffic was light, so it was easy for Keith to drive past the arrival area for United Airlines. Uncle Chris was standing near the curb by the taxi stand. He still dressed in a Miami Vice style that included a jade-colored silk T-shirt, tan slacks, and brown huaraches sandals. The outfit was topped-off with a light brown, cotton-silk blend jacket with the sleeves pushed up on his forearms. Chris threw a brown duffle bag in the back seat and was in the front seat putting on his seatbelt before the airport policeman could reprimand them for stopping so close to the area reserved for taxis.

"How's it going nephew?" Chris said. "Any news from the hospital?"

"No. They didn't call last night," Keith said.

"No news is good news," Chris replied and pulled out a pair of sunglasses from his front pocket. He put them on to cut down on the blinding glare of the sun. Arizona heat was ridiculous, but California sun was just as bright. Chris settled down into the passenger seat as he thought about his brother lying in the hospital, *This better not have anything to do with that money I owe Smitty or heads are going roll.*

Chapter 7

"*I* was headed to Night Train," Nichelle said protesting to the driver when the car kept going straight down Western Avenue past King Boulevard.

"Night Train," Phillip said. "There's always trouble at that club, so I'm taking you back to where you were picked up."

Nichelle groaned. There was no reason not to show off her new outfit somewhere tonight. "Can't we stop and get somethin' to eat first? I'm still hungry."

Phillip considered her request. He really couldn't call the soggy sandwich and chips they gave her earlier a decent meal, but that was when she was a person-of-interest having been with Wade Dennis twice on the same day he was shot. Without a word, Phillip turned the wheel of the State issued navy-blue Chevy and drove into the driveway of a fast food restaurant at the end of the block.

Nichelle gasped and exclaimed, "*Burger King*! Come on, man. I didn't get fitted to go through a drive-thru."

Phillip parked the car in the last empty space, "We're not on a date Nichelle. You know the game. I give you something and you give me something." She must have recognized him from the old neighborhood because he hadn't been called 'Philly' since they moved away. After Nichelle wrote him a note asking if the holding room "had ears," he deduced she wanted to tell him something in confidence. What she didn't know was that he already read her file. Nichelle Evers was always bending the rules and trying to get something for nothing. Phillip was no fool she could hustle and he wasn't having it.

She softened her tone. "All I'm saying is I would like to go somewhere a little nicer. There's a Sizzler at the Baldwin Hills mall and it's only a few miles from here."

"It's closed, but I'll spring for Downtown Buffet."

"Okay," Nichelle answered quickly.

"Okay?" Phillip said and turned to look at her. "Don't you have something else you want to tell me?"

"How did you get this gig Philly?" Nichelle said.

Phillip sighed. He didn't have the patience for small talk. A police officer's life was hanging in the balance. "Look Nichelle, either tell me what you want me to know or I'm taking you home right now."

Nichelle nodded. Nerd-boy was trying to be hard. "All I know is after I stopped by the 99cent store and was headed back down King, I was standing at the red light on Denker Avenue and saw a woman in a long dark trench coat come running out of the inside parking lot of the police station. The lady looked around and was hugging her arms around herself like she was hiding something. The light changed and I crossed the street. When I looked back, I saw her headed down Denker toward Vernon."

"What time was this?" Phillip asked.

"About 6:15. I know because it takes twenty minutes for me to get home and *The People's Court* was already on and it starts at 6:30, just before it gets dark."

"Describe the lady to me."

"She was light skinned, kind of like Tisha Campbell's color, but with long dark brown hair. I was too far away to tell if it was hers."

"How long was her hair?"

Nichelle touched her arm midway between her shoulder and her elbow, "To here. It was kind of straight and fly-away. It looked natural, but it could have been a weave. It would have looked better with highlights."

"How tall was she?" Phillip asked sticking to the facts.

"She looked to be around five-seven or eight, but I couldn't see if she had heals on because of the long coat. I think she was slim, but the way the coat covered her up, it's hard to say."

"How old did she look?"

"Humm…I'm not good at judging ages. If I didn't know you from the old neighborhood, I'd a thought you were a lot older than me, but I guess she was around thirty to thirty-five years old."

"Did she seem distraught?"

"She seemed crazy because of the way she was looking around like someone was going to see her. She looked guilty. Can we go now? I'm hungry," Nichelle said.

Phillip started the car, "While we're on the way, let me know if you think of anything else."

Nichelle nodded, but if he wanted anything else out of her it was going to cost him. *After all a girl's got to eat and pay her bills.* "I was serious when I asked about how you got this job. You and your father moved away all of a sudden and I never saw you at Miss Bessie Mae's again."

"My father and Bessie Mae weren't married and she isn't my mother, so when Shayla was born looking like old man Baldwin from the grocery store, my father packed us up and we moved out of state. I'm sure all the neighbors talked about that for months."

"Yeah, they did but no one knew where ya'll went and disappeared to."

"We went to Galveston, Texas where my father's parents live."

"You never came back to L.A.?"

"No. Not until I moved back a few years ago. According to my father, my mother divorced both me and him. She had dreams of being an actress not a wife and mother. Anyway, after we left Bessie Mae's, we moved in with my grandparents. From the time I met my grandparents, they felt like my real parents. They put in the time with me, whereas my father was always working. My grandparents were strict, but I liked the routine. They attended Good Shepherd Baptist church on Sunday and Wednesday night, rain or shine. He was a deacon and she was an usher, so sometimes we went to church every day, but whenever I wanted to do something like play ball, they let me as long as I kept my grades up. My father hooked up with an old girlfriend, and later that year, he married my step-mother, Leslie. I was so close to my grandparents, my father let me stay with them and he and his new wife got started on a new family. Now I have three younger brothers and a sister."

Phillip stopped a red light and stopped speaking for a moment, seeming to be lost in his memories. When the red light turned green, he focused on the present and continued his story.

"After high school, I went to college and majored in political science. After graduation, I applied to the police academy. I worked my way up to Chief Detective and planned to settle down in Galveston, but my grandfather needed a special surgery and treatment only offered at UCLA hospital. Fortunately for me, LAPD was hiring, and I was offered a job a few weeks after I completed my final interview with them. My grandparents packed up, sold the house, and the three of us came to Southern California. We couldn't afford a house in Westwood near the hospital, so we settled for a nice duplex in Inglewood near the 405 Interstate." Phillip turned into the parking lot of the Baldwin Hills Mall. He parked and turned the ignition off and said, "And that's my story."

After being seated in a booth at Downtown Buffet, the waiter took their drink orders. Nichelle filled two plates with food wanting to sample everything. Phillip went to the grill and waited for the raw meat and fresh vegetables he selected to be stir-fried. When he returned to the table, Nichelle was already eating. Phillip whispered a quick prayer over his food and he and Nichelle ate in silence.

When she finally looked up from her plate, Phillip asked, "So, what happened with you, Nichelle? Did you move away from the Eastside?"

Nichelle took a sip of her iced tea. "We moved alright…downstairs into a three-bedroom in the same building. I thought I was finally going to get my own room and that's when my mama's two sisters moved in with us; Ella Dean and Angelene. It was more crowded because my aunts had a room, my sister and me had a room, and mama had the big room with the bathroom. I was mad. Why does one person get the big room and the private bath and the rest of us have to use one little bathroom?"

Nichelle looked at Phillip like she wanted an answer. He shrugged. He never shared a bedroom in his life. Even in college his assigned roommate, Herb Danberry, stayed off campus with his girlfriend Rita Union for four years.

Nichelle finished the last of the crab legs on her plate then resumed the conversation. "My sister was bussed to Torrance and went to school with the white folks. She graduated from Torrance High two years ago. She went to Southwest College and got her AA in Secretarial Skills or somethin'. She's holding down a gig for some big company downtown."

"What was her name Haven, Heaven?"

"Heavenly," Nichelle said, not pleased he remembered. She wanted his focus to be on Nichelle. "As for me, I used a friend's address and caught the bus up Slauson Avenue to Crenshaw High School, C-house!, and that was all the school I needed."

"What have you done with your time since high school?"

"I worked here and there," Nichelle said.

You've been fired from every job you've ever worked and never worked anywhere longer than a year, Phillip thought while drinking the last of his diet-Coke.

I can't let him think Heavenly is doing better than me, Nichelle said to herself at the dessert bar. When she sat back down she told him, "Last year I took a class to become a home health aide. I had to complete a first-aid and CPR class. I was fine with first-aid, but I wasn't about to do no putting my mouth on and breathing inside of someone I don't personally know, but they used dummies in the class. I still don't know if I could actually save anyone. I would figure it was their time to go. I don't want to get the HIV virus and get AIDS and the person I'm trying to save dies and I die a slow painful death too cause I put my mouth on them. That is not how I want to go."

"I see," Phillip said as he was grateful he was in good heath and wasn't dependent on Nichelle to save his life.

"So, Philly, I see you doing real well," Nichelle said. "I wish I could say the same."

Phillip was careful not to let her see he had cash in his wallet. He placed a credit card on top of the check in the black tray. His cell phone rang, and he answered it. Nichelle scowled because Philly didn't take the bait, but she had his business card. She would call him later and tell him she remembered something about the case. It would be good for at least another meal and maybe a few dollars. While he was talking, Nichelle slipped the five remaining chocolate chip cookies from the plate into a napkin and stuffed them into her little purse. They would taste real good later on tonight as she planned to dip them in hot chocolate while she watched a new episode of *Cheaters.*

$\mathcal{C}$hapter 8

$\mathcal{K}$eith was torn. Should he stay or leave the hospital? His father's condition was stable. He was breathing on his own, but the medication in Wade's system kept him in a deep sleep. Keith wanted to stay at his father's side, but he and his uncle had been at the hospital all day. The waiting around was exhausting, plus they needed to eat. Uncle Chris was sleeping in the second guest chair next to the bed.

Keith stood, stretched and went out to the nurse's station. It was empty. He stood there, and in moments, a nurse returned. During the shift change, the new nurse arrived. She hung up her sweater and put her purse under the desk

"Can I help you?" She asked. 'Catherine' was the name on her nametag.

"Yes," Keith said. "The doctor was supposed to come at 2:00 today and see Wade Dennis, Room 504."

Catherine typed a few letters on the keyboard in front of her. "His nurse was Belinda. Doctor Nunez was scheduled to be here at two o'clock, but he had an emergency. I'm sure he'll be here to check on the patient sometime today."

Keith looked up at the clock on the wall in the nurses' station. It was almost four o'clock. "I need to leave and get something to eat. Can you ask the doctor to call me with an update?"

"Of course," Catherine said. She scrolled through the notes on the computer screen. "You are?"

"Keith Dennis, Wade's son."

"I have your contact number as 541-555-6375."

"That's right, and here's my Dad's home number where I'm staying...." Keith said ready to recite the number.

"It's already in the computer," Catherine said. "You probably filled out some documents when you came in."

It was all a blur to Keith. "We're going to leave now, since there's no telling when the doctor will come. If my Dad asks for me, tell him I'll be back tomorrow." He left the nursing station and went back into room 504 to wake up his uncle.

Both were ravenously hungry, but neither man was known for his cooking skills. Chris suggested they have dinner at First and Ten, a trendy sports bar and restaurant in the area. Keith parked in the self-parking section of the parking lot and they stood in a short line to add their name to the waiting list. The hostess told them the wait to be seated for dinner was approximately twenty-five minutes. Chris convinced Keith it would be worth the wait and led him to the bar. Keith was a social drinker and the beer on his empty stomach went straight to his head. The alcohol helped ease some of the tension of the day, and he felt his body relax.

He wanted to talk to Trish, but not the Trish of this morning who was probably cheating on him with her neighbor. He wanted to talk to the Trish he met a year ago, quite by accident. They started seeing each other at the mid-week movie matinee or on the jogging path. Before long, they were making plans to hang out on the weekends. She invited him to be her date at a formal dinner-dance for her sorority. Keith was mesmerized when she came out in a long burgundy dress with her hair swept up and wearing make-up that enhanced her big blue eyes. She didn't look like his cute little running buddy anymore. They took pictures and were comfortable together, like a happy couple, even before they had their first kiss.

He liked getting to know Trish as a person and thought this was the way two people were supposed to grow together. Keith could definitely see Trish in his future. Her plans were to be a doctor; his to be a lawyer. It was perfect. She would understand the long hours he needed to spend studying and why he would sneak away for an afternoon movie matinee just to chill and be around people and feel normal. Keith let out a deep sigh.

Chris had been watching the Cardinals play the Dodgers on the television over the bar. He turned to face his nephew, "Thinking about your Dad?"

"He's always on my mind, but I was thinking about my maybe/maybe-not girlfriend." Keith told his uncle about the incident with Trish when he called her that morning.

Chris nodded and didn't say anything. He didn't trust women, but he didn't want to pass his cynicism on to his nephew. Chris believed the girl was bumping uglies with the neighbor and was dumb enough to let the guy answer her phone. "I don't know Trish, but you don't want to jump to conclusions."

"Yeah, but being so far away from her..."

"Are you in-like or in love with her?"

"I thought we were on the same page. We were supposed to move to Palo Alto together."

"That sounds serious," Chris said, glad he didn't express his real feelings on the matter. "Maybe she is telling you the truth. She might be using the neighbor to help her move her stuff." *Yeah right. I bet he's moving it up and down and in and out.*

Keith didn't respond. He wanted to think Trish was faithful, but why hadn't she called him all day? This was the biggest crisis of his life and she was miles away probably giving it up to *Doug* and laughing it up with this guy about me, the sucker.

Keith took his phone out of the case and looked at it. The screen was black. He forgot to stop by Verizon and get the charger. Maybe Trish *had* called him. It was going to be a long night because he couldn't call her from the house phone either because he hadn't memorized any of her telephone numbers. Once they were programmed into his cell phone, he thought there would never be a need to remember them.

"Phone dead?" Chris asked.

Keith nodded and jammed it back into the case.

"Not to worry, kiddo. Uncle Chris has magic fingers. Come on, our table's ready." Chris put his arm around his nephew's neck, but his eyes followed the swaying hips of the hostess.

When she stopped at their table, Chris asked for her name, and with a wink, he told Debby he would be back to see her. Debby Curtain was a man-magnet and the perfect eye-candy for First and Ten. She had the total package, and tonight, she was dressed in an off-the-shoulder floor length black dress that exposed her flawlessly smooth shoulders and toned upper arms. The rest of the dress hugged her curves. Debby's pretty face, friendly personality, and perfectly proportioned body guaranteed return customers. Debby was accustomed to men flirting with her, and she played the part of their 'dream girl.' She found it humorous because anyone who thought she was a dainty little female would be shocked to discover she'd studied various forms of martial arts and taught a kickboxing class on the weekends.

In contrast to the hostess attire at First and Ten, the waitress uniforms consisted of a black and white striped referee shirt, black slacks, black *Nike* walking shoes, and hound's-tooth-patterned baseball cap with the

First and Ten's logo on the front. A few minutes after the Dennis' men were seated, their waitress came to the table to take drink orders. Chris ordered another beer, and without looking up, Keith asked for orange juice. When the waitress returned, Chris ordered a Double Decker Po-Boy sandwich with curly fries. She turned to Keith and when he lowered the menu her face brightened in recognition, "Keith?"

Keith looked up at her. The baseball cap pulled down over her forehead was hiding most of her beautiful face. Kimberly! He gave her a slow smile. Kimberly McMillan was his first girlfriend when they were going into the 9th grade. They drifted apart at the end of the summer before high school because her family moved away when her father, an assistant minister, was offered the pastorate of a church in the San Fernando Valley. During their senior year, Keith and Kimberly's paths crossed again, but since Kimberly was never without a boyfriend, Keith had to be content to be just her friend. He stood up and gave her a cordial hug.

"I can't believe it's you after all these years," Kimberly said. "Let me take your order and I'll come back and sit with you on my break."

Keith pointed to the Friday Night special--chili bean soup and roast beef sandwich on sourdough, then he and Uncle Chris watched Kimberly walk away. She was tall and thick in the right places. Her dark hair was spilled down her back in a massive curly ponytail. When she turned the corner Chris turned back and grinned at his nephew.

"What?" Keith asked.

"My man," Chris said and grinned while nodding his head up and down. *Trish who?*

Chapter 9

$\mathcal{K}$imberly McMillan-Miller rushed to the employee lounge, opened her locker and grabbed her purse. She dug around in the bottom for a comb and groaned when she looked up into the mirror affixed inside the locker door. After running the comb through her hair, she rubbed lotion on her hands and over her hair to smooth down any stray hairs that insisted on sticking out at odd angles. She reapplied lip gloss and let a peppermint dissolve on her tongue.

Just last night she told her best friend, Donna, that Keith Dennis was the one who got away. Life didn't always give you second chances and she hoped he was still single and available. She debated on removing her wedding band. These days she wore it to keep stray men from hitting on her, but the ring was a reminder that a wedding ring didn't make you married. Wesley J. Miller taught her that.

She met him on a Saturday afternoon seven years ago when she was walking along a picturesque beach in La Jolla shores. Kimberly didn't realize she was walking fast until Wesley caught up with her and asked her why she was in a rush. He was barefoot and wearing khaki cargo pants rolled up to his ankles and a black tank shirt. He was obviously in the military, something Kimberly could easily discern having been born and raised in Southern California. She explained to him how walking alone and thinking was one of the ways she relaxed.

"But look," Wesley said as he looked out at the waves crashing against the shore. He placed his hand lightly on her shoulder, and in that moment, he seemed so taken with the beauty of the ocean, Kimberly didn't mind that a stranger was touching her. Kimberly saw the scenic view through his eyes, and the more Wesley talked, the more she was drawn to him. He was not traditionally handsome, but six-feet tall and he exuded a confidence that intrigued her.

Wesley had already traveled the world, and while they strolled along the beach, he told her stories about exotic places he'd visited and dangerous situations he'd survived. At thirty-years old, Wesley had already served in the U.S. Air Force for ten years. Kimberly was impressed with his education; degrees in Aviation Operations and Professional Aeronautics. In contrast, she possessed a month old high school diploma and hadn't chosen a career path. That was one of the reasons she was walking along the beach, to commune with God and to get a hint about the direction she should take. Kimberly was a sheltered PK, a pastor's kid, still living at home, and helping her parents with their calling. As she compared her normal, boring life to Wesley's, there was no reason for her to speak other than to ask him questions, because he knew so much about so many things.

The day after Kimberly met Wesley, he returned to where he was stationed, Columbus Air Force Base in Meridian, Mississippi. Wesley called Kimberly that night and every weekend to talk for at least an hour each time he called. From the start of their telephone communication, Wesley always asked her to come visit him. Kimberly knew her parents would never agree or understand. They seemed to want to keep her in their cocoon, keep her close, and keep her a child. Three months later, the weekend of her nineteenth birthday, Kimberly informed her parents she was going to a woman's retreat in Tennessee. After enjoying her usual birthday dinner and cake with her family and close friends, Donna, her best friend, took her to the airport. When Kimberly checked in at the American Airlines ticket counter, she changed her final destination from Memphis, TN to Meridian, MS. Wesley met her at Meridian Regional Airport. He'd rented a car and a motel room, and instantly, he surprised her with a marriage proposal.

Kimberly was thrilled to be asked and to know she wasn't going to be an old-maid. She did feel bad knowing her parents set aside money in a special account for her dream wedding, but Wesley must truly love her to want to marry her even before they slept together and at this moment, making Wesley happy mattered more than any of her own reservations. Harvey and Gwendolyn McMillan knew Wesley's name, that he was in the military and that Wesley called Kimberly on a regular basis, but they had no idea their daughter was completely head-over-heels about this man. Kimberly navigated her teenage years and the drama of high school so well that they didn't worry about her being sensible when it came to men or dating. Over the years, Kimberly introduced them to several boyfriends, and on more than one occasion, she told her mother the reason she broke up with a boy was because he was pressuring her to become more intimate with him. There was no reason for them to believe her relationship with Wesley was any different especially now that she was older.

One month after the secret wedding and weekend honeymoon, Wesley was granted a two-week leave for Christmas. He assured Kimberly he could hardly wait to see her and spend all of his time in California with his bride. Kimberly was proud to bring him home to meet her family, but the visit was a total disaster. Harvey McMillan wasn't impressed with Wesley and thought the young man was self-centered and prideful. Some of the stories he told them sounded farfetched or had to be outright fabrications. Gwendolyn pulled Kimberly aside. She thought Wesley was far too worldly and not a good influence on her. The evening came to a crashing end when Wesley announced he and Kim were married and her parents might as well get used to the fact their daughter was now his wife, so her father and mother's concerns didn't matter.

Kimberly walked around shell-shocked the rest of the evening. She packed a bag and left with Wesley because she did not know what had just happened. The newlyweds spent Christmas together, alone at a hotel. It was the most miserable holiday Kimberly could ever remember; there were no family or friends or parties or special food and festivities, and worse of all, by spending so much time alone with Wesley, she began to realize he wasn't interested in anything she had to say. When Kimberly thought nothing could hurt anymore than what happened in the last two weeks, Wesley told her that her parents were fools for participating in organized religion. He was quick to lay down the law as her husband: he would never allow his wife or any child of theirs to go to church or be around those hypocritical grandparents on a regular basis.

Wesley returned to the base after the Christmas holidays. He left a heartbroken and depressed wife with her friend Donna. Kimberly was too embarrassed to go back home and face her parents who were still reeling with the knowledge that 'the devil was in the camp,' and their baby was married to a heathen. *Where had they gone wrong?*

On Sundays when Kimberly knew her parents would be at church, she went back to their house to get more clothes. She was careful to leave before they returned. On the last Sunday of the month, Kimberly went into her bedroom to pack some clothes into a suitcase when she noticed an unopened envelope on her pillow. She realized then she wasn't fooling anyone. Her mother must have known Kimberly was coming to the house when they were gone.

The return address on the envelope was Wesley's address and she tore it open. His unit, the 32nd Air Refueling Squadron, was probably already on their way to Iraq. The letter confirmed it, but she gasped when she read the last paragraph.

Things aren't working out between us Kim. Your lack of education, and because of your parents brainwashing you all these years, has ruined any chance of you being the kind of wife I need, so consider this time apart our official separation. I'll file for divorce when I get back Stateside or you can get the papers started. Take comfort in the fact that you'll get over this and over me and marry some drone like your father. Our first six months together were fun. That's what I'll remember. Wesley

Kimberly was so angry she couldn't cry for several minutes. When the tears finally came they were hot, angry tears. She understood why a person would commit murder because if Wesley J. Miller was in her presence and she had a weapon, she would not have hesitated to end his life. Everything her parents and friends said about him was true and Kimberly felt violated and used. Wesley knew what he was doing. He took her mind, then her virginity. He didn't love her at all. She was the stupid sheep going to slaughter, and he was the crafty wolf in sheep's clothing. It was all crystal-clear to her now. Divide and conquer. Separate her from her loved ones. He wasn't the devil, but she could hear the devil laughing at her. Kimberly was still thinking about what she was going to write in answer to Wesley's letter when the doorbell rang.

Her first thought was to pretend no one was home, but her car was in the driveway and it was time to stop hiding. Kimberly wiped her eyes and hurried downstairs to answer the front door. Just like in the movies two men dressed in uniform stood on her parent's porch.

"Hello ma'am. I'm Sergeant Crawford. This is Sergeant Long of Columbia AFB. We're looking for Mrs. Kimberly Miller?"

Kimberly opened the screen door and stepped outside. "I'm Kimberly." She showed them to the wicker chairs on the wide porch, and they all sat down.

The men gently and politely told her that her husband, Wesley Johan Miller, had been killed in the line of duty. Kimberly only heard parts of the rest of what they told her, but as his wife, she was Wesley's next-of-kin and beneficiary.

Wesley gone? Dead? She was angry with how he treated her and wondered what she would say to him when she saw him again. But now, that would never happen. She hadn't wished him dead (except by her own hand in retaliation). While the men talked, Kimberly twisted her white gold wedding band.

Since the young widow seemed to be taking the news very well, the soldiers gave her details about when and where the body would be returned. Apparently, Wesley had no other family and the only burial instructions he gave were that he was to be cremated and his ashes spread at sea in the Gulf of Mexico. Kimberly thanked the officers for coming, accepted their condolences, and she remained on her parent's porch trying to absorb and process the events of the last hour.

Ignoring her nervous excitement, Kimberly slid into the booth next to Keith. "Keith. It's so good to see you." She turned to the man sitting across from them, "I'm Kimberly."

"My pleasure Kimberly. I'm Keith's uncle Chris," Chris said and shook her extended hand.

"I think I met you a long time ago at the Dennis' annual beach party…It was a birthday party that year."

"Yes. I was there. That was in my surfing days," Chris said and began telling them behind-the-scene stories about the day of the beach party. He and Kimberly kept the conversation going especially when she mentioned being a Lakers' fan. Chris was a die-hard fan of the Boston Celtics. The trash talking continued until they turned to Keith and asked him which team was better.

Keith smiled, leaned back and put his arm around the back of the padded booth and said, "No question. The L.A. Lakers."

Chris sneered while Kimberly clapped her hands and grinned at Keith. Chris pretended to be disgusted and got up from the table, "I'll be back." He walked toward the restrooms that were located near the hostess station and Debby, the cute little hostess.

Keith downed the last of his orange juice then turned toward Kimberly. His blue-green eyes took in every detail of her face, "What have you been doing these last six years?"

Kimberly smiled, "A lot has happened since we last talked." She sighed took a deep breath and said, "I met a military man, we dated briefly, got married…"

Keith stifled a groan. He finally noticed the wedding ring on her hand.

"It wasn't working out, but before we divorced, he was killed in Iraq."

"I'm so sorry," Keith said. *Kimberly, lonely widow or much sought after hottie?* She was even more beautiful than he remembered, and he had to stop himself from staring: olive colored skin …warm brown eyes.

"Thank you. It was strange how it happened and how you never know the last time you'll talk to some one is really the last time. He wasn't a Christian…"

"What?" Keith exclaimed. The Kimberly he knew was a sold-out Bible believing Christian and daughter of a Christian pastor, "What did your father say?"

"My parents were disappointed of course, but not more than I am to be almost twenty-five years old and just starting to get back their trust. What did I know then? I was young. Career-wise, I've fallen behind because the whole situation depressed me for so long I couldn't concentrate in my college classes, so I stopped going. I ended up working minimum wage jobs for a few years. After listening to me complain about my boring and unfulfilled life, my parents sat me down and we had a serious talk. They helped me see I was the one who needed to change, and that I was the only one in charge of my life. They've really been great about everything, so after the talk and lots of prayer, I made a plan and went back to school. I stuck with it and now I have my Associate Arts degree in Liberal Studies from Los Angeles City College."

"Congratulations Kim. That's a very good start," Keith said. "What are your plans now?"

Kimberly looked away, overcome with emotion. Keith had always been a good listener. He really cared about her. She smiled up at him and wondered why his face flushed before he broke eye contact.

"I volunteer at View Park Library and on Saturdays I teach an ESL class, that's English as a Second Language. I found that I love teaching adults, so I'll be back in school at Cal State LA in the fall and after I graduate, in a couple of years, I'll be a credentialed teacher."

"Impressive," Keith said. "I'm glad you're back on track but I wonder…"

"What?" Kimberly asked.

"What about guys, boyfriends? You haven't sworn off men after one bad relationship have you?"

Kimberly laughed and shook her head, "Not exactly."

"Are you dating anyone special?" Keith asked touching her ring finger.

"The question should be am I dating at all and the answer is no," Kimberly said. "I have a hard time trusting anyone especially someone I don't really know. I just keep all men on a friendship level. I wear my wedding bands to keep strangers at a distance. Not that I have much time to go out. Working here and at the library sums up my social life. I spend the rest of my time studying or helping out at the church."

"Are your parents doing well?" Keith asked trying to ignore the heaviness crowding his heart.

"They're great. How is your father doing? I really like him," Kimberly said.

Keith told her the story of the last twenty-four hours, and he was careful to leave any mention of Trish out of the conversation. Kimberly was visibly shaken by his news.

"Why didn't you tell me this at first?" She exclaimed and pulled her cell phone out of her shirt pocket. After talking to her mother she set the phone on the table. "My Mom said to tell you they're starting a prayer chain right away to pray for your father's recovery. It's almost six o'clock. I'm telling you personally that I've seen prayer change things. Just remember that and give me your telephone number, so I can keep in touch."

Keith obeyed, relieved he didn't have to bear this burden alone and glad someone else was concerned about what was weighing on his heart. Uncle Chris was with him, but he was even more lost than Keith when it came to spiritual matters. Kimberly leaned in close to Keith to give him a hug to comfort him. She held onto him a few heartbeats longer and he rested his cheek on her head with his arms around her. He could have held her like this all night. Kimberly felt safe in his arms, and she believed he could be trusted…with her heart.

She sat back up just as Chris came back to the table. "I have to get back to work, but see me before you leave. My Mom wants you and your uncle to come over for lunch or dinner or both."

"Okay," Keith said. He thought of the Rev. and Mrs. McMillan with fondness. "Tell her thank you for me." He was feeling much better; a complete turnaround since he got the terrible news that his father was shot and his life was hanging in the balance. Kimberly made him feel, no matter the final outcome, that they were in this together.

Chapter 10

Phillip Covers watched Nichelle while she walked up to her front door, unlocked it and went inside. When the porch light flicked on then off, indicating she was safely inside, Phillip drove away slowly observing the quiet and peaceful atmosphere of the middle-class South Los Angeles neighborhood. It was hard to believe that a few blocks away was gang territory just like it was to believe that Nichelle and Heavenly Evers were related, much less sisters, because Nichelle was all hood and Heavenly was all lady.

Through no fault of her own, Heavenly possessed a body that aroused or resurrected the fantasy life of most men. She was one hundred percent female with a husky voice that could thrive on late night radio. Oddly enough, Heavenly didn't date very often because her regal charm intimidated men from CEOs to thugs.

If Heavenly remembered Phillip Covers, she never let on, but she would direct him to the elevators in the same professional manner as always, but each time Phillip heard her sultry voice, he broke out in a cold sweat. Heavenly was good at her job because she made it her business to know where every office was located in the high rise. It didn't bother her to go to lunch by herself every day because most of her female co-workers were jealous of her effect on the opposite sex. That was their problem.

At twenty-one years old, Heavenly was proud to be holding down a desk job and making enough money to afford the lease on an apartment in a newly renovated up-and-coming area near downtown. The apartment was on the second of ten floors and came partially furnished because the last tenant left in a hurry.

The landlord was glad to forgo the expense of hiring movers to remove the living and dining room furniture and having to either sell or store it, after Heavenly told him she would keep the furniture. When she agreed to clean the place herself and paint the walls, he waived the twenty-five dollar-a-month cost off a reserved parking space. In spite of the furniture looking new, Heavenly sprayed the couch and loveseat with *Febreze*, and then she covered both of them with solid black slip covers she purchased from *Bed, Bath and Beyond*.

She loved the high ceilings and exposed brick in her apartment's entry way and chose sophisticated colors for the other walls—black and roast coffee brown. Her signature color was pink. Heavenly bought black, brown, and pink fabric from Joann's Fabric store and made throw pillows for the couches and a matching runner for the dining room table. She used her fifteen percent-off *Michael's* coupon to buy picture frames and covered them with the leftover fabric using her glue gun to secure the ends. After studying the walls, she chose just the right unframed art to put into her frames and the result was splashes of color throughout the apartment.

Her favorite room was the bathroom. Even though the walls and cabinets were plain white, this room housed a Jacuzzi tub and separate shower. This was her sanctuary, so Heavenly made it as girly as possible with pink and white accessories.

Heavenly painted three of her bedroom walls white. The remaining accent wall was painted cocoa brown. This was the wall where she put her new bedroom set from *IKEA*. When she was a girl, Heavenly dreamed of having a sleigh bed and when she saw the perfect bedroom set in white-washed pine, on-line, she ordered it in Glazed Blonde, queen size. Heavenly was saving up to buy lamps to put on the nightstands, but until then she accessorized the furniture using large white candles placed in crystal vases. The bedding she purchased from *Anna's Linens* was a pink, brown, and white comforter set that coordinated and pulled together all of the colors in the room.

Even now, seven months after moving in, Heavenly thought the room was feminine enough for her, but not so much that it would make a man feel uncomfortable. That is, if she ever invited one back to her place.

She liked living among the white folks, where it was quiet and the neighbors, for the most part they kept to themselves. There were so many rules about noise and guests that any party in this building would have to be pretty dull. The one exception was the annual meet-and-greet Independence Day party for new tenants. It was held on the roof of the building every 4th of July. Tea lights were strung all around the perimeter and lawn chairs lined the four walls. Soft music from a few strategically placed speakers served as background noise and a hosted bar in the middle of everything kept the bartender busy. A long buffet table next to the bar was covered with a table cloth that looked like an American flag. It was filled with platters of hot and cold finger-foods along with red and blue paper plates, matching cups and white plastic forks.

While the sun descended toward the horizon, fifty-or-so tenants of the building milled about or sat around and talked. The tenants were more diverse than Heavenly originally thought. She noticed three other Black people, four Hispanics, two Asians, and ten other people that if she had to guess their ancestry, it would have been a mixture of the previous four. The majority of the rest were 100% white and most looked to be of social security age, from the era when full retirement was age sixty-five and the parting gift from the company for a job well done was a gold watch.

Heavenly met a few of her neighbors then wished she hadn't because they proceeded to tell her all of the building's gossip including scandals of people who were no longer living in the building. Heavenly wanted to live away from problems, heartaches, and headaches. She didn't have to pretend to not feel well after the non-stop talking of two women who'd been in the apartment building the longest and felt it their duty to share with the newcomers.

Because their building was positioned at the top of the street, it had an awesome view of the city and it was fun to see, from their vantage point, the firework displays in the distance, in miniature. When it was totally dark and most of the tenants were looking at the lights in the sky, Heavenly left the gathering early and was back inside her own apartment in time to finish reading the Book of Esther in her *Bible*, then turned on the television.

Heavenly was a list maker and kept several lists in a 3-ring binder she called her Goal Binder. The bold and bright colored binder was probably intended for pre-teens, but it was perfect for keeping her lists organized. While listening to the monologue of *The Tonight Show*, she turned the pages until she got to the letter M for Man of My Dreams. This list was memorized, but Heavenly enjoyed going over it because she believed someday her dream man was going to walk through her front door. She had never met such a man growing up, but over the years, she saw enough trifling men in her life to know what she didn't want. Bold letters with the words 'HE WILL' were on the top of the front page and on the list was: Have a good job, a place to live, a decent car, an education past high school, know how to dress, like to dress up (sometimes), talk nice, know how to pray, know what the Bible says, enjoy church, love God, want kids, love his mother, love me. The backside of the page was the words 'HE WON'T'. She read the back side too in case there was something she needed to add. He won't be lazy, stingy, a gambler, a player or ghetto fabulous, raise his voice to me or talk rough, cuss in my presence, drink too much, fight, smoke, cheat on me, or want me to be less than I am.

Satisfied with her list, she closed the binder and thought about her own mother. Janine Evers, who never seemed to have a man of her own and was willing to accept a piece-of-man from time to time. She did try to protect her daughters as much as possible by never allowing any of her acquaintances, no matter how well she thought she knew him, to be alone in the house with her girls. Janine would have been appalled to know how many times her so-called man-friends stopped back by the house when she wasn't home. Nichelle and Heavenly never opened the door, but they did talk to whoever it was through the mail slot. In spite of what they were promised, the girls knew the person was lying if he told them their mother said it was okay for him to come inside and wait for her to get home.

If the man persisted, Nichelle would go to the telephone and call their neighbor, Miss Bessie Mae Baker. Miss Bessie Mae would poke her head outside the door across the hall and stare the man down. He would either leave or sheepishly give the older woman the gift he brought for the girls. Sometimes it was candy or ice cream or money, but Heavenly never liked taking anything from them. Intuitively, she knew something was wrong with the man's intent because of the queasiness she felt in her stomach. Nichelle gladly took the whole "gift" and sometimes paid the price after eating too much chocolate or ice cream. Heavenly would go to her room and do homework or read a chapter in her favorite book to take her mind off the incident. Sometimes she would start dinner and make a salad or heat up a can of green beans on the stovetop because their mother cautioned them about using matches to light the ancient stove, especially when Janine wasn't there.

In Heavenly's opinion, life was better when the aunts came. It was the year she turned ten-years old. Janine knew she had to do something because her girls were growing up fast and she saw how Heavenly was taking after her side of the family and developing physically much faster than her older sister. Nichelle at twelve-years old wasn't happy having to share a bedroom with her sister and complained that three was a crowd and five was way too much.

Ella Dean and Angelene moved in with them after Janine moved into a bigger apartment on the ground floor. It was an eye-opener and education in the lives of the two young girls, and Heavenly began to dream big. Aunt Ella Dean had buried two husbands and had lived in a house she and her last latest husband bought. Heavenly was very impressed that her aunt had been a homeowner for several years before her last husband died. Then some fast-talking financier talked the widow into refinancing her house and pulling all of the equity out of it so she could put the money to work for her.

Since the house was paid for and valued at four hundred thousand dollars in 2006, Ella Dean put the money in a bank account that was set up to automatically pay the new mortgage while drawing interest on the remaining balance. It was a good plan as long as the economy was in an upturn, but in 2008, the value of the house dropped to two hundred fifty thousand dollars. The variable rate increased to double digits and Ella Dean could see her mortgage payment was going to drain her bank account of all the money, and she'd still owe the balance on a house that wasn't worth the balance of the loan amount.

Aunt Angelene worked for several years as a pastry cook at San Marino's Family Restaurant. She lived next door to the restaurant in a small two-bedroom cottage owned by the San Marino family. This was convenient in more ways than one since Angelene was having an affair with the restaurant owner, Simon San Marino. In 2008, Simon's wife, Clara San Marino finally had enough of her husband's adultery and stabbed him. The affair between Simon and Angelene abruptly ended after Simon recovered from the stab wound and decided he wanted to live more than he wanted a mistress, so he tearfully fired Angelene and sent her packing. Angelene moved in with Ella Dean. The dilemma of what to do about the house still loomed over the sisters because neither of them was working.

Ella Dean decided to put the residence up for sale, but offers came in well below what was owed on the house. Their younger sister Janine told them a 3-bedroom apartment had just been vacated in her building. If they could come up with five hundred dollars a month, they could move in with her and help her care for their nieces. Ella Dean had never worked outside the home, but she was a great organizer. She and Angelene could start a baking business. Angelene could make all kinds of fabulous pastries, pies, cakes, cookies, and cupcakes while Ella Dean would package the products and sell them door-to-door and to local businesses. Ella Dean estimated they could make a thousand dollars a week and would net a seventy-five percent profit.

Ella Dean closed her bank account and used the money to open a joint account with her sisters at the Southern California Credit Union. She informed the holder of her mortgage that the house now belonged to them and she had no forwarding address.

Ella Dean put all of her furniture in storage, and while the new apartment was empty, she supervised the patching and painting. Most of the rooms were freshly painted white, but she struck a deal with the landlord and was allowed to put different colors on the walls. The kitchen was brightened up with a buttery soft yellow. The living, dining room, and second bathroom were painted soothing ice-blue. The girl's new room color was mauve, a compromise of the purple Nichelle liked and Heavenly's favorite color, pink. Their mother's room was already light tan, a color Ella Dean approved, but the master bedroom and adjoining bathroom got a fresh coat of paint anyway. The room the aunt's shared ended up with a relaxing shade of pale green called First of Spring.

When the paint was dry Ella Dean organized a yard sale and sold all of Janine's old furniture. She filled the new apartment with antiques and expensive furniture and window treatments from her storage unit.

While Ella Dean was a master decorator and planner, her sister Angelene took over the kitchen and cooking duties. She was known for her baking, but Angelene cooked all food with a Southern flare. Butter, eggs, and whole milk were staples, as was homemade gravy smothered over pork chops, ham hocks to season collard or mustard greens, and at every meal, yeast rolls, biscuits or corn bread, made from scratch. Angelene at five foot-five inches tall was an even unashamed, three hundred pounds. As far as she was concerned, she could cook better than any woman who starved herself skinny, and that the way to a man's heart was through his stomach.

While Angelene was making a peach cobbler, Janine sat in the kitchen with her while lamenting over Heavenly needing a D cup already. Angelene personally grew out of triple D's during high school over thirty years ago and in her book a D cup was practically flat-chested.

She laughed and held up her rolling pin, "She only needs *one* D? Please. I'll take her with me to Margene's. That woman can measure you and make a bra to fit. She can get girdles and shapers too. Not that I need one. This is my shaper." Angelene held up the pie tin and then set it down and placed the thin butter-filled crust inside.

Remembering how it was to grow up with her aunts made Heavenly smile. Being around them boosted her self-esteem even before she knew her self-esteem needed boosting. Ella Dean helped her know what was coming as far as men folk were concerned. She took her nieces to church with her on Sundays and sometimes Bible Study during the week. Angelene taught the girls to cook and told Heavenly to not let anyone make her ashamed of what God gave her.

Miss Margene wasn't making ladies underwear anymore, but Heavenly stopped by her house to say hello whenever she found herself on the eastside of Los Angeles.

Chapter 11

$\mathcal{G}$wendolyn stood at the window and watched the young man park his car at the curb in front of their house. She clasped her hands, "Keith! Honey, its Keith Dennis."

Harvey folded his newspaper, set it down and went to stand next to his wife who was gazing at Keith with joyous rapture. Harvey wouldn't admit it to anyone, but he was excited to see Keith too. It had been part of his daily prayers for his daughter to have a good, loving, Christian young man to be apart of her life and of all the boyfriends, Kimberly ever introduced to him, he genuinely liked Keith the most.

"It's Keith!" She said again.

"I know dear. I can see him," Harvey replied.

Gwendolyn couldn't take it anymore. She opened the screen door and hurried down the front stairs to greet their visitor. She hugged him tightly for a moment before holding him at arm's length. "I'm so glad to see you. Oh, you poor boy. How is your father doing today?"

"Hi Mrs. Mc; Sir." Keith said. "My father's condition is stable." She walked him up the stairs and back toward the house with her arm wrapped securely around his.

"Hello, son," Harvey said. Rather than extending his hand, Harvey embraced the two of them briefly then he turned to open the screen door. "Come on in."

"My uncle might join us later," Keith said.

"Oh, don't you worry about that. It's a shame Kimberly has to work or she would be here too," Gwendolyn said. She let his arm go so he could sit down in one of the Queen Anne arm chairs. "When Kim told us she saw you I could hardly believe it. It's been years since we've seen you."

"Yes, ma'am. I haven't been home very often. I've been away at school in Oregon," Keith said.

"Go Ducks," Harvey said, "although I'm not happy they beat USC last season."

Gwendolyn waved her hand at her husband. "You can talk sports later." She turned to Keith, "Tell me about your studies."

"I graduated from the University of Oregon two years ago with a BA in English."

Gwendolyn looked away from Keith to her husband. "Harvey, Keith has his bachelor's degree in English," Gwendolyn exclaimed.

"Yes, dear. I heard," Harvey said.

"I just completed my Masters in Conflict and Dispute Resolution."

"Harvey!" Gwendolyn said.

"Yes, dear. He has his Masters."

"And…"

"There's more?" Gwendolyn asked. Her voice was an octave higher than normal.

"Yes, ma'am. I've been accepted at Stanford Law School, and I start in the fall," Keith said.

Gwendolyn burst into tears, "I'm just so happy for you." She stood up and hurried from the room.

Keith looked at Harvey who shrugged.

"She'll be alright," Harvey said. He was accustomed to his extremely excitable wife—the original drama queen. She would cry and praise God for a while then be back to serve lunch. The men continued talking and catching up on their lives.

"You're still doing summer camps?" Keith asked.

"Yes. I enjoy spending that one-on-one time with the youngsters," Harvey said. "It gives them a chance to see me as just a man instead of a reverend in a robe."

Keith nodded. It was true. It was the church sponsored summer camp Keith attended which helped him realize the pastor and his family were regular people. That was the summer he and Kimberly got to know each other very well. Thirteen-year old Keith started hanging around the McMillan house almost every day, so much that when he didn't come over, they called his house or sent Kimberly over to the Dennis house to make sure everything was okay.

Kimberly agreed to be Keith's girlfriend at the end of that summer after Keith assured her that he only expected a kiss from her and only when they were alone. He really wanted to keep her away from other boys who talked about all of the kind of nasty things they wanted to do with and to girls. Keith only expected to kiss her cheek or hand, but after her verbal commitment, Kimberly surprised him with a full lip-lock. The kiss was sweet and exciting at the same time. What she started, he finished by grabbing her head in his hands to lock her into a position, so they could keep on kissing. After a minute of passionate bliss, she fell limp in his arms.

"I didn't know…you could kiss…like that," She panted. Like what? Keith didn't know what he was doing other than what felt natural. Kimberly must have mentioned the kiss to her noisy friends because several girls at school started to smile at him. Not regular smiles, but knowing looks and winks when Kimberly wasn't looking. Keith didn't like it. His guy friends slapped him on the back and asked him what it was like. They were so immature, but as long as they didn't mention Kimberly's name in their sleazy conversation, he wouldn't have to pound any of them to a pulp.

That year, Reverend McMillan was transferred to another and larger parish and moved his family to the San Fernando Valley to the Church of Christ of Santa Clarita. It was almost fifty miles away from Los Angeles. Kimberly and Keith talked on the phone and by e-mail, but both were active in sports and afterschool clubs at their respective high schools and eventually their communication dwindled to every other month. They never formally broke up, but it was implied, as the two of them let the priorities of their high school activities superseded their relationship.

"You both look well," Keith said. "The longer I stay in town the more I miss it and the people."

"We missed seeing you too," Harvey said. "I guess Kimberly told you about her deceased husband?"

"Yes. I was shocked when she told me he wasn't a Christian," Keith said.

Harvey nodded. "She was young and naïve and Wesley was a fast talker."

It still didn't make it right and Keith wished he could have put his fist in Wesley's face for hurting Kimberly.

"Are you dating anybody special?" Harvey asked.

Keith couldn't look him in the eye, but he knew better than to lie to God's man. "I was. I'm not sure," Keith said and told Harvey about the telephone call to Trish that he made earlier. While Harvey talked, Keith replayed the call to Trish in his head.

"Have you been trying to call me?" Keith asked.

"No. I was waiting for you to call me back," Trish replied. "Remember you said you were going to call me. So how is your father?"

"He's stable right now. My uncle Chris is here with me." *And if you loved me you would be here too.*

"I'm glad you're not alone."

"Are you alone?" Keith asked.

"What do you mean?" Trish said.

"Just what I said. Are you alone? Have you been with anyone since I've been away?"

"I don't like what you're insinuating."

"You didn't answer my question."

"Are you interrogating me?"

"Trish, do you really want to move with me to California?"

"Where is this coming from? Don't you want me to move with you?"

"Why are you answering my questions with other questions? Why can't you answer me?"

"Keith," Trish said, choosing her words carefully, "I know you're upset about your father. I would be too, but I think you're misplacing your anger and frustration and directing it to me."

"Maybe I am, so we'll talk later," Keith said and ended the call.

"Just like you were shocked when Kimberly married a non-believer, don't you think God feels the same concern about you?" Harvey asked. "You know what the Word of God says about cohabitating with a woman who isn't your wife, so why would you make plans to do it?"

Keith sighed, "It seemed like the next logical step in our relationship. I thought we would be compatible roommates, and maybe get married some day."

"That's fine for the world, son. They don't know any better. You accepted Jesus Christ and were baptized years ago. You helped teach Sunday school, so I know you know the Word teaches us not to be unequally yoked with an unbeliever. Your job is to be the salt and light and to tell others the truth. By living like the world, you are not letting your light shine," Harvey said.

Keith nodded. He looked the pastor in the eye knowing he wasn't judging him. Keith accepted the righteous instruction imparted to him from a man he respected.

"You're taking the broad, easy way by planning to live with her and ignoring the narrow, straight path."

"You're right, sir."

"You don't seem to trust this young lady either..."

"Are you two ready for lunch?" Gwendolyn reappeared. She had calmed herself and was ready to resume her role as hostess.

Harvey smiled at his wife and told Keith, "We'll talk more later."

The men washed their hands and came to the table. It was already set with white china and crystal goblets. Gwendolyn was in her element and served their plates heaped high with oven-fried chicken and garlic mashed potatoes. The string beans and corn were from her garden.

After her husband blessed the food, she filled their glasses with ice and fresh squeezed lemonade. Gwendolyn passed the gravy boat and platter of toasted garlic bread. Dessert was a slice of *Mrs. Smith's* Dutch Apple pie warm from the oven and topped with a scoop of French-vanilla ice cream along with ice coffee served in ice cream sundae glasses. After dessert, Gwendolyn set out bowls of watermelon slices and grapes while she cleared the table. Keith insisted on helping with the dishes while Harvey fell asleep in his lounge chair.

"I have a dishwasher, but I still prefer to wash the dishes by hand when I have the time," Gwendolyn said. She put on a pair of bright yellow rubber gloves. "I like to look out over the garden." Their house was built on the edge of a half acre of land. One-forth of an acre was set aside for Gwendolyn's vegetable and flower garden.

"It's just like I remember when I was a kid," Keith said looking out of the kitchen window. "You always did have a green thumb."

Gwendolyn beamed. "I like taking care of the plants, but I sure don't miss having to take care of the animals." She grew up on a farm, and even after moving to the city, she kept a rooster and a few chickens to have fresh eggs and meat. "I shop at the local Farmer's Markets, so I can get food fresh from the farm. It's a shame what they sell in stores today and call food. Young people even know what real fruit tastes like."

Keith smiled while she talked and carefully dried each dish. His mind drifted to his own mother and how she never got to see him grow into manhood. She was thirty-one when she died. So young. Too young. He mentally shook himself before his mood turned melancholy. It was stressful enough to stay positive while dealing with his hospitalized father. Keith's cell phone vibrated in his shirt pocket.

"Excuse me, Ms. Mc," Keith said and put the dry towel on the empty drainer. "Hello? Yes. I remember you Nurse Catherine."

Gwendolyn stopped cleaning the baking dish and took off her gloves. She set them aside and left the room to give Keith some privacy. She went into the living room and sat on the couch across from her sleeping husband and sent up a quick prayer for Wade Dennis and that his son was receiving good news.

After a moment Keith stood in the doorway. "I'm going back to the hospital."

Gwendolyn gripped the arms of her chair and sat forward.

At the sound of Keith's voice Harvey awoke and sat upright, "Is everything alright?"

"Yes, sir. My father is awake. They took him off life support this morning and he's conscious," Keith said. He smiled and Gwendolyn rushed to him and gave him a hug.

"Thank God," she said.

"Thank you, Jesus." he replied.

"I'll drive you," Harvey said. He didn't ask, just walked directly into the mud room off the kitchen and grabbed his jacket from a hook on the wall.

"Oh yes. Drive him," Gwendolyn insisted. "I'll be on the phone calling the prayer warriors."

Keith followed obediently. Once he was seated inside the Lincoln

Town Car, he called his Uncle Chris and left a message to meet them at the hospital. Thank God they would soon see Wade Dennis living and breathing on his own, but the question remained: *Who shot him?*

Chapter 12

Nichelle threw her lottery ticket in the trash can. It was frustrating to know that none of her numbers came up. She would make a great winner for the commercial and throw the best party in L.A. with her first check. All the Big-Baller-Shot-Callers would be invited and she would hold court in the VIP section. Nick Cannon could come in but not his wife, that Mariah "too much cleavage" Carey.

Digging inside the box in Glenda's closet again, she pulled out a two-piece lime green linen Capri set. It was a size 8 with the tag still attached. Perfect. She would have something new to wear when she met with her friends Charm and Brandi at the *Bridge de Lux* movie theater near Fox Hills. Charm, like her name, tried to talk Nichelle into using Glenda's car to pick them up, but Glenda was funny about her car. She actually kept track of the mileage on the 2002 Cadillac Fleetwood, and Nichelle had a feeling Glenda would be showing up back home sooner rather than later and Nichelle didn't need to be job hunting because Charm wanted to ride in the Lac.

It was hard to miss the shiny gold everything Charm was wearing. Her gold lame jogging suit complete with a hood, hugged her hour glass figure like it was designed for her. Being four inches shy of six feet tall, Charm could get away with wearing gold ballet slippers and still look long and sleek. Her long gold-colored fingernails were freshly applied from *Perfection Nail Salon* and she styled her honey blonde hair with a French roll in the back and curly blonde bangs over her forehead.

Brandi was always on a diet except when she went out with her friends or late at night. She always dressed conservatively in jumpers or women-size pants. Her friend, Charm, would always get by on her looks, savvy nerve and as a bonus she was light skinned. Nichelle could eat anything and stay skinny, so she could rock any style of clothes, but Brandi's oversized body needed dark colors, so as not to highlight her girth. It wasn't fair except she was the voice of reason and thought of herself as the brains of the group; more sophisticated and smart than Charm or Nichelle.

"Oh, girl. I like that," Charm said when Nichelle approached them.

Nichelle model-walked past them a few times, so they could check her out head to toe then took an empty seat at the outside table. She picked up Charm's Styrofoam cup, took a sip because Brandi would have a cow if you touched her food.

"What's up bitches?" Nichelle said.

Brandi frowned, "You know I don't like that word."

"Then why'd you answer?' Nichelle replied and she and Charm laughed.

Brandi said nothing, but picked up her cup of chocolate malt. She looked away pretending not to care that Nichelle got the better of her. That was the way it went with the three of them, but before the day was over, they were going to need her.

"Are you going to the Hoodie Awards?" Charm asked. "It's in Las

Vegas in August. If we buy our tickets to the awards show, we can get a cheap room somewhere else. With the money we save from that expensive hotel package, we can gamble and if we play enough the hotel will give us an upgrade on our room."

"Or we can meet some single guys and let them foot the bill for being in our company," Nichelle added, and then looked at Brandi, "Well, a couple of us can."

"They have outlet stores in Vegas too," Brandi said ignoring the dig.

"How would we get there?" Charm asked.

It was a good question. It was an oxymoron to travel to Las Vegas looking fabulous on the Greyhound bus and if they flew in, it meant no spending money once they arrived.

"Don't you know anyone else going?"Nichelle asked her companions. She took their silence as a "no."

"Maybe we could go on a turn-around trip," Brandi said. "I've seen some trips where you pay twenty dollars and take a bus with a bunch of other people. The bus stops at gambling spots along the way. We could get off at our hotel and just not get back on the bus."

"That's a good idea Brandi. Your Mama should have named you Brainy," Charm said.

"Or half-brain." Nichelle said. "How are we going to get back?"

"We could find a way back. We could hitch a ride…" Charm said.

"No!" Brandi and Nichelle replied together. It was the one thing they could agree on. No more hitching rides. The last time Charm flagged down a car, it ended up in a high-speed chase. The car was stolen, and they almost spend the night in jail. After they convinced the police they had nothing to do with the stolen car, they were released but Nichelle sued the City of Bellflower for the injuries sustained when the police officer, who was chasing the driver on foot, pushed her out of the way and she fell to the ground. The case was settled out-of-court and provided Nichelle with tax-free income for a year. She wanted to cry when the automatic monthly payments ended.

"I don't mean stand on the strip and hitch a ride," Charm said. "While we're at the awards we can ask around. With all those people coming in to Vegas for the Hoodies, and I'm sure we can find someone coming back to L.A."

"Maybe," Brandi said.

"Damn. I might not be able to go," Nichelle said. Philly told her to let him know if she left the city. Not the state, the city. Unless she told him it was work related and she was going to see Glenda. No. That wouldn't work because Glenda wasn't supposed to be in Las Vegas either. But if Glenda was in Las Vegas on vacation and her home health aide was needed...

"Come on," Charm said. She stood up from her seat and walked quickly toward the movie theatre. Without question, Brandi and Nichelle followed.

The front theater walls were made up of forty foot high glass panes. A man dressed in a dark blue jumpsuit stood on the inside by one of the doors. When they reached the front of the theater, he opened the door and stood aside. Nichelle had never formally met the guy, but Charm told her he was her play-cousin Trey and that's all she needed to know. Trey worked on-call for the janitorial and maintenance crew at the Bridge theatre. He was the man to know, when his supervisor wasn't around, because Trey was willing to let his friends and special acquaintances sneak into the movies for free.

They ducked into the first theatre. Previews were showing. Charm led the way and they stopped in the middle of the stairway. As their eyes adjusted to the darkened room, Charm could see her favorite seats in the dead center were taken. She went up a step and into the isle right behind the person who had "her seat." She would find a way to cross her legs several times and kick the seat in front of her to punish them unless the movie was good enough to distract her.

As the previews continued, Charm nudged Brandi. "Go get us some snacks."

Brandi frowned, "Why me?"

"You keep saying you want to exercise and get in shape. I'm trying to help you," Charm said.

Nichelle snickered.

Brandi scooted to the edge of her seat, "I only have ten dollars."

Charm pulled some money out of her pocket. "Here's a five. Remember I got you in for free. I saved you ten dollars so this five is like I'm giving you fifteen."

"What about her?" Brandi said motioning to Nichelle.

Nichelle didn't know why Brandi was so cheap. She had a decent job as a teacher's assistant at Thirty-seventh Street School and worked in a classroom full of fourth graders. It would be the perfect job if it weren't for all those kids. Brandi still lived at home with her parents and younger brother all of whom were working full-time jobs. Their household income had to be over five thousand dollars a month and here was Brandi nickel-and-diming her for stupid snacks at a movie that she got into for free.

"Here," Nichelle said. She reached across Charm and pressed some currency into Brandi's hand. Nichelle dared Brandi to say something about it once she saw the amount. "Bring me lemonade or fruit punch and some popcorn. Put lots of butter on mine."

While standing in line pouting, Brandi studied the menu boards. She decided on a number 3-combo, a large Diet Pepsi with nachos and cheese for herself. It made her smile too, after buying two kid-packs consisting of a small bag of popcorn, a small drink and a small bag of gummy chews for her friends. If Charm complained, Brandi might share the giant-size Snickers bar in her purse because Charm did get her into the movie for free, but for two dollars, she was bringing back Nichelle more than she deserved.

Nichelle took the kid-pack, and she didn't complain because she knew it would bug Brandi more than if she had. Nichelle was the genius of the group because she only spent two dollars for a movie, popcorn, drink, and a snack. And to top it off, Brandi went and got it for her. Charm didn't appreciate Brandi's cleverness, but she ate everything but the gummy chews. Half way through the movie, Charm smelled the *Snickers* bar Brandi managed to quietly open. Charm stared at her until Brandi offered her a piece. Charm took the whole candy bar and gave Brandi her bag of gummy chews.

"Less calories," Charm whispered to Brandi before she could protest. Charm always lived up to her name. She was the brains of the threesome and knew Nichelle and Brandi needed her.

After the movie, they walked through *Nordstrom's Rack* and tried on clothes. Nichelle told them in fabricated detail about the man she talked to at the police station who was shot. According to Nichelle, she was a key witness and might not be able to go to the Hoodies. However, her master plan was to wait until her friends booked and paid for the hotel room then show up at the hotel on Friday night after they checked in. A bigger matter was talking Glenda into letting her drive the Fleetwood to Vegas, but since part of Nichelle's job was to take and record Glenda's blood pressure and blood sugar levels and submit an accurate report to the home health agency, Glenda might agree. After doing her job, Nichelle could spend the rest of the weekend partying with her friends, and if they acted right, Nichelle would offer them a ride back home in Glenda's caddie.

Chapter 13

"If you want me to come, I'll come," Trish said, "I just don't want to come all the way to Los Angeles then you verbally smack me every time I open my mouth."

Keith tossed in his sleep while the last conversation he had with Trish interrupted his rest. Problem was, he didn't want Trish to come. He wanted to spend time with Kimberly. He wanted the fact that his father was shot to be a nightmare and not a reality. His perfectly planned life Keith thought he was running had spun out of control.

Keith always thought of his father as being strong and healthy. It was surreal to see him lying face up, with tubes attached to his body. Doctor Nunez informed Keith that because of the drugs and pain medicine, his father would probably not remember anything for a while. While Keith was in his room, Wade opened his eyes for a moment and Keith thought he saw recognition before they closed again in sleep. Thank

God that Wade was breathing on his own, and he would be moved out of ICU into a private room. The multitude of plants, cards, and flower arrangements filled the square table top next to the bed. Most of them were from co-workers at the police station, the largest was from the Church of Christ of Los Angeles.

Kimberly instructed Keith to write down the color or type of flowers on the cards and bring them to her. The Hospitality Group at the church would use the information to personalize thank you cards they would address and post for Keith on behalf of his father.

Was this what it was like to have a wife? Keith mused as he signed the cards. Trish would have been too busy to help him like this. Keith rubbed his hand over his face. He wasn't being fair to Trish. Other than a strange man answering her cell phone, she never gave him any reason to believe she wasn't in his corner.

Rev. McMillan hadn't condemned him, but Keith wrestled with his own guilt of having drifted away from God and a life dependent on faith and prayer. Kimberly could be helping him because of the situation with his father and not because of any romantic feelings being rekindled. Keith sighed. He wasn't being fair to Kimberly either because he hadn't told her about Trish and their plans to live together. When had his personal life turned in to such a mess?

Uncle Chris thought the whole thing was amusing. He often referred to his nephew as Player-Player or Pimp Daddy, which he knew annoyed Keith, but it was fun to watch his nephew trying to take the high road when what he really wanted to do was nail Kimberly. The dork would probably have to marry her though because of his principles and conscience. It was a shame too, because if Chris possessed Keith's innocent face and hard body, he'd keep Trish in Stanford and Kimberly in Los Angeles and certainly a few more females on the line as backups.

As it was, he was juggling Jazmine in Phoenix and Judy in Scarsdale. At twenty-eight years old Jazmine was twelve years younger than Chris, but she energized him with her youthful enthusiasm. Jazmine liked to dress up and go out. Party and be seen. She didn't want any kids and was a career woman employed by Phoenix International Airport as a payroll supervisor. Her goal was to be the Director of Human Resources before the age of forty.

Judy retired from the Scarsdale School District five years ago. She had been a school bus driver who injured her back at work and could no longer continue her job duties. There were no other work options that didn't require sitting for long periods of time so she stayed on disability and retired on her fifty-fifth birthday. Judy's three grown children were gainfully employed and living in other states, so when Chris stopped by to see her, Judy was content to stay at home and watch a good movie on television. She didn't cook very often, but she would order take-out and she and Chris would enjoy a quiet evening together at her home. Chris was the common denominator in both relationships and with no pressure for a deeper commitment from Jazmine or Judy, he enjoyed the best of both worlds.

Back in Oregon, Patricia "Trish" Glover wasn't sure what to do. Keith's father was in the hospital recovering from a gunshot wound. She had a lot on her mind including reasons why Keith kept their relationship a secret from his father, especially since they had dated exclusively for the last six months. Trish hated having to meet his father for the first time under these circumstances, but she was beginning to regret her decision not jump on a plane with Keith when he left for Los Angeles even though it all happened so fast.

Trish had a new problem. She was left alone to deal with her neighbor, Douglas Brown, who lived in the apartment building across from her duplex. Doug wanted more than friendship even after Trish made it clear to him she had a boyfriend. Her neighbor wasn't exactly stalking her, but he always seemed to appear out of nowhere when she left her house or returned home. Trish hoped that by moving to California with Keith, any problems with Doug would go away, but now she wasn't sure the move was going to happen.

*D*ouglas Brown thought Patricia Glover was the perfect woman. She was a smart, beautiful, and was a future M.D. They were so right for each other. The fact that her boyfriend was no longer around meant that Douglas Brown and Patricia Glover were destined to be together. There was nothing he wouldn't do for her. Patricia was his world. Even his hard-to-impress mother admired her, and if Patricia moved to California, Douglas would follow her. He was sure that the day would come when she would understand how much he cared for her and fall completely in love with him. Nothing would stand in their way.

Douglas arranged to have flowers delivered to Patricia's doorstep every week from now until their wedding. He shivered with anticipation knowing how happy Patricia would be to get them. Everything was on schedule and going as planned.

$\mathscr{C}$hapter 14

$\mathscr{D}$onna and Kimberly were at the end of a long work day. They sat at a table in the employee lounge. "Have you asked him yet?" Donna asked. Donna was a chef at First and Ten since it opened several months ago. She was a teacher's assistant at the high school and Kimberly an incoming eighth-grader when they were paired together during the annual Big and Little Sister Tea, a gathering sponsored by the PTA to help the middle school students adjust to life on a high school campus. It was a new role Donna cherished since she was the youngest in a family of five children. After graduating from college, Donna went to culinary school, but she kept in touch with her 'little sister.' She wrote a personal recommendation for Kimberly after her fiasco of a marriage and it helped Kimberly get hired as a part-time waitress at First and Ten.

Donna was sorry she was the one who drove Kimberly to the airport the weekend her friend was supposed to be going to the women's conference, only to find out Kimberly went to Meridian instead and married Wesley. Donna met Wesley Miller the day before the fateful Christmas dinner at the McMillan's. She told Kimberly what she thought of him but the newlywed was under the spell of her beloved's influence and couldn't comprehend the advice. Donna considered talking to Kimberly's parents, but she decided it probably wouldn't matter. Kimberly could be stubborn and had already made up her mind about Wesley.

After Wesley returned to Mississippi, Kimberly came to Donna with a broken spirit. Donna saw that Wesley was a control freak, and if she were in Kimberly's shoes, the marriage would be annulled. Kimberly listened to what Donna had to say, but in her heart, it was too late. They took sacred vows and Kimberly meant every word she said; for better or worse, and she couldn't see how anything could be any worse. Donna was no marriage counselor and didn't blame Kimberly for her decision to stay married. What right did Donna have giving her opinion anyway when she'd never been down the isle?

Donna never told Kimberly about her admiration for Keith when she was in high school and completely understood why Kimberly wanted him back now. Keith Dennis was handsome and sweet and just the kind of guy that would fit well in any situation, especially around family. He was balanced; being a man's man and a woman's dream. He was athletic and followed college and professional football, basketball, and baseball, but he wasn't obsessed by it. Keith was attentive and curious about new subjects and didn't feel intimidated if a female proved better than he was at playing card games to knowledge of sports or cars. He was always respectful to females and didn't have a clue that they saw him as sexy and irresistible. Keith left swooning females in his wake never realizing the effect he had on them, which only added to his charm.

In keeping with the look of an up-and-coming attorney, he stayed clean-shaved and wore his dark blonde hair stylishly short. Keith also kept his fingernails clean and trimmed and used cologne or after-shave every day. He preferred to dress in classic-contemporary style clothing, typical of the fashions showcased in a *Macy's* or *Nordstrom's* ad.

"I haven't asked him if he has a girlfriend" Kimberly said. "I really don't want to know if he does, but I'm hoping he'll forget all about her and only want me."

"But Kim, he's going to Stanford which is no where near Los Angeles," Donna said.

Kimberly frowned. "I know. I'm just dreaming; hoping. I don't want to put pressure on him now especially since his father is still in the hospital."

Donna sat forward and put on her coat. "I understand how you feel. Keith is a great guy, but ever since I've known him, he's always had his life planned out. I don't want you getting your hopes up and ending up disappointed. You know he's slow…"

Kimberly grinned and raised one eyebrow, "Sometimes slow is sexy."

Donna shook her head, "Don't go there Missy. Come on. Let's get home. I need to feed the dog."

"Okay," Kimberly said. She waited until Donna stood up and took out her keys to stand up. They said their goodbye's to two members of the cleaning crew who had just arrived. Donna locked the door behind them and walked toward the parking lot. Kimberly and Donna took turns driving to work and this was Donna's week. Donna believed in driving the best car she could afford, which at the moment was a leased 2010 BMW 750. The car came with all of the latest technological gadgets, handled beautifully and it was a pleasure to ride in.

Kimberly sank down into the warm leather seats and turned to her driver, "home Donna." She said raising one hand with dramatic flair.

Donna rolled her eyes, started the engine and backed out of the space. She hit her brakes when a silver Camry passed them going in the opposite direction.

"Is that Keith?" Donna asked. *I'd know that handsome profile anywhere.*

Kimberly perked up. The car looked like Wade Dennis' Camry. Donna made a U-turn in the practically empty parking lot. They saw Keith get out of the car.

Kimberly pushed the window button down. "Hi. We're closed."

Keith rewarded her with a dimpled smile. "Hi, Kim. Donna. I just came by to see if you wanted to grab a bite to eat."

"We were just on our way home," Kimberly said.

"Let me take you out to dinner," Keith said. "You'd be doing me a favor because my uncle went back home to Arizona today and it's lonely in that house."

"Follow us home, so I can get changed," Kimberly said.

Keith's eyebrows furrowed, "Changed? Why? You look cute in your referee outfit. Plus we'll get better food if they see us with a chef."

"You want me to come?" Donna said.

"Of course. The invitation is to both of you. Just like you are," Keith said with a smile. Kimberly blushed and tried to smooth her hair back out of her face.

"Bless you," Donna said. "You can even drive my car."

Kimberly's head snapped around; had she heard right? Donna never let anyone drive her baby. To prove her intent, Donna opened the driver side door and for the first time, climbed into the back seat.

Keith was ecstatic to be allowed behind the wheel of such a performance vehicle and thanked Donna several times during their ride over to Anthony's On-the-Pier. Kimberly took of her work shirt and was grateful for the white blouse she was wearing underneath. She wore layered tops because the temperature at First and Ten was usually too cool for her comfort even though she was in constant movement during most of her shift. In less than twenty minutes, Keith stopped the car in front of the restaurant. He handed the keys to the valet. Since they had no preference as to dining inside or outside, they were immediately seated at a table outside near large outdoor heat lamps. Light from covered candles flickered on the wood table top and the sound of the ocean waves crashing on the beach helped Kimberly and Donna relax to the soothing rhythm.

Keith ordered a hot-spiced tea and a seafood appetizer platter to start them off. They talked, ate and enjoyed the view of the tall ships docked in the distance. A few of their friends from high school, Davis, Brooke, and Keisha, were seated at the table across from them, and while they ate, they chatted and caught up on what each person was doing.

Davis was a real estate agent and complained bitterly about his disappointment with the downturn in the market. The sale of single-family houses had been the source of his greatest commissions. Brooke, a stay-at-home mom, had left her three young children at home with her husband and was thrilled to be out of the house and taking part in an adult conversation. Keisha was an insurance broker. She didn't want to think about work, but when Davis passed out his business card, as he did at every opportunity to drum up business, she followed suit.

When the others were deep in a conversation about the economy Kimberly leaned over to Keith, "Is your father able to have visitors?"

Keith automatically smiled at her, but there was sadness in his eyes. "He can but he's not talking much. The drugs have him sleeping most of the time. I hope he'll be more alert tomorrow."

Keith noticed Donna looking at her watch. She liked to feed her French bulldog, Pixie, no later than 8:00 at night then let her out to "do her business." This schedule usually rewarded Donna with a good night of uninterrupted sleep.

"I think we need to call it a night," Keith said. "I practically kidnapped these ladies." He and Davis took the tab to the cash register. The ladies left a generous tip in cash on their table for the waiter then, after freshening up in the restroom, they met the men outside the front door of the restaurant. The temperature had dropped fifteen degrees since the afternoon high of seventy-six degrees Fahrenheit and the cold air flowing from the ocean made it feel colder. The group said their good-bye's and all agreed they should get together again soon, but no one committed to where and when. Davis, Brooke, and Keisha hurried to the self-parking lot where Davis' car was parked.

Keith insisted Donna and Kimberly go back inside and wait for him in the restaurant lobby. He gave his parking ticket to the valet. After the BMW arrived in front of them, Keith got behind the wheel and turned on the heater. When the car was warm he signaled for the ladies to get in. The parking supervisor nodded his approval at Keith and held the car doors open for the ladies. When they arrived back at First and Ten, Keith began to dread the end of the evening. He kept up a positive front for his companions but hated the thought of going home alone. Keith gave himself a pep talk about being grateful for having had one night out with friends and away from the hospital and his problems. Thank God his father was out of the ICU, and it was time for him to start thinking about work and the upcoming employee orientation for his new job.

When Keith pulled the BMW next to his car, Donna and Kimberly thanked Keith again for dinner. He got into his car and started it up just as the ladies drove off. In less than twenty minutes, he was home and stunned to see Donna's BMW parked in front of his father's house! He pulled the Camry into the driveway, parked and quickly got out of the car anxious to see what was wrong. Before he could ask, Kimberly got out of the Beamer, closed the passenger-side door and Donna waved and drove off. Keith still didn't have a clue.

"What's the matter?" Keith asked as the BMW taillights disappeared around the corner. "I guess it's not car trouble…"

Kimberly walked up to him and stood looking up at him, her brown eyes sparkling from the glow of the overhead street light. "I've wanted to do this for the longest time." She held his face in her hands and pulled him down toward her until her lips were pressed against his. Keith's knees felt weak. He pulled back. It took a moment for him to process what just took place. Then without thinking, he took over and grabbed a hand full of her hair. He lightly pulled her head back, so he could position himself over Kimberly and return the kiss she started. Keith pressed his other hand against her back to hold her upper body close to his and gave her the kiss he'd been thinking about doing since he saw her at the restaurant that first time. When he finished there was no doubt what they both wanted to do next.

It was like their first kiss all over again and Kimberly lay limp in his arms. "My God, Keith," she said breathlessly, "how do you do that?" She was no expert, but Keith Dennis was gifted. Keith wrapped his arm around her waist and guided her into the house. He attributed her weakness to keeping her out late after work. Once the front door was closed and locked, he turned to face Kimberly again.

"Are you sure about this?" He asked. His voice was strained. He stood very still. His arms at his sides, but his hands were balled into fists making muscles in his arms jump. She started it, but if she changed her mind, he would have to respect her decision and Keith would have a chance at winning his internal battle between his flesh and his spirit.

What Kimberly saw was disciplined control and knew it was taking everything he had to hold back. She couldn't look away from the intensity of his eyes that appeared dark blue in the dim light of the room. They needed to talk because there were many unanswered questions but tonight she was going to be selfish and satisfy her curiosity. She had no doubt he wanted her, but Keith would never force or coerce her. She had to give herself to him of her own free will.

In a bold move, she slowly unbuttoned the top button of her blouse. Keith staggered back a step, his eyes fixed on her fingers. She smiled at his reaction and unbuttoned the next button and the next one until the lacy top of her white bra was visible. She stopped and took a deep breath that forced her top open even more. Keith's mouth was dry. He was transfixed to the place where he stood. It was the sexiest thing he'd ever seen.

Kimberly ran her fingers around the waistband of her pants and stopped at her belt buckle. She slowly pulled the end of the belt from the front loop and rested her fingers on the top button of her jeans. Keith couldn't have moved if he wanted to. His own pants were feeling tight. Kimberly unbuttoned the top button and lowered the zipper. She wiggled her hips and the jeans fell to the floor. Keith couldn't take it anymore. He ran at Kimberly ignoring the panic in her eyes. He lowered his shoulder and picked her up so her rear end was up in the air. He held her legs with one arm and walked deliberately into his bedroom carrying her like a man with one purpose in mind. He would make love to her later, but right now, she was asking for something else and he was just the man to give it to her. It no longer mattered she hadn't verbally answered his question. By her actions she'd unleashed a basic need—sex.

Chapter 15

*P*hillip Covers exited the hospital after having visited with Wade Dennis. Wade seemed to recognize him, but he was so medicated that he only stayed awake a minute at a time. Phillip felt awkward bringing another man flowers or candy, and he knew better than to bring a box of cigars to a hospital patient, so he signed his name to a get-well card and slipped two crisp twenty dollar bills inside before sealing the envelope.

Phillip viewed the security video, and just as Nichelle depicted, a woman was seen hurrying out of the side door of the police station around the time of the shooting. She held her head down, so her face was difficult to see clearly. None of the people in the surrounding area would admit to seeing this woman, and most of them who saw the photograph, asked why the lady was wearing a long coat in the summer time. The fact that she was wearing a long coat on a hot day convinced Phillip that someone had to have seen her but chose not get involved with law enforcement. It might be time to sweeten the pot and offer a monetary reward.

Phillip made the decision to call Nichelle Evers and see if she remembered anything else about the day of the shooting or the woman in the long coat. As expected, Nichelle suggested he buy her dinner before she was willing to remember anymore details. Phillip told her to be ready at 5:00 pm. He almost didn't recognize Nichelle when she came out of Glenda's house and walked up to his car. She was dressed in a nice fitting pair of dark blue jeans with a matching cropped jean jacket, a white tank top and a pair of white sandals. Her hair was styled in a conservative bob, accessorized with a navy blue headband. She looked normal.

Not sure how she would take a complement, Phillip thanked Nichelle for being on time. To subliminally reward her conservative appearance, he decided they would go to a nicer place, the sports bar and restaurant, First and Ten.

Nichelle was not happy about her look, but with such short notice, she slapped on a wig and hurried outside so she wouldn't keep Philly waiting. He seemed so impatient and always worrying about the time. She chose the jean set because it was cute and looked good on her. Nichelle bought it on Crenshaw Boulevard from a guy selling clothes out of the trunk of his car in the parking lot of *Krispy Kreme* donuts. It was a good deal for twenty-five dollars, but Nichelle talked him into giving her two identical sets for forty dollars. She was sure she could sell the second set to someone else for at least thirty dollars and profit from her investment. Since it was near the end of the day and the guy was ready to shut down his operation before a donut-loving lawman would do it for him, he agreed.

When they arrived at First and Ten, Nichelle almost asked Philly why he didn't bring her here the last time they were together, when she was 'suited and booted'; but that was not the conversation to have *before* he paid for dinner. Once inside, Nichelle knew this was the kind of high-class place her sister would like. It had big screen televisions strategically placed all over the room, and it was filled with mostly men who looked like they came directly from an office. Nichelle was going to like the place a lot better once she had a few drinks in her. After being seated, Phillip let her order a cocktail and immediately wanted to know what else she remembered about the "incident."

"Remember when I said I was standing on the corner at Denker waiting for the light before I saw the lady come out of the building?"

"Yes."

"Well, before she came out, I happened to look down Denker Street and saw a car."

Phillip kept his eyes trained on her, and when the waiter brought Nichelle's drink, he held it right in front of him. Nichelle rolled her eyes. What was wrong with this man? Alcohol was supposed to loosen people up.

"I saw a Chevy Impala parked at the curb. It was black. It stood out to me because first of all, I like Chevy Impalas and second of all, the license plate was covered up. It must have been a rush job or last minute because just as I was crossing the street, the paper covering the license plate flipped up." Nichelle illustrated the motion of the paper with her hand. "A car passed by and it kind of flew up then back down."

Phillip pushed the glass toward her, but he didn't let it go. Nichelle resisted rolling her eyes this time, but this Negro was due a lot of attitude because she was cooperating and giving up valuable information.

"I didn't see the license plate, but I do know it wasn't a California plate."

Phillip let go of the glass, and Nichelle reached for it. She took a big gulp and set it down. The whiskey burned going down, but it gave her a quick mellow high right away. She smiled, "All I saw were the colors white with dark green in the middle and dark blue numbers."

"Are you saying the same woman you saw come out of the police station got into the Impala?"

"I am not saying that I saw her get inside, but I saw her walk toward the car. The lady stepped off the sidewalk and into the street like she might be getting in the driver's side, but when the light changed, I crossed the street, so I didn't actually see her get into the car. It was a nice car though." Nichelle said and took another sip from her glass.

"Did you notice anyone else in the car?"

"The windows were dark. Tinted. I couldn't see inside the car at all. It was black on black baby," Nichelle said. "The only thing missing was rims. I'd a floated that bad boy on dubs, but this car had the standard rims that come with the car."

Phillip took out his cell phone, punched a button and instructed the person on the other end to gather all of the state license plates with a combination of the colors white, blue and green. He gave a description of the car, ended the call and slipped his phone back into its case. "After dinner, will you come to the station and see if you recognize the license plate?"

"I'll look, but like I said, I only saw it for a second," Nichelle said.

Nichelle ordered fried chicken wings and potato salad. Phillip chose the Philly steak sandwich and coffee. While waiting for their food, Nichelle noticed the restaurant got busier. The food must be good because the atmosphere was boring. She knew Phillip was more interested in watching the basketball game on the big screen than listening to her, but that didn't stop Nichelle from talking. She had nothing against sports, but she had never watched a whole game all the way through—even the Super Bowl. The commercials were the best part of watching the game and Nichelle always picked her favorite team by the color of their uniforms.

After eating dinner, she was puzzled as to why people were standing in line to get in. The food was okay, but in a cook-off, *Roscoe's House of Chicken and Waffles* or *M&M's Soul Food* would beat this place every day, cause whoever heard of serving chicken wings without hot sauce? Phillip seemed perfectly comfortable in this environment. She could see

Heavenly with a guy like this. They could nerd-up together and have little brainy nerdy kids.

"What's so funny?" Phillip asked when he noticed Nichelle chuckling.

The buzz from her second after-dinner-whisky was right on time. "Nothing Philly. I was just thinking…you didn't mention a wife. Are you single?"

Phillip frowned. Maybe Nichelle was reading too much into him taking her to First and Ten, "Yes. Happily."

"I was wondering…"

Phillip felt a bead of sweat forming on his forehead, a dead giveaway he was feeling anxious.

"My sister Heavenly is single and would like coming to a place like this. How about I set you up with her?"

If she had sucker punched him, Phillip couldn't have been more surprised; a date with Heavenly Evers? He wouldn't bring her here. No way. He would take her some place special, a quiet classy restaurant where they could talk and he could show her a good time. "What makes you think your sister would want a date with me?"

Nichelle shrugged, "Why not you? As far as I'm concerned she's going to stay single because Heavenly doesn't put herself out there. She won't go clubbing with me. She just goes to church, to work, then sits in her crib way downtown, all alone and makes lists."

Phillip was pretty sure Nichelle was single too, but instead of asking about that he wanted to hear more about her sister. Lists?

Nichelle looked around the room, "Heavenly would like a place like this. She needs to do something besides sit at home on the weekends waiting for Mr. Right to knock on her door." She leaned toward him conspiratorially and added, "You and me both know the chances of that happening…slim and none."

"You have my card," Phillip said. He desperately held back a grin. This was so unexpected, "Call me with her number if she's okay with me calling her."

"I'll do you one better," Nichelle said. She took a pen and wrote on a napkin. "This is Heavenly's home number. I already talked to her about you Philly. She said it's okay if you call her. She'll be glad to go out with a guy like you."

As their dinner dishes were being cleared Phillip's cell phone rang. He left the table to take the call and when he returned he smiled brightly at Nichelle.

"Good news. You don't need to come to the station. We've identified the owner of the black Impala. Thank you, Nichelle. We were just about to offer a monetary reward for more information, but I think you saved the department and the city quite a bit of money, at least ten thousand dollars."

If looks could kill it would have been the last day on earth for Phillip "Philly" Covers. Fortunately, he was scanning the dessert menu and missed the eye-daggers of his companion. He was too busy thinking about the name, Heavenly Covers.

Chapter 16

Keith didn't want to think about Trish at all while he ravaged Kimberly, pulling the remains of her blouse off her shoulders and kissing her neck, but he kept hearing Trish's voice and another voice. *Flee fornication.* Keith hadn't meant to rip the blouse, but the fabric was keeping his mouth from the soft tender flesh underneath and it had to go. *The spirit indeed is willing but the flesh is weak.* In the next agonizing moment, he realized Trish's voice was coming through the telephone answering machine.

"Keith. It's me, Trish. I'm here at the airport. LAX. I don't know if you're still at the hospital, but I took a chance and came to Los Angeles to support you. I'm sorry I didn't come with you before, but I'm here now. I guess I should have called to let you know I was coming. I just want to talk to you in person…well, call me when you get this message…bye Keith."

Kimberly was still breathing hard. Her eyes were closed as her chest rose and fell in a hypnotic rhythm, but she hadn't moved from where she lay. Donna was right. Of course, Keith had a girlfriend or maybe a wife. Kimberly had not asked because she didn't want to know. She just wanted Keith.

He rolled off of her onto his back and put his arm across his forehead. *Could his luck and their timing be any worse?* Ever since he spoke with Rev. McMillan, scriptures kept popping into his head. Not that they were able to stop him from almost sinning against his own body. Keith was totally embarrassed because he should have told Kimberly about Trish, especially before ripping her clothes off. He heard the mocking voice of Uncle Chris in his head -*Player-Player*. Keith groaned and after turning on his side, he looked right into Kimberly's face.

She reached out and rested her hand on his arm, "I know what you're thinking Keith and it's not all your fault. I share the blame because I should have asked you if you had a wife or a girlfriend, but I didn't because I was being selfish. I wanted you."

"Don't try and let me off the hook Kimberly, I should have told you about Trish. I should have told Trish about you before we…"

Kimberly touched her index finger to his lips, "We haven't done anything."

Keith leaned his head forward and opened his mouth to draw her finger inside. She closed her eyes and enjoyed the sensual exploration of his magic tongue. Warm. Soft. Sweet. Then he held the same hand against his chest and she felt the rapid beating of his heart. Without words, he explained to her they *had* done something—opened Pandora's box. They were way past the puppy-love stage.

Keith closed his eyes. This very week, her pastor/father admonished him to live up to the Christian principles that were at the core of his life. How could he explain away his carnal desire to become one with the pastor's daughter and a woman who was not his wife?

Kimberly stroked his face. "I know you Keith, and I don't want you to beat yourself up about this." She sat up and picked up her tattered blouse.

"Dang-it, I'm sorry. I'll buy you a new one," Keith said. He got up, went to his closet and picked out a long sleeve t-shirt. He came back to the futon and reached for the blouse to exchange for the shirt.

Kimberly held the blouse to her chest and smiled. "Oh no. I'm keeping it for a souvenir. This might be as close as I come to getting to know the real you."

Keith threw his t-shirt at her head. Giggling, Kimberly dodged it. "This is my special shirt." While teasing him she balled up the former blouse and stuffed it inside her purse.

"At least let me see the size," Keith said. He had to replace it. He planned to look at the tag while she pulled his t-shirt over her head, but he couldn't look away from watching how she filled out his shirt. Keith never thought of a t-shirt as sexy, but on Kimberly, it ended right below her rounded bottom. Did it tease or taunt him? Both. *Lusting after a woman in your heart is like already having committed adultery.* He left the room before he was tempted to murder another innocent shirt.

In his father's bedroom, he called Trish back. Keith's guilt was multiplied after talking to Trish because she sounded so glad to hear him. After the call ended, he found Kimberly in the living room standing in front of the fireplace examining framed photographs on the mantel. Keith walked up behind Kimberly and wrapped his arms around her. She smiled and leaned back against him. It felt good. It felt right. He had to get his body under control. After a moment Keith whispered in her ear, "I'm going to drop you back off at home and go pick up Trish. I'll have to explain to her that it's over between us."

Having his lips so close to her ear made a shiver go through Kimberly. She reached around to stroke his face, "You are so scandalous."

He knew she was teasing and that if the call hadn't come when it did, their relationship would have gone to a totally new level. He held her a few minutes more then kissed her on the top of the head, released her and reached for the keys to the car.

When Kimberly opened the door to the house she shared with Donna, she tried to come it quietly but Donna called her name.

"Kim. What happened? I can't believe he turn you down," Donna said, her words slurred from being awakened from sleep.

"Not exactly. He seemed very interested, but his girlfriend called right after Keith ripped off my blouse."

"What?" Donna said. That last comment rendered her totally awake.

Kimberly went directly into Donna's room and sat on the corner of the bed knowing her roommate would want details. Donna turned on the lamp by her bed and sat up. Pixie, who had been asleep in the corner of the room in her dog bed, figured it was a slumber party and joined them on the opposite side of Donna's full-size bed. As Kimberly filled Donna in on everything that happened, including details of Keith and Trish's relationship and the guy who answered her phone, Pixie lay her head on her paws and went back to sleep.

Donna stretched her hands over her head. "One day my knight-in-shinning-Camry is going to come into my life and rock my world."

"Make sure he's not in the castle kissing any other princesses, silly," Kimberly advised.

"You better keep quiet about Keith and his gift," Donna warned.

"I am. I'm only telling you as my mentor. I learned to keep my mouth shut back when I first kissed Keith when we were going to the 9th grade. I made the mistake of telling Alia Peterson and before I knew, it was all over the school. By the time I got home, a couple of parents already called my mother, but by then, the story was that we went all the way. I told my mother what happened, and thank God my parents believed me, but I learned my lesson."

Donna yawned, "I think Keith is going to dump that Trish girl. If he loved her, he would have introduced her to his father already. I have a feeling you two are getting back together."

"I wouldn't mind," Kimberly said. "My parents love him. They don't say it, but all the other guys I brought home for them to meet over the years never seemed to measure up."

Donna scooted down in her bed. "Keith Dennis is the kind of man any normal parent would want their daughter to be with. As a matter of fact, I wish he had a twin."

"Me too. Then I could send the twin to the airport to pick up Trish, and I'd be in heaven right now with the original." Kimberly said. She got up from the bed and turned out the lamp.

"Sweet dreams," Donna said.

"Shut up," Kimberly replied before closing her bedroom door. It was going to be a long, lonely night.

$\mathscr{C}$hapter 17

$\mathscr{K}$eith circled the airport arrival level again. It was his third time around and he still didn't see any sign of Trish. He finally turned into the parking lot, parked his car and walked to the arrival area. He scanned every face, but Trish's was not among them. Before having her paged, Keith pulled out his cell phone and discovered he had a voicemail message waiting.

"Keith. It's Trish. I decided to go to a hotel. I'll call you when I get settled." Trish must have called him while he was walking Kimberly to her door. He couldn't resist getting one last kiss, but he made it a quick one. Keith was in enough trouble with himself, with Kimberly, with her father and especially with the Almighty. He played the call back a second time wondering why Trish changed her mind about him picking her up. Maybe it was the cosmos at work making sure he didn't mess up. Keith was ready to be pissed at the cosmos, for leaving him hanging, literally, when he was almost in paradise with Kimberly.

Keith drove from LAX with no particular destination in mind. He wouldn't be able to sleep for hours, so there was no reason to go home. He also didn't want the memories of what almost happened in that house, in his own bed, to haunt him. There were several 24 Hour Fitness' within a thirty mile radius of the airport and working out would help use up the adrenalin that was keeping him hyped up. Keith ended up driving to Country Club Drive, the street where Rev. and Mrs. McMillan lived. He knew what he had to do.

"Come in, son," Harvey McMillan said when he saw Keith on his front porch. He opened the screen door.

"I'm sorry to stop by so late," Keith said and entered the warm, cozy living room.

"Nonsense. You're always welcome; in fact, I just missed you at the hospital today when I visited with your father. He's looking much better."

"He does and Dad is staying awake longer. The doctors think he's out of danger. Once they release him, they showed me the diet and exercise plan that will help him get to a healthy weight."

"Wonderful. I'll be sure to let the intercessory prayer warriors at the church know the good news."

"Who is it dear?" Gwendolyn asked. She peaked around the corner. Her hair was tied up in a colorful scarf and she held her summer robe closed around the neck with one hand.

"It's Keith Dennis."

"Keith! Oh, I'll be right out," Gwendolyn said. She pulled the scarf off her head and hurried back to her room to spruce herself up.

"You're like a celebrity in this house," Harvey said.

Keith grinned. "I hope I'm not keeping you up. I wanted to talk to you."

"Of course. Are you taking care of yourself, getting enough rest?" Harvey asked.

Gwendolyn entered the room, her hair combed and lip-gloss applied, "Keith. What a pleasant surprise. No, don't get up. I'll hug you right where you sit."

"How are you doing Mrs. Mc?" Keith said after embracing the older woman who smelled like *White Diamonds* perfume.

"I'm fine. Are you hungry? We have leftover chicken and dumplings."

"No, thank you. I'm at a crossroads in my life and I've come here for wise counsel," Keith said. He turned to the pastor. "Sir, I'm going to breakup with Trish. Our relationship is not based on the right things."

"Harvey!" Gwendolyn said. "He's breaking it off with the girlfriend."

"Yes, dear. I heard," Harvey replied.

Keith continued, "My feelings for your daughter Kimberly have grown into mature love…"

"He loves Kimberly!" Gwendolyn said. She grabbed at her robe and hugged her arms around herself, "Harvey, Keith loves our Kimberly."

"Yes, dear." Harvey said.

"And I wanted to ask you, sir, well, both of you…" Keith said.

Gwendolyn sat up on the edge of her chair. "There's more?" Her voice was barely a whisper this time.

"Yes ma'am. I want your permission to court Kimberly and if she's willing, ask her to marry me."

Gwendolyn stood up and raised her hands to heaven. "Oh, my God. Harvey, honey, did you heard what he said?" She began dancing her own private holy dance in a circle. Then she maneuvered her way backward in to their bedroom where she could really let loose.

Harvey smiled at Keith. "Son, are you ready for a mother-in-law that can't hide her feelings?" He extended his hand.

"Yes, sir," Keith said and shook his hand. "Ever since I saw Kimberly, it's like a light went on in here." Keith pointed to the center of his chest. He told Harvey how different he felt in his relationship with Trish compared to Kimberly. Trish wasn't a bad person, but what they had in common was their drive and ambition. It was a relationship of convenience rather than true passion or love and certainly not based on Christian principles. "When I saw Kimberly at the restaurant, it was like we hadn't been apart for more than a day, much less, seven years. If there was such a thing as a soul mate, mine is Kimberly. I can't imagine the rest of my life without her."

"How does Kimberly feel about you?" Harvey asked.

"We haven't talked about it, but I think she feels the same way I do," Keith said.

"Keith. I've known you since you were a boy. I had the privilege of leading you to the Lord. I know you started out with a firm foundation and have moved away from it, but God is all about second chances. First John 1:9 says, 'If we confess our sins, He is faithful and just to forgive us our sins and cleanse us from all unrighteousness.' If the Lord forgives you, that's all that matters. You do your part and He'll do His. Personally, I believe you'll be a good provider for my daughter. You've always been focused and committed to being successful; however, I expect the man that marries my daughter to be the spiritual head of the household and love her the way we're taught in the Bible, as Christ loves the church. I want my grandchildren being brought up in the way they should go with parents who are on one accord."

"Yes, sir," Keith said. "I want those things, and I'll make sure of it because I want our children to have what Kimberly grew up with; God, first, security and stability."

"What about your plans for your education? Where will you live? How many children do you want? How do you handle money? These are a few of the many questions the two of you need to discuss and have solid answers to before getting married. During your courtship, you need to get an understanding about expectations."

Keith nodded. He and Kimberly needed to plan their future together.

Harvey locked eyes with the younger man. He believed the day would come when Keith and Kimberly would see in each other what he and his wife saw already. Keith wasn't sure what the silence meant. Surely, this wasn't the first time a man had asked him to marry his only child. Harvey probably turned away a lot of suitors. In the next moment, Keith had a flash back of Kimberly seated on his futon in her bra and panties holding her torn shirt. His face flushed and he broke eye contact.

"What is it son?" Harvey asked.

"I want to do right by God and you and Kimberly," Keith said. I love her. I've always loved her, but how do we keep from uh…coming together?"

"Short engagement," The pastor quipped.

His comment relieved the tension Keith was feeling, and he smiled.

"Seriously Keith, I know you're battling your flesh. You're both young, healthy people and you are supposed to have feelings of attraction to the opposite sex, but God's best is for you to enjoy each other, body and soul, in the confines and protection of marriage. In some way, we all battle our flesh every day. Intellectually, we want to do the right thing, but the conversation we have in our mind is what determines our rule over the body. It's the classic battle between the flesh and the spirit, between the old man and the new, between good and evil."

Keith listened and took to heart all Harvey said as he shared scriptures with him. It was calming to know he had options and didn't have to let his body rule his actions. But could he control his body if Kimberly approached him again? They needed to talk.

"I have something for you." Harvey said and disappeared into his den. He came back with a business card and handed it to Keith.

"Pastor Josiah Edmondson is a good friend of mine. I'll call him and tell him you want to join the next series of pre-marital classes. They start with three sessions, once a week. Pastor Edmondson teaches the men, and his wife, Cree, teaches the women. Then the couples come together for joint-group sessions for three more weeks. During that time the couples get one-on-one counseling. By the end of the six weeks, you'll have tools to use to deal with challenges that are common to man and have someone to be accountable to that's *not* your future father-in-law. I'm sure Kimberly will be more comfortable and candid in discussing her issues and concerns as well."

Keith held on to the card. It represented hope. "Thank you, Pastor Harvey."

"I think it will help you to know you're not the only young man dealing with these issues," Harvey said. "So, as Kimberly's father, and on behalf of her mother, you have our blessings. I'm very happy to give you permission to court our daughter. We love you, Keith. I've always looked at you as the son I never had...not that I didn't love my baby girl, but there are some lessons a father can't pass on to a daughter."

Keith nodded. He totally understood. He wanted a son too one day, a boy to mold into a man. But a baby girl meant sleepless nights and catching a case if anyone tried to harm her. He already felt sorry for any guy bold enough to date his daughter, and with that thought in mind, he was glad he hadn't gone all the way with Pastor Harvey's precious girl. Keith's soul flooded his body with strength, and he made a vow to himself he was going to give Kimberly something special. Keith Dennis was pledging his heart, soul, and *body* to one woman forever--his future wife, Kimberly Marie McMillan soon-to-be-Dennis.

Kimberly, however, was not of the same mind. The next morning, she sat in the kitchen and watched the sun come up. Pixie walked into the kitchen and looked up at her.

"Hey girl." Kimberly said. She leaned down and rubbed the head of the dog that slowly wagged her tail in appreciation, but when Kimberly didn't move to let her out, Pixie continued to the back door. The dog stood in front of it and looked over her shoulder at the human. "Okay," Kimberly said. She stood up and went to open the back door. Pixie ran outside, and at the same time, cold air blew inside. Kimberly took a deep breath of fresh air, and then quickly, closed the door. So much for the heat wave. As usual, the Southern California weather had changed drastically from the day before. Kimberly started a pot of coffee and made it extra strong. When the coffee was ready, she let Pixie back inside and filled her water dish.

"Thanks," Donna said when she entered the gourmet kitchen. She never expected anyone else to take care of her dog, but she was grateful when it happened. Donna pulled two skillets down from the overhead hooks. She opened a deli package of thick sliced bacon and filled the first skillet with several strips. While the bacon fried, she whisked some eggs, mild cheddar cheese and her own mix of seasonings in a bowl. By this time, Pixie sat at attention next to her dinner bowl willing a morsel of food to fall to the floor. Donna trained her dog to sit in the service porch, out of the way when she was cooking, so Pixie could not interfere while anyone was eating. Pixie learned as a puppy that any wining and begging would result in being put outside.

Kimberly watched Donna cook. She sipped hot coffee while her stomach growled. Even though Donna cooked for a living, she still enjoyed fixing food her own way in her own kitchen. Kimberly usually washed the dishes, but today, she was going to put everything, including the skillets, into the dishwasher.

"Okay Sweet-pea," Donna said and put a plate of food in front of Kimberly. "I know you're probably depressed this morning."

"I couldn't sleep," Kimberly mumbled.

Donna spread apricot marmalade over her toast. "Why don't you take the day off? Maybe you'll get some sleep during the day and maybe Keith will call with an update?"

Kimberly nodded. She was not going to be a good waitress with Keith and Trish on her mind. Kimberly finished her breakfast said good-bye to Donna who was leaving for work and went to take a shower. In the shower, she washed her hair and later blow-dried it. While getting dressed, Kimberly noticed how much better she felt with a full stomach and now that the caffeine had kicked in, Trish or no-Trish, she was going after her man.

$\mathcal{C}$hapter 18

"$\mathcal{D}$addy, what's going on with Mom?" Kimberly asked when she was alone with her father in his office. Her mother had been so weepy all day. At first, on the telephone when Kimberly called to see if her parents wanted anything from the Farmer's Market and later when she and Donna dropped off the groceries.

Harvey smiled, "She's fine. You know how emotional your mother can be."

He was sitting at his desk, having just completed his outline for the upcoming Sunday sermon. Kimberly was across from him seated on the leather couch with her legs drawn under her.

"Sure, but she seems so…I don't know…happy and sad at the same time."

Her father smiled and closed his Bible, "Kimmie."

Kimberly smiled back. He hadn't called her that little girl name in years.

"I'm speaking to you as your father right now."

Uh-oh.

"Your mother and I are so very proud of you. You didn't let one setback keep you from pursuing your goals and now you're back on track."

"Thank you, Daddy. Without you and Mommy's belief in me, I don't know how I would have coped."

"You're stronger than you think," Harvey said. He rubbed his eyes. "Kimberly…"

Here it comes.

"There's going to come a day when a young man comes to your mother and me and asks for your hand in marriage."

Kimberly smiled at her old-fashioned father. Guys these days didn't do that kind of thing anymore.

"If it's the right man, who has his priorities in order, he'll get our blessing, but you need to make sure you're ready."

What? Me?

"You need to spend some quality time with God and let Him guide you in your conduct. I'm speaking as your pastor now," Harvey said. "Your husband, whoever he is, deserves a virtuous woman."

Had God told her father about her wonton ways with Keith and her plans to have him by any means? Kimberly couldn't look her father in the eye anymore. She studied her hands while he spoke and was convicted deep in her soul because, in her heart, she knew her intent. Keith had a girlfriend. Trish was a person with feelings, and Kimberly was willing and eager to disregard those feelings, so she could have her own way. Did God lead her to her parent's house today? Kimberly's heart was heavy and feeling camaraderie with the first man, Adam, in the garden after the fall, she wanted to cover herself and hide her sin. Sinning came so easy and natural; it had snuck up on her.

After Wesley, Kimberly spent hours of alone time talking to God and studying her *Bible* to rebuild her self-esteem and plan her career. There was no reason to pray about men or having another husband or boyfriend because Kimberly promised herself that she would stay unmarried and celibate for the rest of her life rather than go through another bad relationship. At the time, Keith was the only man she considered worthy of her time and attention, and she hadn't seen him in years. What were the chances that he would come back to Los Angeles, then to the restaurant during her shift and be seated in her section? It was a dream come true, and the feelings they had for each other had intensified. Unlike when they were kids, they now knew what they were doing and to stop at kissing would be impossible after unleashing the floodgates of passion. Kimberly shamefully pretended God was looking the other way and not paying attention to her actions. But, she knew better. Kimberly twisted her hands together, her eyes brimming with tears. She was exposed. Guilty as charged. Thoroughly chastised.

"You're right, Daddy." Kimberly said.

Harvey was back in Daddy-mode and couldn't handle Kimberly crying, so he left her alone in his office, so she could deal with the emotions of the two-edged sword of being verbally chastened and convicted in her own heart.

Chapter 19

$\mathcal{D}$ouglas looked at the flowers piling up on Patricia's porch. His mother told him all ladies like token gifts, especially flowers. If it weren't for Keith Dennis, Patricia would have loved his surprise. Douglas went on-line and paid for Winslow Florist.com to deliver a bouquet of flowers to her home every day for a week and now she was gone. His eyes narrowed. Patricia must have followed that pretty boy to California. Keith must have some sort of hold on her. It wasn't her fault. She was so beautiful just like the flowers he sent her. It was Keith who ruined it for her, for them. Patricia needed freedom from that tyrant. He didn't deserve her, but somehow, Keith Dennis made her leave home. Keith Dennis. What a stupid name.

Doug's anger escalated to a boiling point. He ran out of his front door, across the courtyard, and grabbed the first bouquet. In a rage, he pulled the red roses out of their glass vase and he flung them across the porch. Thorns pierced his skin and he grimaced in pain while blood began to stream from his hand. He stared at a drop of blood until it descended from his fingers to his sleeve. This injury was Keith's fault too; in fact, Keith Dennis was the cause of all of the pain in his life. Keith drew first blood, and now he would pay.

$\mathcal{C}$hapter 20

$\mathcal{M}$r. Bill Baxter was Keith's new supervisor at the Law Offices of Becker and Snowden-Los Angeles aka LOBS-L.A. Baxter arranged for a new employee orientation for Keith on Tuesday morning, so Keith could shadow a group of seasoned attorneys. There was a gentlemen's agreement with the Stanford office partners that Keith would give the Los Angeles office partners first consideration for permanent employment after he graduated and passed the bar.

Keith arrived at 7:45 in the morning on his first day at LOBS-LA. A very attractive receptionist directed him to the elevators that would take him to his first appointment with Jill Beckman, director of Human Resources. Keith would remember the receptionist because of her professional and friendly manner, melodic voice, voluptuous body, and the unusual name on her identification badge. On the elevator, he mentally chastised himself for noticing any other females. Didn't he have enough problems with Trish and Kimberly without adding Heavenly to the mix? His focus needed to be on his new job and impressing the partners.

The orientation lasted four hours. Attorneys, Tia Chen, Bo White, Derrick Pond and Ned Denton, spoke with him individually about what a typical day in the office would entail. They answered Keith's questions about his assignment and gave him a tour of the entire twelfth floor. Keith left a message on Trish's cell phone every hour when he was allowed a ten minute break. She still hadn't called him back. They really needed to talk.

At the end of orientation, Keith was sure he'd be able to handle working part-time in the law library and continuing his education, but where? If his father needed assistance at home, while recovering, he could hire a home health aide. However, in his heart, Keith couldn't leave Los Angeles until he knew his father was receiving the care and attention only a family member would give him. Then, there was Kimberly.

Cast all your cares on me because I care for you.

It was funny how life threw curve balls especially when he thought it was all planned out. Keith desired a J.D. from Stanford University law school since his first year of college. He visualized himself graduating with a prestigious law degree and passing the Bar while working for a prominent law firm like Becker & Snowden. A few years later, he would open his own practice and marry Trish, who would be at the point of starting her residency. They would find a five-bedroom house in the suburbs, and after five years start a family. He thought a boy and a girl would be perfect for them, but Trish convinced him two of each would be better. Two kids or four, it was all good. There never was a plan B, but that was then. Ever since the shooting, his life was divided into two segments; before his father was shot, when life was planned out and easy; and after, when each day brought uncertainly and he had to contain the turmoil with prayer. Keith was forced to face the reality that a degree from Stanford might not happen. He had to consider applying to law schools in Los Angeles, and it being this late in the year, he might not be accepted for the fall semester. Without having a Stanford education, the partners of Becker & Snowden might not honor their offer of employment. His master plan was unraveling, and he still hadn't broken the news to Trish that their relationship was over.

A feeling of dread came over him. What if Kimberly didn't want to get serious right now especially since her first marriage crashed and burned? Kimberly might not want to be tied down with a boyfriend or fiancé, especially one who would be living out of town. What if she wanted to be carefree and saw him as a one-night stand? Did she still want kids? He really needed to talk to Kimberly.

As soon as he arrived back home Keith bowed his head and prayed. He fought against allowing his feelings of helplessness pull him into depression.

Trust in the Lord with all your heart and lean not to your own understanding. In all your ways acknowledge Him and He will direct your path.

He smiled and welcomed the words bubbling up from his heart.

Come unto Me all who labor and are heavy laden and you will find rest unto your souls. Take My yoke upon you and learn of Me; for My yoke is easy and my burden is light.

Keith held onto those words and released his cares into the hands of the Lord.

Chapter 21

$\mathcal{P}$hillip looked around the room before checking himself out in the full length gilded mirror. Even the restrooms of Chi Boulevard Restaurant were classy, a step above any of the other five star places he'd patronized. Phillip was wearing his best suit, a tailored Kenneth Cole, black tuxedo. The cut of the suit and the tuxedo stripe down the leg of his trousers added to his long, lean look. The freshly starched eggshell tuxedo shirt was new but the black patterned tie was his favorite accessory because P. Diddy himself wore a similar one worn at a recent awards show. A pair of black leather *Stacy Adams* dress shoes completed his ensemble. Earlier in the day, his barber, Tracy, from the Best Cuts Barber Shop trimmed his fade and removed any other objectionable hair from his neck up. Phillip wore his favorite and most expensive *Casio* watch, his college class ring and a single 1ct. diamond stud-earring in his left ear.

He considered buying flowers and candy to present to Heavenly, but he knew too many people with allergies and on diets and decided against it.

The cost of dinner at the restaurant alone should make her forget any token gifts because this was *the* place to dine, according to his friend, Bob Flagg, an assistant trainer for the Los Angeles *Clippers* pro-basketball team. This place was so exclusive; dinner was served not by reservation, but by invitation. Everything was planned in advance, including the music that would accompany the meal. Phillip spent two hours answering questions at the concierge desk a few days ago so the evening would be as perfect as possible. There were five amazing views from the dining room and Phillip chose a view overlooking the city with the Pacific Ocean as a backdrop.

When Phillip returned to their table, a photographer was taking a picture of Heavenly. She was unaware of being photographed and was leaning forward for a better look out of the picture window. She looked amazing. Her white halter dress was fitted at the waist, and flowed down over her hips ending just below her knees. The glow from wall sconces reflected light on one side of her face, softening her serine but thoughtful expression. A waiter, hardly noticeable, stood nearby ready to respond to any request. The night was going just as he planned it.

Heavenly smiled at Phillip when he returned to the table. She was surprised when he told her they were going to Chi Boulevard because a few weeks ago, she overheard two of the senior partners from the law offices of Becker & Snowden discussing the difficulty of getting an invitation.

The restaurant décor was stunning and the service, unsurpassed. Heavenly felt confident in her full skirted jersey dress. It was a bridesmaid's dress she purchased last year and wore in a college friend's black and white themed summer wedding. She splurged on a white Rampage Faux-snakeskin handbag and a pair of strappy sandals called *Sheer Flowers* by designer, *Ann Taylor*. Her jewelry was simple; large silver hoop earrings and two silver bangle bracelets. First lady, Michelle

Obama, inspired her hairstyle that was flat ironed straight with a side part and curled under.

"Are you enjoying yourself?" It was the third time since they arrived at Chi Boulevard that Phillip asked her that particular question. He wanted to stop himself, but he was so nervous that the same words kept coming out of his mouth.

"I don't have words to describe this place," Heavenly said. She looked around at a colorful mural painted on the walls.

He loved the sound of her voice and was intrigued by the tiny tattoo of a star on the inside of her ear near the top. Heavenly was saying the words he wanted to hear, but something about her body language and the lack of expression in her eyes gave him the sinking feeling she was trying to spare his feelings and make it through dinner, so he could take her back home.

After all of the seven courses had been served, the waiter poured them a cup of coffee with a splash of rum for their after-dinner drink.

"Can I be honest with you?" Heavenly said once they were alone.

Oh no. "Please do," Phillip answered. *Here comes the brush off. Will it be a headache or some forgotten appointment?*

"Phillip, I don't date very often. It's not that I don't get asked out, but I don't attract the kind of man that can see past the outside."

He didn't know what to say. Her luscious curves, sensual smile, and bedroom voice is what got his attention in the first place.

"But when I agree to go out on a date, I want to get to know the person and I want him to get to know me."

"So do I..." Phillip said, but Heavenly reached over and touched his hand to let him know she wasn't finished. Phillip stared down at her hand on his. At least she touched him of her own free will before the night was over.

"But what almost always happens on my dates is...guys try to impress me. I don't mean flowers and candy. That's cool. It's nice and appropriate for a first date, but I've been flown to San Francisco...just for dinner."

She paused for effect. "I've been taken on private yachts rented only for a few hours. One time, I was picked up in a limo and taken to a concert… in a helicopter. All these were *first* dates. The worse one was the guy who used a month's salary to take me out for a few hours on a single night. We sat courtside during an NBA playoff game. I felt guilty because I know he was doing something he couldn't afford. He was trying to make me see him as something he really wasn't. Most of those guys seemed to be nice guys, but I'll never really know because they were so busy making sure the date went as planned they never relaxed. They weren't being real with me and showing me who they really were. They spent all that money and weren't really having a good time, so I couldn't relax and enjoy getting to know them."

Phillip felt stupid. He'd fallen into the same trap of trying too hard. He looked down then back up at her and she continued.

"Even if I were to go out again with any of those guys, how could they top the first date? If we start seeing each other on a regular basis how can we look forward to a special occasion when our first date was an airline flight to another city for dinner? What's next? A trip to the moon? Don't get me wrong. I work every day. I know the value of a dollar and I like going to nice places, like tonight. But anyone who knows me knows I'm not what they call a high-maintenance woman. I'm a working girl. This place is awesome, wonderful, but I know *I* can't afford to come here on my own even with an invitation and even if you can, I don't have enough nice clothes to come to a place like this on the regular." It was true. She dipped into her savings account to buy the cashmere shawl to match her dress and to get a professional manicure and pedicure, a luxury she usually reserved for her birthday or the Christmas holidays. It would be weeks before she made up the deficit to her savings.

Phillip nodded in agreement. "Heavenly, I hear what you're saying and you're right. I was trying to show you a good time and take you somewhere you'd never been before, but I should have asked you what you wanted to do. I apologize."

Heavenly smiled, "Thank you."

"But, in my defense, I hope you won't hold it against me for taking you to Chi Boulevard. I really do want to get to know you better."

"Then why didn't you ever ask me out before now?"

Phillip frowned, "When?"

"The times you came into the Enterprise building and stopped at my desk," Heavenly said.

Phillip stared at her unable to speak. He must have misunderstood, "You noticed me?"

Heavenly looked down then coyly up at him and his heart expanded in his chest. He had always been attracted to women with deep chocolate complexions and Heavenly Evers topped the list.

"Yes. I noticed you, but you never seemed to remember me. You always came in and asked directions and walked away."

"You were at work…I didn't want to keep you from doing your job and get you in any trouble."

"I do get breaks and eat lunch everyday, Phillip."

Phillip laughed at himself, "You know you're right, but my goodness girl, after I talked to you, I could barely think. I really do like you Heavenly."

"Prove it," Heavenly said and sat back in her chair.

Phillip laced his fingers on the table in front of him and looked across at her. "Heavenly?"

"Yes."

"What would *you* like to do on our next date?"

She rewarded him with a grin and leaned toward him. "I really want to go to a place like you took Nichelle."

It was his turn to lean back. "First and Ten? The sports bar?" He could afford to take her there twice a day, every day!

"It's a restaurant, too."

"Yeah, yeah, it is," Phillip said. "Why there?"

"Because I grew up in an all female household and I don't know the rules of sports. I want someone to teach me about basketball and football and what the heck is a first and ten?

Phillip could hardly believe his ears; a second date with Heavenly to teach her about sports? His confidence soared. He could easily impress her with his knowledge of sports especially since she wanted him to teach her. "We could do that. When would you want to go?"

"How about next week, maybe Friday or Saturday night or what day are the games played?"

Phillip chuckled, "Baby, there's always a game on somewhere."

Baby. She liked the sound of that. "Okay. Call me tomorrow, and we'll decide on the time."

"It's a date," Phillip said. This night was going better than he ever imagined.

"What kind of things do you do when you're not working?" She asked.

"I don't have much of a life outside of work. I haven't been out on a date like this in months, but when I'm off, I usually run errands for my grandparents including taking them to church." Heavenly was mentally checking off the items on her list of HE Will's while Phillip entertained her with stories about his Papa and Nana and what it was like to sit around the dinner table and have them explain how it was in the olden days.

"I bought them a cell phone and they keep it on the coffee table like an accessory."

"On the coffee table?"

"Yes, and one day, Nana told me the phone wasn't working. I came over to check it out and she was right. I wasn't working because they never plugged it into the charger."

Heavenly stirred her drink while she listened. "I think it's sweet for you to take care of your grandparents. It says a lot about the kind of man you are."

He shrugged, "They're like my parents."

Heavenly smiled and thanked the waiter for filling her water glass, then looked back at Phillip, "Do you want to know what else I like?"

Phillip swallowed hard. God she was beautiful. "What else do you like?"

"I like to cook."

Cook? "Really? What do you like to cook?"

"All kinds of food. I watch the Food Channel whenever I'm home, especially on the weekends, and I buy a lot of different spices to make all kinds of exotic dishes but…"

"What?"

"I'm not sure I always make it right. I wish I had someone there to taste the food right after I make it and tell me if it's really good."

"If this is your way of inviting me over to sample your cooking, I'll be glad to sacrifice my taste buds."

Phillip grinned when Heavenly responded by laughing out loud the first time that night. To him, the sound was just like her name, heavenly.

Chapter 22

Chris Dennis looked at the clock in his dashboard. He was going to give his nephew another hour before letting himself into his brother's house even if he had to break a window. Chris never cared to live in Los Angeles, but that was before being run out of Arizona. Not literally, but L.A. was looking pretty good about now especially after the last horrible twenty-four hours. Fortunately, he was a month-to-month renter of a furnished apartment, so it was easy to pack his clothes, remove his flat screen from the wall and put everything inside his Jeep. After filling up his gas tank, Chris made his way to the 10-Interstate and headed west.

During the long drive, he had a lot of time to think about how quickly his life moved from being great to total humiliation. Chris went from juggling three females to wondering if any woman would ever date him again. Judy seemed to take it all in stride but Jazmine showed him a vengeance that, up until now, Chris believed was reserved for the Almighty. Jazmine contacted the cable network show 'Cheaters' and she and Chris were going to be featured in a thirty-minute episode next season. It was so one-sided. One minute he was having a nice dinner with a foxy lady from California, and the next, he was moving out of state. How did the *Cheaters* people know Jazmine wasn't guilty of cheating too? They just took her word for everything and followed him around for a few weeks. They showed Jazmine some video of him going to Judy's house and confronted him while he was out on a date with Debby.

He and Debby Curtin, the hostess he met at First and Ten Restaurant, had been outrageously flirting by telephone and e-mail and Debby on a dare, flew into Phoenix to spend the weekend with him. Chris promised her a good time and a night she'd never forget but being busted by the *Cheaters* people, on camera, was the last thing he had in mind. If it wasn't embarrassing enough that an angry female crying crocodile tears was in his face, along with the host of the show (Joey Grekco) accusing him of cheating, Jazmine thought she could push petite, little Debby around. Debby smiled at the camera while she pulled Jazmine into a headlock. It took all of the *Cheaters* security and the host to convince Debby not to snap Jazmine's neck. To top the night off, the head of the security team actually offered Debby a job on the show because of her skills in self-defense.

Chris sunk a little lower in his seat. Debby told him he certainly kept his end of the bargain. It was truly a night she would never forget. She seemed to think it was amusing as she rode off in the taxicab still being filmed by a *Cheaters*' videographer. It astounded Chris that she was still speaking to him.

His brother, Wade, was doing a lot better and there was talk of him coming home to fully recuperate. Chris already planned to return to California for another short visit, but now he was going to take a leave of absence from Arizona Electronics, Inc. and look for a new job somewhere in Los Angeles County. If he lived with Wade until the doctors released his brother to return to work, Keith could go back to Northern California and attend Stanford Law School. This could be a win-win for all concerned.

Keith recognized his uncle's forest green Jeep parked in the driveway and pulled the Camry behind it. Chris got out and opened the hatchback. He carefully pulled out his big screen television that was wrapped in a blanket. "Hi." He said over his shoulder.

Keith reached for the other side of the big screen. "Hi, Unc. It looks like you're moving in."

"Yeah, looks like it," Chris said.

They emptied Chris' car of his possessions and piled them up in the guest room.

Keith leaned against the dresser. "Do you want to go to the hospital and visit Dad?"

Chris lay face down across the bed, "No. I'll go tomorrow. I'm exhausted."

"Maybe when you wake up, we can go back to First and Ten…"

Chris found the strength to lift himself up on his upper arms. "No. Not there. I'm going to sleep until tomorrow. Then we'll go see my brother, okay?"

Keith shrugged, "Sure. Talk to you tomorrow." He closed the door behind him. At least he wasn't alone in the house, although in a way, he was still by himself. When his stomach growled, Keith went into the kitchen and looked inside the refrigerator. Disgusting smells accosted his nostrils. He propped the door open and looked inside looking through various containers to find the source of the offensive smell.

It took twenty minutes, but Keith emptied the refrigerator of everything and washed each shelf and the bottom drawers. Once the inside was clean, he replaced a head of cabbage, a carton of eggs, jars of condiments, a few aluminum cans of assorted sodas and lite beer, and a gallon of bottled water. Keith opened the freezer and saw a three-pound roll of ground beef, four bags of frozen vegetables, a package of T-bone steaks, a half-empty carton of chocolate chip ice cream, and a variety of *Hungry Man* dinners.

He selected a couple of beef sirloin microwavable dinners because he liked the corn and mashed potatoes with gravy sides. Following the package directions, he put the dinners, one at a time, into the microwave. While the food was cooking, Keith went through the house and emptied all of the small trashcans into the big trashcan in the kitchen; then took the kitchen trash bag outside to place it inside the city garbage can.

When he lifted the lid of the large black garbage can he heard a loud pop, then loud beeping from the Camry. Something set off the car alarm. Keith dropped the trash bag on the ground and ran to the back gate. It was dark, but he was able to make out two people running away from the rear of the Camry.

"Hey!" he yelled, but by the time he unlatched gate and ran past his uncle's Jeep, the runners had jumped into a waiting car that was idling in front of his driveway. As the car sped off, Keith ran out to the side walk and looked up and down the street to see if any of the neighbors were outside that he could enlist as witnesses.

Chris stuck his head out the front door, "Are you alright?"

Keith started to nod then he noticed the writing on his car. Under the street light it looked like maroon colored paint.

"Where are the keys?" Chris asked because the Camry's car alarm was still sounding.

"My room, on the dresser." Keith shouted.

In seconds, Chris returned and pointed the car alarm remote at the Camry and silenced the alarm. He walked outside in his socks to see what was holding his nephew's attention. Chris stood next to Keith and leaned down to get a closer look. Then he backed away pulling Keith by the arm. "Go inside and call the police."

Chapter 23

"S-T-A-Y. Any idea what this could mean?" Detective Sloan asked Keith.

They were sitting in the living room after photographs of the writing and samples of the stain were gathered as evidence. Another detective retrieved the shell from a .45, as well as a single bullet, lodged in the bumper of the car. Both items were already on their way to the crime lab for analysis.

"No, sir," Keith said. "I didn't know it was gunfire or I would not have run out front. I think I may have scared who ever it was away when I yelled."

The detective looked at his notes. "You saw a couple of people running away…"

"I really didn't get a good look at either of them, but I'm sure it was a Honda insignia on the getaway car. The car was a dark color, I think it was black. I couldn't make out the model, but it looked to be the size of an Accord or Civic."

"Do you have any enemies or know of anyone who is angry with you?" Detective Sloan asked.

Keith was quiet while he debated on sharing his concerns. To his surprise, Chris spoke up about his experience of being caught by a girlfriend that he insisted was really an acquaintance.

"Do any of these women have weapons, specifically guns?"

Chris rubbed his chin. Debby's weapons were her hands and strong body. She didn't need a gun. Jazmine was too proper to dirty her own hands with a gun. Lights, cameras and exposing him to the whole world were her weapons. Judy didn't seem to give a damn if he was in her life or not, which hurt his pride after knowing of her lackadaisical attitude. Chris shook his head, "No. I've never seen any of them with or talking about weapons or guns."

"Do you think any of the three women would follow you here?"

"I didn't think any of them knew about the other, but that theory is all shot to hell. I'm the *last* person who knows what a woman might do."

"I'm worried that Patricia Glover, from Eugene, Oregon called me from LAX more than a week ago, and I haven't heard from her since." Keith said.

"Is she a friend or relative?"

"Trish was my girlfriend and she came to L.A. to support me. She called me after the plane landed, but when I went to pick her up, I couldn't find her at the airport. I checked my cell and she left a message that she was going to a hotel and would call me later. I've been calling her for days and leaving messages, but she hasn't contacted me again. I'm getting really worried. I called her job and they said she took a two-week emergency leave, so they don't consider her missing."

Detective Sloan wrote down Trish's full name and other descriptive and personal information. "We can track her from the airline passenger manifest and there are security cameras all over LAX. If she went from the airport to a hotel she most likely either used a hotel limo or a rental car. I'm sure we can track her whereabouts at the airport. Do you think she might have anything to do with the message STAY on your car?"

"I really doubt it. Trish isn't the type to pull a stunt like that. She's very level-headed and sensible. She sounded happy when I talked to her, the first time anyway." Keith retrieved both messages from the answering machine and his cell phone and played them for the detective.

Detective Sloan wrote down the date and time of the incoming calls. "Make sure you don't delete those messages. Anything else you can think of?"

"What about that Doug guy?" Chris said to Keith.

Detective Sloan looked at Keith, "Who is the Doug guy?"

Keith cut his eyes at his uncle. He didn't want his own insecurities known all over town. "He's nobody; one of Trish's neighbors. The day after I got here, I called Trish to let her know how my Dad was doing and Doug answered her phone."

"Has she mentioned any problems with Doug?"

"No. She told me he was just a neighbor and she asked him to answer her phone. It had never happened before."

The detective noticed Chris raise an eyebrow but remained silent. *Jealous boyfriend?*

"Do you know Doug's last name?"

"No. I've never met him," Keith said. "Didn't know he existed until he answered Trish's phone."

The detective put his pen in his front pocket and closed the leather portfolio that held his notepad. "Okay. I have enough for now. We'll patrol the area in unmarked cars through the night and contact you in the morning." They all stood.

"By the way, how is your father doing?"

"Very well," Keith said and gave him an update.

Inside, Keith felt relieved. Until now, no one else seemed concerned that Trish had vanished. In order to break up with her, he had to find her, and Keith definitely didn't want to be responsible for any harm coming to Trish, especially since it was his fault she came to Los Angeles in the first place. Once Trish was located, he would have the breakup talk with her, and then he could focus guilt-free on Kimberly. He wanted Trish to have a good life and hoped she would accept the reality that she was no longer part of his future.

Chris looked through an opening in the draperies and watched as Detective Sloan walked to his car and drove away. Tomorrow, he and Keith would cut the tall hedges that ran along the property line. Then it would be easy to see any one in the front of the house.

Several neighbors were standing in their front yards but not because they heard the noise from the gun and the car alarm. Those who heard anything thought it was a car that backfired. The residents on Country Club Drive felt safe, especially living on the same street as a police officer, but tonight several police cars invading their quiet street interrupted their tranquility.

Ironically, Mrs. Buss, the little old lady from down the street, missed hearing gun fire because she wasn't wearing her hearing aid. She was just about to sit down to dinner when her dogs ran to the front of the house and started barking frantically. Mrs. Buss followed the dogs to the living room window, looked out and waved over Mr. Tan, who lived two doors down. Mr. Tan filled her in on what had happened and together they walked up the street to see Wade Dennis' silver Camry being placed on the long bed of a tow truck and driven away.

In spite of the extra patrols promised by the police, both Keith and Chris didn't figure on getting much sleep that night. Keith met his uncle in the den with a couple of sodas and a jar of roasted peanuts. Chris turned the television to ESPN news, and before the thirty-minute program ended, both were asleep on the comfortable sofas.

Several miles away, Nichelle and Brandi huddled in the backseat of Brandi's 1999 *Honda* Accord. Charm drove east on Century Boulevard past Prairie and made a right turn into the shopping plaza parking lot.

She found a parking space in the high trafficked area between *Chili's* and *Red Lobster* restaurants.

Charm looked at the two friend/enemies in the rear view mirror who, if it were possible, would be white as sheets and said, "Calm down you two. We're okay. I'm sure we weren't followed."

"We were shot at!" Brandi said. She wiped away a few stray tears with the back of her hand. Nichelle agreed with Brandi for once. Tonight had been a catastrophe. After Nichelle complained non-stop to her friends about the ten thousand dollars she missed out on because she gave up important information to Philly for a few drinks and a dinner that wasn't all that good, Charm came up with a plan to get that money.

Charm said they could graffiti the shot police man's car, but not with spray paint but actual blood from her "job." It sounded like a good idea at the time. Charm was in the process of completing eighty hours of community service at a health clinic. This was her penance for driving without a license and pleading poverty. Even the judge raised her eyebrows at her plea because Charm stood in the court room dressed in a designer suit retail priced at nine hundred dollars.

"Is that St. John you're wearing?" Judge Lillian Hart asked looking over her glasses.

"This?" Charm said. "I didn't buy this from St. John's. It came from Women-to-Work, a non-profit organization that gives gently-worn suits to women who can't afford nice clothes to wear to job interviews."

Of course it wasn't true. The suit came from William, a security guard who boosted it from the St. John's warehouse and sold it to Charm for two fifty-dollar bills. Judge Hart gave Charm the benefit of the doubt because she couldn't prove otherwise.

Brandi looked up Wade Dennis' address on the Internet. The threesome figured it would be easy to "plant" evidence and at just the right time Nichelle would reveal it to Philly. Nichelle would be rewarded the ten grand for her help and the money would be divided up accordingly. Brandi would get a thousand dollars for looking up the address, buying paint brushes and holding the vials. Charm's cut was a thousand dollars for coming up with the master plan. They all thought it was a clever move to use actual blood instead of spray paint. Since Charm was already doing community service for driving with no license, because she would stay calm no matter the situation, she was assigned to drive. That alone was worth another grand. Nichelle would be in the money again; seven thousand tax-free dollars. It was almost like winning the lottery.

They waited until the sun was almost down, and Charm drove down the street past the house just in time to see the silver Camry pull into the driveway. This was the third time the threesome staked out Wade Dennis' house. It was a nice, quiet street except for a nosy neighbor who walked her two dogs every night. The old lady with white-hair stared at the *Honda* Accord, and she walked over to the car to inquire if they were lost. Charm rolled down the window and explained they were considering buying in the neighborhood and were just checking to see what it was like at different times of the day. The old lady seemed satisfied with that explanation and continued walking her dogs.

When it was dark, Nichelle and Brandi got out of the car and walked a half block to the Dennis' house. They stooped down between the car and the tall hedges, and Brandi opened and held the vial of blood while Nichelle painted. The message was supposed to be 'Stay Away' but after Nichelle wrote the first word a burgundy car pulled up and stopped in front of the driveway. The passenger side window came down, and a shot was fired. Nichelle and Brandi wanted to scream. They were 'stooping ducks' about to be murdered in the driveway of a man who had enemies that wanted him dead. Instinct told them to flee in the opposite direction, but someone else was coming from the backyard. Mercifully, the car with the shooter sped away and was replaced by Brandi's *Honda* Accord. Nichelle and Brandi ran to the car, flung open the back door and piled into the back seat. They stayed down while Charm, who witnessed the drive-by, drove them to safety.

Nichelle chewed on her fingernails. Damn. Now that they got away, how could they explain their presence at the scene of the crime? The police were going to ask all of the neighbors if they heard or saw anyone. *Old-lady-white-hair* was sure to gab about seeing three black females in a black Honda Accord. Why did bad stuff always happen to her? "Let's get something to drink."

"Yeah, I feel you," Charm said. "Come on, Brandi."

"Why me?" Brandi replied.

"I need you because Nichelle is shaking like a leaf," Charm said. "You know she can't act like nothing unusual happened. I need you to order for us while I go to the ladies' room, then we'll figure out what to do next."

Brandi wanted to stay in the back seat and pull a blanket over her head, but Charm finally noticed her ability to play it cool and think on her feet. Brandi didn't want to disappoint her by refusing, so she gathered her wits and got out of the car.

Nichelle was glad to be alone. She needed to think. After closing her eyes, she took a few deep-cleansing breaths. No one thought their plan could fail, so there was no plan B. First thing they needed to do now was to get rid of the blood and paint brushes and park the Honda in the garage. When her friends returned to the car, Nichelle would tell Brandi to take this car to *Earl Shieb* on Crenshaw and Slauson. For a couple of hundred dollars, she could get a paint job; any color, but black. After Nichelle had some alcohol to calm her nerves, they would decide their next steps. Nichelle wished she told them to bring her back something to eat. She opened her eyes and tried to look away from the bright light before realizing it was the spot light from a police car. The sound of a low-flying helicopter seemed louder than normal. Then came an all-too-familiar sound from a police bull horn.

"You, in the *Honda* Accord. Open the door very slowly and show your hands!"

Chapter 24

Wade Dennis was finally awake and somewhat alert. He'd been kept in a drugged stupor for so many days that he had no idea if it was still the month of August. He did remember being in his office, talking to his son, hearing a noise. Then pain scattered through his arm and he fell, in slow motion, backward in his chair. He must have been on the floor a long time, and he could remember the strong smell of dirt mixed with carpet cleaner.

After a while, there were voices, people shouting and finally he was in an ambulance. Everything else he remembered were parts of weird dreams and strange noises. He was sure Keith had been in his hospital room and maybe his brother Chris, but the memory was foggy, because at times, his dead wife Julie was there too. Looking around the room, Wade hated all of the flower arrangements lining his window sill because they reminded him of Julie's funeral.

A small Filipino woman entered his room through the open door. "Good morning, sir. I'm Belinda, your day nurse. Can you tell me your name?"

Wade cleared his throat, "Wade. Wade Dennis."

"Very good," Belinda said. She seemed genuinely pleased. Belinda took his vitals and recorded the information in the computer next to the bed. "Ninety-nine degrees is your temperature; not bad, and your blood pressure is one thirty-four over eighty, could be better."

Wade felt like he'd been in a fight with Mike Tyson when Tyson was in his prime. He ached all over, but most of all, the shooting pain in his right arm radiated through his whole body. "When was the last time I ate?"

"Breakfast is on its way," Belinda said. "Then you'll get a sponge bath and…"

Wade frowned, "Not from a lady!"

Belinda stopped and looked at him, "Oh. I didn't know you were shy Mr. Dennis. After a week and a half, I was starting to feel we were friends, but if you prefer I'll have Juan bathe you."

"I prefer to bathe myself," Wade said. Talking was making him tired. He laid his head back and closed his eyes.

"How's the pain?"

Wade kept his eyes closed, "Doing its job."

Belinda was not deterred, "On a scale of one to ten, if one is no pain and ten is the worse pain you've ever felt."

"Fifteen."

"Okay. I'll be back with your pain medicine," Belinda said and left the private room. Minutes later, she returned and added a vial of morphine to Wade's IV. He slept through breakfast and woke up when Dr. Nunez came in to examine his wounds.

Wade didn't say anything when Belinda cleaned his wounds and the surrounding area because the doctor was present and it seemed unmanly to complain. After the doctor left his room, Belinda brought warm water in a plastic bowl, a washcloth, and some liquid soap to his tray. Without asking, she carefully washed the rest of Wade's upper body then his legs and feet. The nurse emptied the bowl, rinsed it out and brought it back to him with more warm water and a fresh washcloth along with a toothbrush, a sample size bar of soap, toothpaste, and mouth wash.

"Let me know when you're done," Belinda said. She discretely pulled the curtain around the bed to block the view of his bed from the corridor.

Wade was grateful the nurse didn't listen to what he said earlier about wanting to bathe himself because he was already exhausted. Wade washed his face and private parts as best he could, then yearned to take a nap. He fell asleep several times while brushing his teeth. When he finally woke up, it was lunch time. All of the cleaning supplies were gone, and magically, he was wearing a clean hospital gown. He didn't remember the nurses, Juan and Belinda, changing his sheets or taking his vitals again either.

The main dish on his lunch plate was sliced beef with a serving of mashed potatoes and mixed vegetables. A dinner roll was separately wrapped in clear cellophane and a small green salad with a packet of Italian-lite salad dressing was in a Styrofoam bowl. The rest of the meal consisted of a small banana, a serving of orange juice, and a cup of sugar-free gelatin.

Wade tasted the beef. It wasn't bad, but after not eating solid food for days, any food would have tasted pretty good. It took effort, but he managed to put a little margarine on the dinner roll and took a bite. In twenty minutes, he finished everything except the banana and the gelatin. Eating was exhausting. It was time for another nap.

Chapter 25

August Lord sat inside Chili's Restaurant with his back to the door. He didn't like this set up. It was too wide open and easy for someone to come in and hold the place up. He should know, he was a son of Storm Lord one of the most notorious gang leaders in Los Angeles' history and founder of the Storm Lords gang. August wore dark sunglasses to keep his eyes hidden to not let the people around him know he was watching their every move. The black knit beanie he wore pulled down over his forehead was too warm for Southern California, but August was raised on the east coast, so warm or not, he wasn't going to change his style.

August was a big man. Although his actual height was five-eleven, he seemed taller and he projected a no-nonsense aura such that no one, unless they had a death wish, would want to challenge him. Prison wasn't nothing, but a family reunion and sometimes, the only time he ever saw his male relatives. It was mentally demanding to always being on guard, to have to choose his words carefully and never be able to trust anyone. He spent the last first day of August, his thirtieth birthday in prison, contemplating his life.

August fantasized about what it would be like to have a respectable white-collar job and friends he could hang out with who took their family to the park and no violence broke out. What if no fights had to be broken up and the kids could just play and not be knocked over by an adult trying to shield them from gunfire? On the next Monday morning, he would come back to work and talk about what a nice day it was not who was stabbed or arrested or the need to retaliate. That's what came from going to those chapel services. They made August think about how life could be different on the outs.

Becky was working the checkout counter. She didn't want to bother the man in the corner, but his order was ready. She recognized him as a real gangbanger from not only by his fat-shoe laces, camouflage Dickie pants, white sleeveless cotton U-neck shirt, and a dark green Flack jacket, but by his position while seated. In spite of his being seated, this man was poised, ready for whatever went down.

"Number fifty-three," she said and tried not to look too long in his direction.

August stood, walked over to her, and laid the stub on the counter, "Is there forks in there?"

Becky wasn't sure, but she handed him a pre-packaged utensil packet that he tossed inside the bag. He indicated his thanks by a slight lift to his chin and left the building. Outside of the restaurant, August stood near the curb and scanned the parking lot. Now that he was on the outside, he had to get used to normal traffic without wanting to keep close to the walls. His homeboy, Short Dog, let him drive his car, and August backed into a parking space in the middle of the lot, so he could drive out. He sat in the car while he ate and thought about where he could hang out for the rest of the night. August didn't have his own spot, but he could stay at several of his friend's and acquaintances places in South Los Angeles. He only had to mention his last name and it opened doors. No one wanted to offend Storm. At last count, Storm had fathered twenty children by half as many baby-mamas. August was somewhere in the middle.

His mother, TaWanna, tried to raise him right and keep him interested in school and away from street life, but she was a teenage mother with few life skills to equip her son, and with a father like Storm, it was hard for the boy to reject the lure of the streets, especially when there was no man around to reinforce what his mother told him. TaWanna died last year; the victim of a drive by—a senseless act of being in the wrong place at the wrong time. August was in prison and was not allowed to attend her funeral until Storm, who was in the same prison, got wind of it. Storm had a talk with the warden, and August was allowed out for two hours, heavily guarded.

August didn't like to think about how he disappointed his mother. TaWanna only wanted what was best for him and always told him about what life could be like if he would stay out of trouble and stay in school. August dropped out in the eighth grade. As the son of Storm Lord, he could hang out with the older guys to smoke and drink. Other kids his age admired him because thugs and members of the Storm Lords gang accepted August as an equal, a possible heir. The first time August was arrested it was for drug possession, and he was sent to a juvenile court school camp. Since there was nothing to do but to attend school in the camp, August completed enough credits to finish the 8th grade, so he was returned to regular school after his sentence was served. This became a pattern for him until he turned eighteen years old and was finally tried as an adult and sent to prison for 'possession of cocaine with an intent-to-sell.' August was six credits shy of finishing high school.

In prison, being Storm's son was a blessing and a curse. It was a blessing because the older, bigger, sicker men left him alone, but it was a curse because he was a target for everyone else, so when the guards could get away with it, they treated him like he was less than human. It was okay though because August was tough. He would remember their faces and promised himself if ever a day came he met one of them on the street, August would be the only one to walk away.

August saw the black *Honda* Accord pull next to him. At first he thought the light skinned girl was alone, but after a few minutes another big-boned, dark skinned girl got out of the back seat, and they walked toward the Red Lobster. He was almost finished eating when he noticed a police car moving slowly through a row of cars in the next isle. He remained motionless, fully alert, watching. The movement of the police car reminded him of a snake slithering through the grass. In seconds, two other police cars with flashing red and blue lights blocked his only means of escape. Two bright lights, one shone overhead from a helicopter that appeared out of nowhere and the other was the spot light from one of the police vehicles.

"You in the *Honda* Accord. Open the door very slowly and show your hands!"

August knew the drill. He set his food on the dashboard keeping his hands in view and slowly turned moving his hands outside the open window of the driver side door. He was inwardly startled when he looked into a pair of frightened dark brown eyes and saw a pair of skinny arms reaching out of the car toward him. What the…?. What was the chance of two black *Honda* Accord's parking next to each other like this? Who did they want?

The police had never encountered this scenario either. Two officers cautiously approached the cars with their guns drawn. "Ma'am you get out first. Keep your hands up."

Nichelle did as instructed. How did the police find them this fast? Where were Charm and Brandi? She wasn't going down for those traders.

Officer Jones holstered his gun, "Do you have identification miss?"

"Yes. It's in the car," Nichelle said.

The second officer held his gun on August. "Get out of the car and keep your hands in sight."

August kept his movements smooth and slow. He assumed the position by placing his hands on the front of the hood, leaned slightly forward and spread his legs. Officer Getty patted him down and visibly relaxed when no weapons were found on him. "Do you have identification?"

"In my inside jacket pocket," August said. He was so calm and speaking in a normal voice that Nichelle strained to hear him.

"What else will I find in your pocket?" Officer Getty asked.

"Nothin' man. No drugs, no weapons," August said.

Officer Getty looked at his California driver's license, "Lord. August First Lord. Any relation to Storm Lord?"

"He's my father."

Officer Getty turned to his partner, "Hey Jonesy, we got another one of Storm's kids. This city is overrun with little Black lords." He was the only one who found humor in his statement.

Officer Jones stated, "A man in a black *Honda* Accord just robbed a customer at Chase bank and..." Mid-sentence he paused to listen to the voice coming from his earpiece. "The suspect is traveling west on the 105." Just like that and with no apologies, the policemen hurried back to their respective cars and drove quickly out of the lot heading south on Crenshaw Boulevard, leaving Nichelle and August standing in front of twin, opposite facing, black *Honda* Accord's.

The small crowd that gathered a respectful distance away from the Honda's dispersed. They were somewhat disappointed that the drama ended with no arrests.

"You all 'ight Shorty?" August asked Nichelle.

Nichelle nodded. She liked what she saw. This big, strong soldier wasn't afraid of the police. His status was definitely hood. He favored the rapper Fifty-Cent when he first came out with all those muscles. Nichelle appreciated his gold-capped tooth, ink from his arms to his neck and a swagger that made her one-hundred percent glad she was a female.

Chapter 26

Phillip Covers thought he was acting the same way except for feeling happy and looking forward to a second date with Heavenly. However, his co-workers noticed the sudden change. Out of the blue, Phillip brought donuts to the weekly staff meeting and not the kind in the package from the grocery store; he brought in two-dozen glazed donuts from Krispy Kreme…while they were still warm.

Phillip smiled more than usual, and for no reason at all, he would hum a tune just like a man who hadn't a care in the world. It was disturbing to the group because Phillip seemed to know something they didn't. Rumors began floating around the department that he was leaving. Conventional wisdom was that Phillip was offered a better position, probably in the Major's office because that office was known to have a few vacancies. Why else would Phillip Covers be one of them last week and now walking around as Mr. Pleasant-and-Content with life?

Phillip knew about the vacancies in the Mayor's Office, but he hadn't considered applying for them until after his supervisor asked to speak to him, privately.

Captain John Boswell cleared the last hour of the work-day for a one-on-one meeting with Phil Covers. The walls of his office were floor to ceiling glass, so everyone could see in and out. "Come in Phil," he said after Phillip knocked lightly on the door, "have a seat."

Phillip sat in one of the two straight back guest chairs. These chairs were definitely for looks, not comfort, and matched the other leather furniture pieces in the office, complementing the dark wood of John Boswell's captain's desk. Phillip folded his hands in front of him and looked at his boss. The poor guy had lost most of his hair, but he insisted on combing the few remaining strands over the top of his head. His protruding belly looked like he was carrying twins, which reminded Phillip to renew his gym membership.

John Boswell leaned back in his chair, which squeaked in protest from the redistribution of his weight. He looked up at the ceiling. "Phil, you've been in this department for…"

"Almost five years," Phillip said. He was used to finishing his supervisor's sentences.

"Almost five," John repeated. He looked directly at Phillip. "I've been in this department twenty-five years come December."

Phillip nodded. John Boswell didn't like to be upstaged. He continued talking to Phillip about his own life as a policeman in Philadelphia, and how he walked the mean streets of Pennsylvania and dealt with street gangs and punks who tried to take over the neighborhoods. In the mid-1980's, Boswell was asked to join the Los Angeles Police Force and be one of three leaders in their Gang Intervention Unit.

"I didn't just up and leave my assignment Phil. I went to my superiors and ran the job by them. They were all for me leaving."

I bet.

"They wanted me to spread my wings and show the West Coast what the East Coast already knew. Do you hear what I'm saying Phil?

"Yes, sir. I believe so."

When Phillip didn't offer any more comments Boswell continued. "I know there are openings in certain departments, and it's tempting to reach out to see if you can cut it in another place. The Sheriffs, the Mayor's Office…I'm sure you've heard about those vacancies, but what I want you to do is play it smart and come to me first. Ask me before you accept any of those offers. I know people in both places." He leaned forward and whispered, "I can tell you where the landmines are."

"Thank you," Phillip said. He hadn't thought about leaving his current job assignment, but since these new opportunities were brought to his attention, he would definitely check out the vacancies in both agencies. "I appreciate you taking the time to talk with me."

"Anytime Phil," John Boswell said. Smoking wasn't allowed in the building, but after hours, Boswell often smoked a cigar, and he felt like having one now. Everybody in the department knew where the smoke was coming from because it traveled throughout the ventilation system, but they chose to look the other way and use it as an excuse to exit the building and go home a little early.

Before starting his car, Phillip pushed a button on his cell phone.

"Hello Phillip. What's up?" Heavenly asked.

"Hey Baby, can I stop by after work and use your computer?"

"Sure you can. I'm going to fix Chinese food tonight."

Phillip could tell Heavenly was smiling and his heart soared.

"Do you want me to bring anything?"

"No. Not really, it's kind of hard to find Vinacafe brand…"

"Girl, I told you to stop selling me short. Your place is right next to Chinatown. I'll find whatever it is. Spell it for me."

"V-i-n-a-c-a-f-e. It's an instant coffee mix."

"Got it. I'm going to check on my folks first then I'll be at your place by 6:30."

"Okay Phillip. I'll see you then," Heavenly ended the call and couldn't hide her grin. Phillip was the perfect man. He was so considerate, always calling before coming by, and always asking if she needed anything. Even when she didn't ask him to bring something, Phillip would come with an exotic spice or a single rose to present to her when she opened the door.

Chuck Dearborn, a financial advisor with an office on the seventh floor was just about to exit the building. "Is that for me?" He asked referring to Heavenly's smile.

"Of course," Heavenly said it in such a way that Chuck wished he was single again; however, using wisdom, he filed the conversation away in his memory, gave her a wink and kept walking.

$\mathcal{C}$hapter 27

"$\mathcal{H}$ave you heard anything about Trish's whereabouts?" Kimberly asked. She was treating Keith to a celebratory lunch at First and Ten wanting to hear all about his new job. His eyes lit up while talking about the huge glass windows in the front of the building. He described the layout of the fifth floor that housed the ten attorneys of Becker and Snowden Law Offices of Los Angeles, and he gave her an overview of his conversations with the junior partners.

Keith really liked the simplicity of their office spaces: big desk, leather chair, floor-to-ceiling bookshelves, state of the art computer and printer stations, and a window to the outside world. He could see himself working at a desk like that someday. Unfortunately, his dream would have to wait because the junior partner offices surrounded an inner space filled with windowless gray cubicles. This was also the workspace of all of the lesser employees: the secretaries, file clerk, and law clerks. The rest of the floor consisted of a break room, copy room, and a room for storage. Across the hall were four meeting rooms of various sizes, the restrooms, and the suites of the senior partners. When Keith grew silent, Kimberly knew something more serious was on his mind.

Keith picked up the small dessert menu and read through it to distract himself from staring at her. He cleared his throat, "According to the police, there is video of Trish at LAX getting into a dark red or burgundy rental car. It seemed to be driven by someone she knew."

"She still hasn't called you back?"

"No, and she hasn't called her parents in Victoria, Canada. They have this standing day they call each other every month, and when Trish didn't call, it's an understatement to say they're worried."

"What's the standing day about?" Kimberly said.

"It's a family thing. Each of them was born on the tenth of different months. Trish is August 10th, her mom's birthday is May 10th, and her dad's is I think October 10th, her parent's got married on June 10th…"

"So when Trish didn't contact them on August 10th, they panicked."

Keith nodded. "She was supposed to come home for her birthday celebration. It's a good thing I already reported her missing because Trish's parents told the police they believe *I* had something to do with her disappearance. I would have called them if I had their phone number."

"Why didn't you have her parent's phone number?"

Keith shrugged, "Honestly, we really weren't that close. We were friends who lived in the moment."

"You didn't love her?" Kimberly asked.

Keith looked her directly in the eyes. "I cared about her, but we were at most friends who became lovers, but I was never in love with Trish. I'm embarrassed that you know I haven't been acting like a saved man. I've done everything, but be a witness to the goodness of God. I took the credit for all my blessings. I made foolish choices and now I'm paying for them."

Kimberly broke eye contact and looked down at the table.

"What's on your mind?" Keith asked.

Kimberly glanced up at him, then back down at the table. "Just wondering if you've ever been in love?"

He didn't hesitate, "Yes."

She looked back up at him.

Keith was watching her. He leaned forward, "Yes."

When he said it the second time looking into her eyes, she knew he was referring to her.

"This is getting complicated," Kimberly said and looked away.

Keith reached over and touched her hand. "I love you, Kimberly."

Kimberly closed her eyes for a moment, "Did you tell Trish you loved her?"

Keith sighed, "I did."

"Then how do I know you won't see me the same way as Trish after some time passes?

A few seconds passed before he answered, "I'm not going to hurt you. I love you Kimberly and I'm in love with you. I'm not Wesley. Don't make me pay for his stupidity."

Kimberly could feel her emotions rising to the surface, "Trust me, Keith; I know you're not my ex-husband…"

"Wesley was never your ex. You were still married to him when he died."

Kimberly paused, "You sound angry…"

"I'm more than angry. I made you a promise to look out for you. I wish I would have been there when you first met that guy."

"I can't hold you to a promise you made when we were just kids."

"I should have stayed in touch with you. We could have helped each other stay on the straight and narrow. If I'd been around you, Wesley never could have come in and hurt you like he did. I hate how he treated you, used you, and tossed you aside. He wasn't even man enough to say it to your face before he left. What kind of husband writes a Dear Jane letter to his wife?"

Unbidden tears sprang to Kimberly's eyes, surprising them both.

"I'm sorry," Keith said. He wanted to end her pain not add to it.

"It's okay," Kimberly said dabbing her eyes with a napkin. "I guess I am holding on to baggage I thought I was over, but thank you for wanting to stand up for me. I was too dumb to know any better."

Keith got up and slid into the booth next to Kimberly. "You weren't dumb honey, you just trusted the wrong person." He gently held her chin to keep her from turning away, "I always wanted to be the man to teach you about love." He gently kissed her on the lips then rested his forehead against her shoulder.

Kimberly held her hand against his cheek, "You already have."

"Oh, isn't that nice," Donna said. She stood next to the table with two white take-out bags. "This little one is your doggy bag, and the big one is for your father. I know hospital food is the pits."

Keith turned to look at her, but he kept his arms around Kimberly. "Thank you Donna. My Dad will love getting home cooked food. I can tell he's feeling better because his appetite is back."

"It's healthy too," Donna said referring to her food. "I used a little olive oil and my own blend of spices for the seasoning, so there is very little salt. The meat is lean ground turkey, and I used whole wheat pasta." Most of the flavor was in the spaghetti sauce Donna made from fresh vegetables picked from the Farmer's Market and that she seasoned with freeze-dried spaghetti sauce mix flown in from Italy.

Keith could smell the wonderful aroma coming from the large bag. "I'll take care of whatever he doesn't eat." He leaned over and kissed Kimberly on the cheek, "I'll call you later. Let me take this food over to the hospital while it's hot."

"Don't worry. There's plenty enough for the two of you," Donna said. When Keith stood up, he leaned toward Donna and gave her a peck on her cheek, picked up the bags and headed to the front of the restaurant.

Donna and Kimberly watched him walk out of the front door. "If you don't marry that guy I will," Donna said.

Chris Dennis came with Keith to First and Ten and had been waiting in the lobby hoping to talk to Debby Curtin. When they arrived, the lobby was bustling with customers, but after people were seated, the crowd dwindled down to just the two of them. Chris stood across from Debby and asked, "How have you been?"

She knew Chris was there, but she looked up suddenly like she was seeing him for the first time. "Well, if it isn't Chris. Chris Dennis," Debby said. "I'm great Chris, but the question is, *how are you?*" Her gray eyes sparkled as she held back an urge to laugh.

Chris felt himself blush. He hadn't blushed since the first time he saw Boyd Ledger's mother come out of the shower in her birthday suit. Chris was twelve years old and visiting at his friend Boyd's house for the first time. The boys were in Boyd's room playing a video game when Chris needed to use the bathroom. Boyd told him to go down the hall and turn left. Chris did as instructed.

Chris was taught to lock the bathroom door when it was occupied. Apparently, this was not the rule in the Ledger home. Mrs. Ledger's mouth formed a perfect "O" when she saw the boy standing and staring. She grabbed a towel to cover herself, then pushed the child back out into the hallway and closed the door. Chris left the Ledger's house and never returned. Years later, he saw Mrs. Ledger in the grocery store. He was a young man of nineteen and knew much more about females than when he was twelve. Mrs. Ledger was the first woman Chris ever saw naked, in the flesh, but decided to let bygones be bygones.

When he walked past Mrs. Ledger she said, "What's the matter Chris? Don't you recognize me with my clothes on?" Embarrassed again, Chris kept on walking and pretended not to hear the echo of Mrs. Ledger's laughter ringing in his ears.

"I'll live," Chris said. "I'm sorry that things got so out of hand in Arizona."

"On the contrary, Chris. I'll always remember that night, and you and I will be watching our episode next season."

Chris groaned wishing he could delete her memory, or better yet, turn back time so there would be no Jazmine or upcoming *Cheaters* episode he'd have to explain or live with for the rest of his life.

Since the lobby was still empty, Debby took it as an opportunity to "take a load off." She sat down in one of the padded benches in the waiting area. "I'll beat out anyone else who has a first date story and have a doozy to share with our grandchildren."

Grandchildren? Did he hear her right? Debby smiled at his puzzled expression.

Chris sat down next to Debby, "Are you saying we're going to have children?"

"Sure. I like kids" she touched his arm. "You aren't too old to perform are you?"

Chris sat up strait and stuck his chest out. "Hell…I mean, heck no!" He grabbed her hand and interlaced his fingers with hers and kissed the back of her hand.

"Of course, you know if you cheat on me what I'll do to you and the floozy, right dear?"

"Me, cheat? On you? Never."

Debby chuckled at his innocent expression. No wonder he got away with stuff. "I think I can work with you." She said, and she went back to the podium to greet the couple who entered the front door. "Welcome to First and Ten. Do you have a reservation?"

Keith stood next to his uncle holding the take-out bags. "How did it go?"

"What?" Chris gaffed. "You don't know who you're talking to boy. I put the Dennis charm on her and she can't wait to get with me again. She's even talking about our grandkids."

Keith shook his head. "I'll never understand women. Let's go Unc. This food is hot and I need to get it to the hospital A-SAP."

Chapter 28

"How does my hair look in the back?" Nichelle asked. Nichelle's dark brown hair just touched the top of her shoulders. It was parted in the middle and styled in soft waves courtesy of Luv hairdressing and conditioner.

Heavenly looked up while stirring the contents of a pot on the stove. "It's cute. You always had a nice head of hair. I like this whole look on you."

Nichelle looked back at her reflection in the mirror. What she saw looked plain, average. She preferred adding a lot of synthetic hair to her head, even though ninety percent of the Black people in America knew it was bought hair, but tonight was special. August mentioned in passing that he liked a female's natural hair and Nichelle was trying to make a good impression on August Lord. She invited him over for dinner at her sister's apartment. Growing up, Nichelle could have cared less about cooking, but Aunt Angelene claimed she could catch any man after he ate three of her home cooked meals, besides that, Heavenly owed her after Nichelle hooked her up with Philly.

Heavenly and Philly had been out on all kinds of lame dates: First and Ten for starters. In Nichelle's opinion, it was a big let down after Chi Boulevard. Then they went to a boring baseball game at Dodgers Stadium. A game they could have watched on television for free instead of paying twenty dollars for parking. Philly must have spent a grip on two Dodger dogs, and not to mention the cost of the other snacks when a whole pack of hot dogs on sale cost a dollar and for what? A free Dodger cap? Nichelle knew a place in the garment district where sports caps cost twenty-four dollars a dozen. Then to top it off, the home team lost to the visiting San Diego Padres. How weak was that?

In contrast, when August invited her to accompany him to the Tenth Annual Real Players' Ball, Nichelle practically swooned. The Real Players' Ball was going to be held in the huge ballroom at Hollywood Park Casino in Inglewood on Labor Day. Nichelle knew all about it after watching a segment on 'BET's *106ᵗʰ and Park*' program. She was glued to the television as the celebrities were interviewed after walking down the purple carpet. Rapper/actor Ice T and rapper Snoop Dogg were in attendance, so to think she was going to be in the same room with them, had her squealing in delight to accept his invitation.

Nichelle already knew there would be television coverage. She would never wave at the camera like she'd seen other people do; like they never been nowhere. She'd Top Model-pose and hold onto August's arm like she was his first lady.

"Nichelle, can you cut up these potatoes?" Heavenly said. One of the side dishes needing preparation was potato salad. The potatoes were already cooked, pealed and sitting in a large bowl on the counter.

Nichelle entered the warm kitchen reluctantly. She needed to stay away from too much heat, so her hair wouldn't 'turn back.' "How do I cut them?"

"Nichelle!" Heavenly exclaimed. "You know what potatoes in potato salad looks like."

Nichelle picked up a large potato in her left hand and a large knife in the other. Before she could slice through both her hand and the potato, Heavenly grabbed the extremely sharp chef's knife from her sister. She handed her another knife that was very dull and could in no way send her to the Emergency Room unless she fell on it.

*H*eavenly took a moment to stir the bar-b-que sauce she was heating in a medium size pot on the smallest front burner. She added mustard, brown sugar, and hot sauce to the pot. Nichelle watched and wondered how her sister knew so much about cooking. It couldn't be that hard.

While she prepared the meal, Heavenly kept one side of the double kitchen sink full of warm soapy water, so the dirty dishes could soak before placing them inside the dishwasher.

A larger pot of mustard greens seasoned with smoked turkey wings was simmering on the back burner, and cut-up chicken parts were baking in a large aluminum pan inside the oven. Heavenly opened a large can of baked beans with her electric can opener. She shook the contents of the can over a large pot and added brown sugar. After stirring, she tasted them then added a few drops of liquid smoke, a pat of butter, a few shakes of Worchester sauce and a tablespoon of mustard. After another stir, Heavenly turned to the mixer on the kitchen table.

All the ingredients to make a pineapple upside down cake were already set on the table. She prepared the cake pan by placing a stick of butter in the pan and putting it inside the oven on the top rack. While she waited for the butter to melt, she mixed pineapple cake mix, eggs, butter, water, flour, sugar, and pineapple juice from the partially opened can of crushed pineapples with the electric mixer. Heavenly took the hot pan of melted butter out of the oven and set it on a cutting board. She turned the baked chicken over in the pan and reduced the oven temperature to 325 degrees.

*A*fter carefully spreading brown sugar over the top of the melted butter she covered the surface with crushed pineapple, then topped everything with the cake batter and set it aside.

"Finished," Nichelle announced.

Heavenly inspected her work. "Good. Start on the eggs." She opened the refrigerator and took out a bowl of six boiled eggs, already pealed and set it in front of her sister. Before Nichelle could comment, Heavenly took out a roll of refrigerated biscuits.

"We're not making bread from scratch?"

We? "These crescent rolls are very good, especially with a little butter," Heavenly said.

"Okay," Nichelle replied under her breath knowing that Aunt Angelene would be turning over in her grave. The old girl passed away a few years ago from complications from diabetes. Nichelle kind of missed her and her cooking, but if Nichelle could ask Aunt Angelene one question it wouldn't be about food it would be: *who was the old Italian man who cried all through the funeral service?* Aunt Ella Dean said the man was Angelene's old boss, and she worked for his family for years, but it didn't make sense the way he seemed more grieved than any of Angelene's family members. He left right after the funeral service in a limo.

Heavenly took the pan of chicken out of the oven and set it on the counter. She made sure it was thoroughly cooked by stabbing the joint of a golden brown leg quarter and pulling up a piece of the tender meat. Satisfied the chicken was done, she placed the cake pan inside the oven and turned the timer on thirty minutes. Nichelle was in the bathroom, probably looking at her hair again, so Heavenly finished making the potato salad. By the time Nichelle returned, the cake was out of the oven and the crescent rolls were baking.

"How does my hair look now?"

Heavenly stopped and blotted her forehead with a paper napkin. "Fine. Now set the table…"

"Just fine? I want to look better than fine," Nichelle said. She turned and walked back into the bathroom.

Sighing, Heavenly took out the lace table cloth her mother gave her as a housewarming gift. She spread it over the kitchen table. From a lower drawer, she pulled out brown woven place mats and black ceramic plates from an upper cabinet. She was glad she decided to buy the eight-piece set of silverware because everything would match. Phillip told her he was bringing flowers for the centerpiece so the table was almost ready.

"Do you like this jean set on me?" Nichelle asked. She was wearing the same outfit she wore when Philly took her to First and Ten. Who cares if he saw her in it before, August hadn't.

"You look really nice Nichelle. I can tell you really like this August person, huh?"

"Wait until you see him. He is so fine," Nichelle said, "and he talk right."

"Come sit down and tell me about him," Heavenly said. She took a bowl of lemons and squeezed the juice from them with a manual juicer while Nichelle told her all of the things she saw in August.

Heavenly had never seen her sister act like this. She was stunned when Nichelle asked if they could have a dinner party at her place to invite the men over. It had never happened before. Heavenly couldn't tolerate Nichelle's friends, Charm and Brandi, so they never hung out together. In the past, Nichelle only kept a man around to use him and eventually the guy caught on and took off, angry, because he'd come to the realization that he would never see again the money she "borrowed."

After rinsing her hands and throwing away the lemon rinds, Heavenly poured two cups of sugar into a large pitcher, added the juice from the lemons and filled it almost to the top with cold water. She stirred while Nichelle told her how much she was looking forward to going to the upcoming Real Players' Ball. When the lemonade was ready, Heavenly added ice cubes and put the pitcher inside the refrigerator just as the timer went off. Heavenly took the rolls out of the oven and turned off the fire under the greens. She gave the baked beans a final stir and covered them.

Nichelle followed Heavenly into her bedroom where Heavenly changed into a new Ashley Stewart solid pink button down shirt-dress. Pink made her feel especially feminine, and the way Phillip looked at her made her feel beautiful. She put on pink pearl earrings and a matching necklace. After another heat wave was projected to last through the rest of the month, so Heavenly decided to wear her hair in easy-to-maintain braids. Her friend Veronica hooked her up with 'individuals,' and after eight hours and three packs of hair, Heavenly was set for the rest of the summer.

*A*s expected, Phillip called to tell her he was a few minutes away. He apologized for not being there already to help, but he had to drop his grandfather off at UCLA hospital after an unusual spike in his temperature.

"Don't you dare apologize," Heavenly told him, "I'll understand if you need to stay with your Papa at the hospital and can't make it."

"What?" Nichelle said. Philly had to come. He couldn't ruin their plans. Leave the old geezer at the hospital. They were used to taking care of sick people.

"Don't panic," Heavenly said to her sister, "he's almost here. Why don't you call August and see if he's on his way?"

Nichelle picked up her cell phone and punched in his number. She already had it memorized. She put the call on speaker. After a few rings, he answered.

"Speak!"

"Hi, August. It's me Nichelle."

"Yo, Baby Girl. What's shaken?"

"I'm cool. I was wondering if you were on your way over. I gave you the address to my sister's place, right?"

"Oh, is that today?"

"Yeah. Right now."

"Oh, wow. I gave my homeboy back his whip, but run that address by me again."

Nichelle gave him the address while Heavenly shook her head.

Chapter 29

armer "Farm" Williams retired from the Los Angeles Police department in 2008 for two reasons. Number one, he had a bad feeling that his luck was running out and sooner rather than later, that he was going to be a victim of the criminal element in Los Angeles that he spent thirty-two years trying to contain. There was no way to eradicate or end wrong-doing during his lifetime, so as a retired police officer, Farm had to be content with keeping the peace, if only in his View Park neighborhood. Farm had been a married father of two children and now, after thirty years of marriage, was divorced. During the thirty years, his kids grew up, moved away and started their own families. In the divorce settlement, Farm kept the three-bedroom single family home, the classic 1965 navy-blue T-Bird, and an apartment building located in Santa Monica. His ex-wife, Tiffany, owned a successful real estate agency and kept the rest of their accumulated assets. They both knew she deserved it, having shouldered most of the domestic duty and parental responsibilities. Over the years, Tiffany used shrewd intelligence and sista-girl savvy to purchase select real estate properties to build an impressive portfolio.

Farm didn't have any hobbies other than watching sports on television and an occasional game of dominos or cards with other retirees. He mostly enjoyed his daily walk through the neighborhood. To the average person, Farm looked like what he was, an older gentleman getting his daily exercise, but in actuality, Farm was a one-person neighborhood watch. He knew the rhythm and flow of the five square miles that he covered on his daily stroll, so when something or someone looked out of place, it stuck out like a bright color on a gray backdrop. Farm would assess the situation while he, nonchalantly, kept moving. If necessary, he would text an ex-co-worker who was a dispatcher at the King Street Police Station. The situation would be contained, such that most of the neighbors never knew the peace and quiet they were enjoying was because of one man's diligence.

The second reason Farm retired was a threat and a promise made to him by Storm Lord. On October 27, 2007, Farmer Williams was scheduled to testify in court the next week because Farm saw Mr. Storm Lord on King and Crenshaw boulevards in the city of Los Angeles on May 23, 2007. Storm was accused of threatening a store-owner with a weapon, and if convicted, he would be sent back to prison. Storm insisted he was out of town on that day and could produce several witnesses who would testify as such. It was Storm and his witnesses' word against that of a twenty-five year veteran of the LAPD. The date and events of the day were etched in Farm's mind because that was the day his divorce was final.

Farm had just completed and signed his last payroll report and was trying to decide where he would pick up dinner, when he looked up and saw Storm Lord enter his office and closed the door behind him. Storm was only 5'-9" tall, but he looked bigger, especially while he stood looking down at the detective. Farm was in good physical shape. He was on the wrestling team in high school, and he briefly studied martial arts in college and worked out regularly since then, but the confined space and possibility that Storm was carrying a weapon changed the game. Farm showed no fear, but he warily watched the infamous Storm Lord who was standing five feet away. Both men knew there was no way out. Storm's salt and pepper hair was plated in thick corn-rows, straight back. He looked Farm in the eye with a black-eyed piercing stare, never blinking. His dominating stance and no-nonsense expression reminded Farm of rapper-turned-actor Ice Cube, before he crossed-over to do main-stream movies.

"Don't testify against me," Storm finally said. His voice wasn't menacing, but it was deep and commanded attention. There was no doubt he meant what he said.

Farm thought of several comebacks, but he thought it was wiser not to respond.

"I don't know who you *think* you saw that looked like me..." Storm put one hand on his chest... "but, I was in San Diego that Saturday. I was visiting a friend." His other hand remained in the pocket of his black-flack jacket.

Farm had never been intimidated by felons and to see the audacity of this one standing in the police station in his office, like he was the President of the United States, took more than gall and bordered on insanity. After a long pause, Farm set his pen down on the desk, "I know what I saw."

Storm broke the eye contact. He stepped away from the door and toward a small metal credenza Farm used to display some personal effects, mostly framed photographs of his children and grandchildren. Farm frowned when Storm picked up a picture frame that contained a family portrait. It was a Christmas photo staged around a Christmas tree, the last picture the Williams' family took together before his son went to college and while his daughter was still in high school. Storm tossed the picture on top of the credenza then pointed his index finger at Farm.

"If you testify against me, *Play-a*, after I asked you not to, I'll come back for you." Storm opened the office door and left as quickly and quietly as he entered.

Farm let out a breath and felt perspiration on his upper lip. How did Storm Lord slip in and out of the police station? Farm never had to testify in court, because the store-owner, who was held up by Strom Lord, dropped the charges. The next week, the store burned to the ground and before end of the year the store-owner moved to Northern California.

When Farm heard about Wade Dennis being shot in his office at the same precinct, the identical feeling of nausea came over him as it did after Storm Lord left his office. Farm followed the Dennis case ever since, gleaning information from former colleagues. Farm was very upset after hearing about the drive-by shooting at Wade Dennis' home and had trouble sleeping that night because there was nothing he could do to help Wade. By morning, however, he'd hatched a plan. Most local thugs never traveled very far from their own neighborhood. Farm owned an apartment building in Santa Monica, and on the next street behind that property, was a vacant house that happened to be owned by his ex-wife, Tiffany Williams.

*W*ade swore he could smell the aroma of authentic Italian cuisine as soon as his son and brother stepped off the elevator. An angel named Donna sent him food a second time, and when he opened the take-out container, it felt like years instead of days since he'd enjoyed her last meal. He slapped his brother's hand when Chris reached for a slice of garlic toast and Wade didn't stop eating until half of the food was consumed. This time the main dish was whole-wheat lasagna seasoned with spicy chicken sausage. Wade moaned and held his stomach because he was completely full. When he went to sleep that night he dreamed he was seated in heaven and an angel served him the same delicious meal.

After the drive-by at the Dennis house and the discovery that human blood was painted on the car door, the case was transferred to the Special Protection Unit of the LAPD. Special Protection Unit (SPU) arranged for Wade to be transferred to a private hospital, Saint Rita's Catholic Hospital in Santa Monica. He was registered under the name: Howard Grant. Security was much tighter at St. Rita's Hospital than at Cedars. The same no-nonsense nun, Sister Ruth, interrogated Keith and Chris each time they visited. Upon leaving, Chris always asked Sister Ruth for a date. Unknown to them, she was secretly amused but always admonished Chris that he would benefit spending his free time in prayer.

SPU arranged for Keith and Chris to move to a vacant house located a few miles from Saint Rita's Hospital. It was a modest two-story craftsman style home on Montana Avenue. Most the neighbors were working class people who were away from their neighborhood during the day, and in the evenings, they were too tired or too busy to notice every time someone moved in or out of the home at the end of the block on their street.

Chris replaced the twenty-inch television in the living room with his big screen and took over the master bedroom and bathroom on the first floor. Upstairs, Keith settled on the next largest bedroom. It came with a full-size bed and matching dresser and a chair. It was all he really needed. The third bedroom housed a set of bunk beds with a tall dresser nestled inside the closet to make room for office furniture. The upstairs bathroom had a shower-tub combination and was located between the two smaller bedrooms. The safe house reminded Keith of living in a timeshare condo except better because the refrigerator and freezer were fully stocked.

Alonzo Rivera was a special agent in LAPD's Special Protection Unit. Agent Rivera moved into Wade Dennis' home, so that an officer would be on the scene should Wade Dennis' property be targeted again. If anyone asked, Alonzo was Al Dennis, Wade's cousin from Louisiana who was house-sitting while Wade recuperated in the hospital.

When flowers came to the Dennis' house for Wade, Alonzo signed for them. If they passed his inspection, he sent them by SPU messenger to Saint Rita's to the room of Howard Grant. The first day Keith delivered the special meal from Donna, Wade instructed his son to give her the fresh bouquet of orange tulips just delivered to him that morning from the United Municipality Employee Union (minus the get well card).

Donna sent food by Keith every day for the next two days. On the third day, Wade gripped his top sheet up to his neck after hearing the news, "What do you mean she wants to deliver the food in person?" He'd just polished off a t-bone steak Donna grilled and seasoned especially for him.

"Donna wants to deliver it herself tomorrow and visit with you." What's the big deal?

Wade rubbed his two-week old beard, "I don't want a woman to see me like this."

"She knows you're in the hospital, besides the nurses see you all the time."

"But have you seen these nun-nurses? Jesus Christ!"

Keith tried to keep a straight face while his father looked taken aback. "They're nice people, but they make Nurse Belinda look like Miss Universe. Why can't you keep bringing me the food? Does she want money?"

"No," Keith said. "I already tried to pay her. She won't take money. Gee, Dad, I didn't know it was going to be such a big deal. I've known Donna for years. She is Kimberly's best friend."

"Have I met her before? What does she look like?"

"I don't think you've ever met her. She was Kimberly's big sister when she started high school. Donna is kind of on the short side, but cute. She's a dog person and very friendly."

Getting to eat the delectable food with no strings attached was too good to be true. Now Wade felt obligated to do something for Donna, at minimum pay her. In any case, Wade didn't want this young, talented woman to see him looking his worse. "Bring me some clothes and a razor." It didn't matter when Rev. McMillan or his brother or son visited. This was a young woman he admired from afar coming to see him. Jeez, what for? He sent her the flowers as a thank you gesture. That should be enough. He didn't mean for it to turn into a face-to-face meeting.

Keith contacted Alonzo to let him know he was coming to the house. He almost laughed when a short, brown-skinned man of Mexican descent opened the front door, because Alonzo didn't look in any way related to the Dennis' family. In his father's room, Keith picked out a pair of tan slacks, a yellow and white striped polo shirt, socks, boxers, and a pair of dark brown Bass shoes. He put everything inside a duffle bag topped with a shaving kit he found in the bathroom.

When Keith explained to Sister Margarita, what the clothes were for, she volunteered to iron the slacks. Sister Mary Clarence, a former beautician in her past life, offered to cut Wade's hair. He agreed to the haircut, and she did such a good job, he let her shave off his beard with a straight razor. It was the first time he ever experienced the work of a female barber, but since she was a nun, in Wade's mind, it didn't really count.

Keith helped his father get dressed and both were surprised at how loosely his clothes fit. Wade pulled on the roomy waistband of his slacks. "The doctor told me I've lost ten pounds already." He was pleased with his overall look and sat in the chair rather than in bed to wait for Donna's arrival. Keith was out of the room when Donna stopped at the open door.

"Wade Dennis? I mean Howard Grant? You look wonderful! I'm Donna. I was expecting a sick person. You must have a strong constitution." She entered the room carrying two large take-out bags and talked to Wade like they were old friends. Wade sat up straighter and tried to look pleasant and alert. Donna was dressed for work in her all-white chef's uniform. Keith was right. She was cute and moved her compact little body quickly and with precision as she set out the food. Her height was only four inches above five-feet, but her outgoing personality was big and infectious, changing the atmosphere of the room.

By the time Keith returned, the pair was sitting at the small round table enjoying a meal of spicy Asian shrimp, mu shu vegetables, wild rice, and white bean soup. Wade was explaining to Donna the kind of bait that was best used to catch cold-water fish. Keith felt like walking out of the room and back in to make sure he was in the right room. Was this the man who didn't want a face-to-face meeting with the chef?

"Come, join us Keith," Donna said, "there's plenty."

"I'm having dinner at the McMillan's tonight, but I wouldn't mind a taste," Keith said. He fixed a small plate and sat on the edge of the bed to eat. It was like being a fly on the wall because Wade and Donna were now in deep conversation about how to clean and cook fresh fish.

Donna pointed her fork at Wade, "I tell you I can fix fish, bake it and make you swear it was fried."

Wade tried to cross his arms, but the pain of doing so reminded him of his injury.

Donna saw his features change, "Are you all right? Should I call a nurse?"

Wade forced a smile, "No. I'm fine. Sometimes I forget where I am… anyway you'll have to prove that to me because I've been eating fish all my life and nothing tastes as good as fried fish."

"It's a deal, but I think I better go now," Donna said. "I don't want to tire you out." She picked up everything she brought in and placed it back inside the take-out bags.

Wade considered standing, but he thought the better of it. "Excuse my seat. Donna, you can come back any time. I really appreciate you sending me some *real* food. You can't imagine what they parade around in hospital cafeterias and call nourishment."

"Sure thing," Donna said, "and thanks for the flowers. You have excellent taste."

Keith walked Donna to her car, "I can't thank you enough for stopping by. You've done wonders for his morale." He opened her car door.

"Really? He seems fine. Was he depressed?"

"I didn't think so, until I saw him having dinner with you."

"That's sweet. Well, I gotta get going." Donna said and got inside of her car. Keith closed her door. She started the engine then lowered the window. "You really favor your father, and I see where you get your charm." Like father, like son except Wade was more seasoned, secure, and settled.

"So, I've been told," Keith said. "Bye, Donna."

"Bye."

Keith watched as she raised the window, opened the sunroof, and exited the parking lot. When he got back to his father's room, Wade was asleep in the chair. A pair of freshly laundered pajamas had been placed on the foot of his bed. "Dad. Daddy," Keith called.

Wade opened his eyes. "Hey, son." He rubbed his clean-shaven chin. "I guess I fell asleep. Do me a favor and call the nurse and ask her to bring me my pain medicine and help me out of these clothes, so I can get back into bed."

Keith watched his father return to his sick bed and hoped Donna would visit again…very soon.

$\mathcal{C}$hapter 30

Dear Keith Dennis,
It's over. I'm breaking up with you. I'm going back to Oregon. There is someone else I care for who isn't ashamed for the world to know he loves me.
This is good-bye,
Patricia

Keith read and re-read the letter sent to his father's house through the U.S. mail. The postmark was from Los Angeles, California. Alonzo dusted all personal mail for fingerprints, and the only prints on the letter belonged to Trish. "It looks like her signature, but Trish is practically a poet when she writes. I believe someone else dictated what she should write."

Alonzo looked at the copy of the original letter. "The salutation is rather formal for a girlfriend or close friend, wouldn't you agree?"

Keith nodded, "And she never referred to herself as Patricia unless a document asked for her full given name but it does look like her signature."

"We're staking out her place in Oregon. Did she like flowers?"

Keith shrugged, "Sure…as much as the next woman."

"I ask because there's a bunch of dead flowers at her front door; it looks like those makeshift memorials people put up when someone's been killed."

A chill went through Keith, "Has anyone contacted the neighbor, Doug?"

"Douglas Brown moved. The landlady said he was vague about where he was going, but she thinks he mentioned moving north to Washington or Canada."

Keith stared at Alonzo, "Trish's parents live in Victoria, very near the Washington-Canadian border."

"It might be a coincidence he moved there. In any case, the department is in daily contact with Dr. and Mrs. Glover."

Maybe so, but Keith had a bad feeling about their safety. His prayers tonight would definitely include intercession for the Glovers and thanks for their protection. Keith would speak to the Lord about keeping everyone safe, and thank Him for all things working together for good.

$\mathscr{C}$hapter 31

$\mathcal{N}$orma Lily deleted the e-mail about retirement planning without opening it. She had been honored this year by her employer, the United States Postal Service, for forty years of service and had no plans to stop working. Over the forty years, Norma had seen people come and go, but she stayed faithful to her job. She was proud to be promoted to a senior manager at a time before affirmative action made it easier for women to advance. Norma had nothing against people of other races, but the physical workplace seemed cleaner and more uniform and the people, neater, before diversity was a priority.

In 1970s, the Postal Service didn't require managers to wear uniforms, but proper work attire for men was a shirt and tie with slacks and jackets in conservative colors like black, dark gray, or brown. Acceptable wear for women was skirted suits, stockings, sensible shoes, and simple jewelry. There were none of these so-called casual days in the name of boosting morale. Norma was against dressing down because casual wear should be reserved for the weekends. At work, people should have pride in their appearance.

In forty years, Norma had never worn a pair of pants or bare legs to work. She heard rumors that her style of dressing and the fact that she never wore pants had something to do with her religion, but they were wrong. Norma just wanted to set a proper example for the others. Someone had to do it since even the department director, Elaine Clarkson, often wore colorful pantsuits like Secretary of State Hillary Clinton. God-forbid! As a card-carrying, registered Republican, Norma had to bite her lip and look the other way every time she saw Elaine wearing pants at work.

In her opinion, the other senior managers, the diversity-training manual described as three Hispanics, two African-Americans, one Asian, and one Caucasian young woman were more concerned about appearance than output. The men wore colorful shirts and ties that any circus clown would have admired. When the women wore skirts, they were too short and their tops too low. Mercy! Norma had very little in common with these people. They hadn't come up through the ranks like she did, but they depended on their "book smarts" and degrees. Little pieces of paper they proudly displayed on a wall in their offices. Well, Norma didn't have all that so-called education, but her department out ranked the others in compliance because Norma's subordinates practiced discipline by routinely following the approved procedures to the letter, or there were consequences.

Norma thought of those she supervised as her children and tried to be patient with new employees during their one-year probation period. Three employees, who'd been supervised by Norma for five years, dreaded the annual performance evaluation because Norma kept notes and files on everyone. It was like she had eyes in the back of her head,

which in a way, she did, in the form of her *special* underlings who gave
her daily reports of what was going on in the trenches. Norma thought
that the current crop of 'kids' were pretty good. Most worked hard, but
there were a few slackers she planned to weed out. Their options would
be to transfer to another department or to be let go before they passed
probation.

Douglas Brown, an accounting clerk, was one of those special
employees who admired his supervisor, Miss Norma Lily, and thrived
when she noticed or praised him. He was thirty-five years old, and like
Miss Lily, he couldn't ever imagine retiring. At work, Douglas stayed in
the background, adding figures, compiling financial data, or filling in
when a co-worker called in sick, but he always keeping his eyes and ears
open to be able to give Miss Lily a 'heads-up.' During Douglas' first
month in this department, his co-workers tried to include him in their
casual banter, but they soon realized Douglas Brown was a social misfit
and left the strange man alone.

After the 2009 service credit recognition ceremony for the current
and retiring employees, Miss Lily invited Douglas to join her for dinner.
Douglas could hardly keep his mind on work that day, he was so excited
and the evening did not disappoint. Miss Lily confided in him that
she noticed how well he completed his job assignments. Whenever she
checked his work, it was always flawless. At dinner, Norma told him not
to tell anyone else, but she thought of Douglas as her favorite child and
that he could call her Norma when they were alone. It wasn't a stretch
for him to start thinking of her as his mother and when he started calling
her Mom during those alone times, Norma didn't object.

"What's the matter Douglas? You seem down," Norma said. She
hadn't received a report from him in a few days. It wasn't like Douglas
not to see her at least once a day. Norma called him into her office in
the afternoon.

Douglas was depressed. He was in his mid-thirties and single with
no girlfriend. He would probably never have one, meaning he wasn't

going to get married or have his own family. It wasn't something he thought much about, until the other staff his age and younger started having kids. Overnight, he became obsessed with wanting a wife and family and it didn't help that every other month someone announced that they (or their wife) was pregnant. There was currently a marriage and baby boom in the office, and he wasn't taking part in either.

"Oh, is that all?" Norma said after hearing Douglas explain his dilemma.

"You don't understand," Douglas said. "No woman wants me."

She saw pain etched into his features and came around her desk to sit in the chair beside him. "Nonsense," Norma said. "You're smart and a hard worker. You've been working here for three years and have perfect attendance. The problem is the women these days not you. Why do you think the divorce rate is so high? These young women think they want the handsome men with the movie star looks. They're overlooking gentlemen like you and your special qualities. Once the right woman gets to know you, and with the right encouragement, she will instantly fall in love. I guarantee it. You are a great catch."

Douglas listened, but he doubted the reality of what he was hearing. Over the years, he asked women to go out with him and most of them turned him down. The one's who agreed to go never wanted a second date; in fact, they asked him not to call again. A few of the women went as far as getting a restraining orders to keep him away.

"You are just what a woman wants," Norma said. "You're smart, but sensitive, and I have a feeling you fall in love too easily."

"What can I do?" Douglas asked. He gripped the arms of the chair with his hands.

Norma smiled at him. She patted one of his hands until he let go of the chair arm and gripped hers. "Let Mommy help you."

After that day, when Douglas came into Norma's office, she closed the door and they role-played different scenarios. According to Norma, Douglas only needed to practice socially acceptable behavior. Norma encouraged him to practice what she taught him with his co-workers and report back to her. After a few weeks, Douglas bragged to Norma he'd been invited to come to happy hour by Joseph and Theo and Miriam. They were the newest recruits to the department, but the fact remained, this hadn't happened since he started with the post office three years ago.

However, Norma wasn't pleased when Douglas told her he had his eye on a special woman. Norma wanted to be the one to find the right girl for him and timing was everything. She had her eye on Shirley Abel as a potential mate for him. Shirley was a billing clerk who was also under Norma's supervision, but when Douglas told Norma about the woman he wanted, Norma changed her mind about Shirley.

If Douglas married a doctor, he would have an intelligent, independent, self-supporting wife and not feel the need to leave the post office or Norma's supervision or influence. This could work out well for all concerned. The doctor-wife would benefit by having a stable, faithful husband who no one else wanted. Norma could help Douglas do things to keep his wife happy. Most important of all, Norma would be the matriarch of the family. She would help the young couple with everything including family planning. There was only one problem. Douglas' future wife had a boyfriend. They weren't engaged, but the boyfriend was still blocking the way to their happiness. The good news was the boyfriend was leaving for law school in another state. The bad news was Trish was planning to follow him. This was unacceptable.

Chapter 32

"Everything is delicious," Phillip said. He was polishing off a hearty plate of barbequed chicken, potato salad, greens, and baked beans.

"Thank you," Heavenly said. She looked around for Nichelle who was out of earshot and whispered across the table. "I don't know what happened to Nichelle's date. She still thinks he's coming."

"Forget him. If I could eat any more, I'd eat this loser's food too." Phillip said.

"Who you callin' a loser?" Nichelle asked. She stood, hands on hips, scowling down at Philly. Who did he think he was? Everybody didn't run they life by the clock. She was a ball of nerves, afraid August wasn't going to show up. The doorbell rang before she could say more and she practically ran to answer it.

"Hey, Chell," August said.

"Hey, yourself," Nichelle said. When she saw him standing in the doorway looking so fine, all she wanted to say about him being late was forgiven.

"Can I go now?" Miracle asked. She was on her way to pick up her son from her mother's house when August said he needed a ride. Nichelle frowned, looking up and down at the female in the Baby Phat, navy velour-jogging suit, with the good hair. If Miracle had the time, she would have asked this buster what her problem was. Miracle was about the same height as Nichelle, with skin a shade lighter brown and twenty pounds heavier. Her naturally wavy hair was pulled back in a ponytail and ended almost to her waist. Miracle knew the skinny girl who was wearing last year's jeans, was jealous of her because there wasn't a day Miracle didn't get up and prepare to look good. Back-in-the day, she would have put this chicken-head in her place, but right now, it was more important that she pick up her son.

"Yeah, hit me back in a few hours," August said dismissing her. Without another word, Miracle turned and walked back to the elevators. August smiled at Nichelle. "I'm here now, Baby Girl," He took a deep breath. "Somebody can burn. Is that mustard greens I smell?"

"Yes," Nichelle counted on her fingers as she recited the menu. "Me and my sister fixed barbequed chicken, mustard greens, potato salad, baked beans, you know, a home cooked meal, but Heavenly used those refrigerator rolls..."

August entered the foyer and paused to look at himself in the floor length mirror. After Nichelle took his jacket, he checked out his reflection, the *Roca Wear* black jeans and long black t-shirt with the latest black, leather, *Timberlands* was the business. His hair was short but long enough to show waves from the wave cap he wore at night. August was undecided on shaving his head bald or letting it grow. Nichelle linked her arm through his and lead him through the living room. The place was tight and August admired the tasteful way it was decorated.

When they reached the dinette in the kitchen nook, Nichelle introduced August to Heavenly and Phillip. After August sat down,

Nichelle started fixing him a plate. Heavenly wished she had a camera to record this phenomenon because never, in her twenty-one years, had she ever seen Nichelle fix anyone's plate but her own.

Phillip and August didn't have much to say to each other. Phillip didn't like August for not apologizing for being late. Furthermore, August came empty handed (except a partially empty forty ounce bottle of beer). He brought no token gift for Nichelle who invited him or for Heavenly whose home and food they were enjoying. The man had no home training plus August Lord looked like a street runner, an ex-con, a gang-banger. In Phillip's opinion, a thirty-year old thug, was verging on pitiful. *Where did Nichelle find this loser?*

August ate his food and ignored Phillip. He liked the crib and wondered if there were any vacancies in the building. He also liked the look of Nichelle's younger sister, Heavenly. Heavenly was built real nice, but unfortunately, she had a man. That fact wouldn't stop August from stopping by some other time to see if she was really into Phillip or not beyond having a man on the side. He could see himself kicking it here, and he had a feeling the down home groceries were mostly Heavenly's doing. He smiled at Nichelle while she topped off his glass of lemonade. Dealing with two sisters was tricky. August had to take it slow or risk losing both of them.

While August was eating dinner and Heavenly and Phillip were enjoying dessert, Nichelle's plate of food was getting cold because instead of eating, she was talking and waiting on August. After Heavenly put the dinner dishes inside the dishwasher, August thought they would play cards or dominos or something, but instead Heavenly took them up to the roof of her building and they sat outside on lawn furniture, looking over the city until sunset.

August really liked the view from the roof and thought about how much he missed being outside when he was locked away. As the sky darkened, the view changed to a show of city lights and a full moon. The head and taillights of cars on the 5 interstate and the 101 and 110 freeways moved in a graceful syncopation. If Phillip wasn't a cop, August would have lit and passed around a blunt he had in his jacket pocket. He had to be satisfied with the buzz from the remainder of his 40-ounce mixed with ice-cold lemonade.

When his cell phone vibrated August glanced at the number. Miracle was on the line. August hadn't seen their two-and-a-half year old son August Lord II in eighteen months. There was no telling when Miracle would let him see the boy again, so he had to go.

Nichelle wanted to walk August to his ride, but he was aware of the negative vibes between Nichelle and Miracle. He wanted to keep the drama to a minimum. After retrieving the plate of extra food from Heavenly's apartment that Nichelle made for him, she walked him to the elevator. August leaned over Nichelle, resting one arm on the wall, "I got your digits. I'll hit you up tomorrow." When the elevator doors opened, he kissed her goodbye and dropped his arm down her back to feel her butt. He stepped inside the elevator, pushed button number one and before the doors closed said, "Thank your sister and you for the invite."

Later that night, Nichelle sat at the table while Heavenly took the dishes out of the dishwasher and put them away.

"So, what did you think of him?" Nichelle said. "August Lord, I mean."

"He's okay, for you, I guess." Heavenly said.

"Did Philly say anything about him?"

Heavenly started wiping down the sink and counters, "Phillip didn't say much about August, but he did tell me something about the Real Players' Ball…"

Heavenly had her sister's full attention, "What?"

"Did you know the men bring a bunch of women to the ball? They call it a stable or harem, and all the girls in the group dress alike. Phillip said there is one guy and seven girls at each table."

"August didn't mention anyone else when he asked me if I wanted to go."

"Maybe you better ask him," Heavenly said. She tried not to make a big deal of it, but she could see Nichelle wasn't looking too happy about this news. "I thought the dinner came out nice once August got here…"

"See there, that's you and Philly's problem," Nichelle said. "Always worried about time. What's the big deal he wasn't here at six o'clock? We all ate. We hung out. And if I want to go to the Real Players' Ball with August and six other females, I will. Maybe, I'll see if I can invite Charm."

Heavenly thought, "You do, and you'll be in the second seat. Charm and August are birds of a feather and deserve each other." Heavenly learned long ago that once her sister made her mind up that there was no talking her out of her decision. It was better to keep her opinions to herself, pray for her sister and wait to see what happened.

The Real Players' Ball was big and Nichelle believed if she invited Charm, her friend would see that Nichelle was the one with the hook up for a change. Inviting Brandi was out of the question. This was something she wanted to brag about to Brandi and take pleasure in driving her off her diet.

Chapter 33

Trish was beginning to lose hope. The first few days after being kidnapped, she tried to focus on details to tell the police after her rescue because she had no doubt she would soon be back home, back on schedule, back to her life. There would be a ransom demand and an exchange. Then she would be freed and her captors, in addition to being felons, would be fugitives. That's when she thought the issue was money.

Her parents would pay the ransom no matter how much it was. Her family's wealth was in the top ten percent of the world. Lack of money was never a concern. Trish's parents inherited their wealth from their parents, grandparents, and great-grandparents. Her father, James Patrick Glover, broke the mold and actually completed medical school after college. As an Intern at Grand View Hospital, James donated his paycheck back to the hospital to support the children's wing, the wing named after his grandfather, Charles P. Glover.

Dr. Drew Peary was a general practitioner. His idea of work was making a few house calls in the morning and playing golf for the rest of the day. When Dr. Peary retired James P. Glover, M.D. took over Peary's practice. James liked the schedule of his predecessor, but he tried to limit his golf games to every other afternoon. He divided his time away from the golf course between house calls of wealthy friends and acquaintances and his own private practice.

After four boys, Sundae Harrington was the first and only girl born to her parents, J.F. and Martha Harrington. When Sundae was two years old, her parents hoped to give her a little sister, the result was another boy and a vasectomy for J.F. Martha dressed her only daughter in ruffled dresses, silk stockings and bows in her lovely auburn hair. Sundae longed to run around like her brothers and play all kinds of games, but she was a girl and girls had to stay clean and be lady-like because it was unbecoming for little girls to behave like unruly boys.

Sundae's life was one of pampering and preparation to take her place in society. It took years, but Sundae finally embraced her destiny and perfected her mannerisms such that her mother, Martha, was proud of and rarely needed to correct her daughter. Sundae's only escape was time spent alone in the family library where she could lose herself in a story and let her imagination soar.

When Sundae Harrington was introduced to Dr. James Glover at a charity luncheon, she thought him beneath her. Her mother expected Sundae to marry royalty (or the equivalent) and show the Brits how it was done. Martha, with little prompting, liked to mention she was a descendent of the Earl of Covington, a cousin of Queen Elizabeth I. She never talked about the considerable distance the cousin was to the Queen, but any ties to the royal family convinced Martha that Sundae was in line for the throne.

When James Glover told Sundae Harrington that he, not only completed medical school but had opened his own practice, she was intrigued. Here was a man who chose to work in a much-needed profession. Every story James shared with her was foreign and exotic, so Sundae started looking forward to spending time with a man who rubbed shoulders with common everyday people and their multitude of problems.

Sundae overheard James' mother, Mrs. Sophia Glover, lamenting about her son's rebellious ways. Mrs. Glover couldn't understand why her boy insisted on working in the presence of sick and poverty stricken people when, if James insisted on being at the hospital, he could serve on the Board of Directors. Sundae began to comprehend why James chose a hands-on profession and admired him for taking charge of his own life. They began meeting in secret.

Their wedding was held in the south gardens at the Harrington Estate in early May. Very soon after the wedding, Martha was informed her daughter was with child. It wasn't the Princess Diana wedding she'd hoped for, but at least the Glover family had a pedigree. Martha was delighted to learn the Glover family tree included an English Duke.

When Sundae gave birth to a girl, the first time out, Martha was overjoyed. This was her chance to improve on her technique of preparing her granddaughter for her destiny. Patricia Elizabeth Glover would want for nothing. However, her mother, Sundae had other ideas. Sundae wanted her daughter to experience the world and indulged Patricia's every request and she enjoyed private lessons from the best instructors in ballet, horseback riding, skiing, gymnastics, acting, rock climbing, and piano. In the summer time, Patricia was enrolled in science or space camp. She also participated in horse shows, went scuba diving in exotic locations, swam with the dolphins and spent a month in a new country every year to learn first hand about geography, history and culture.

Martha didn't approve of Sundae's methods, but she had to admit Patricia was well-behaved and well-rounded. Her granddaughter could converse intelligently on almost any subject but alas wanted to follow her father into the medical profession.

Now a captive, Trish spent her waking hours thinking about her family. She welcomed sleep, hoping each day would bring her closer to freedom. After a week, Trish realized her captors were putting something in her food to make her sleep because it was getting harder to wake up each morning. Trish was given breakfast, usually a boiled egg and a cup of tea then all she wanted to do was go back to sleep. When she woke up again it would be dark. One day Trish woke up enough to hear her captor telling the maid not to make the bed, just to leave clean sheets, because the girl in the bed was ill and recovering from an operation.

If only she had waited for Keith when she arrived at LAX, then she would have her life back, but standing at the curb, Trish recognized the woman in the car. Her neighbor, Doug introduced his mother to Trish a few weeks ago. Mrs. Lily was behind the wheel, when she asked Trish to help her find her hotel. She claimed the GPS in the car wasn't working and she needed Trish's help in reading the directions. If only she had waited for Keith. He was on his way to pick her up. In her waking moments, Trish visualized Keith bursting through the motel door and freeing her, but once she was inside, the car the doors were locked. While Mrs. Lily drove, a young lady named Shirley, who had been hiding in the backseat under a blanket, sat up and showed Trish a gun with a silver handle. She placed the weapon next to Trish's ear and told her to call Keith back and tell him not to come. Trish wanted to protest, but thought it best to cooperate.

Dinner tonight was a Subway sandwich and juice in a cup. "Here," Shirley said. She took her own food to the other bed and arranged it on her lap. Then she picked up the remote control to turn the channel on the television set. The TV was never turned off.

Initially Trish thanked Shirley for the food and tried to engage her in conversation, but any attempts at communication or pleasantry seemed to anger her captor. Trish finally concluded Shirley despised her. When Trish was allowed to take a shower or use the toilet, Shirley stayed nearby pointing the gun at her. If Shirley left Trish alone in the room, which wasn't often, Trish's hands and feet were hogtied and she was gagged then completely covered with the thin rust-colored bedspread. It was the ultimate feeling of helplessness. Trish forced herself to not panic. She counted backward, trying to relax and would finally surrendered to sleep. Her dreams were frightening, but at least she was able to run like the wind or fly away or breathe underwater. She was able to get away from the huge dark cloud that was moving toward her, always over her shoulder. Once awake, the reality of her living nightmare seemed like a dream.

Tonight, while Shirley ate and watched the television, Trish carefully poured the juice, a little at a time, into a box of tissue she strategically hid on the floor next to the bed. At midnight when Shirley dozed off Trish diligently worked for hours trying to untie the rope restraining her hands. Through tears and sweat from the effort at almost the break of dawn she was rewarded when her hands slipped free. Trish was able to think clearly again now that she was free from whatever drug that was being used to sedate her. She slowly sat up in the bed. Her fingers were too sore and raw to untie the rope around her ankles so she left them bound. She had to find a way to get help before Shirley discovered what she'd done.

Shirley slept with the gun next to her, so if Trish's plan failed Shirley would gladly shoot her and the ordeal would be over, but hopefully, the noise would alert someone and they would call the police. Either way, Trish would be free, something she would never again take for granted.

Chapter 34

"Whose baby is that?" Charm asked when Nichelle answered the door holding a toddler on her hip.

"He's cute," Brandi said reaching for him. "Hi, sweetie."

Nichelle reluctantly let the boy go to her, "He's the son of my new man."

"What man?" Charm and Brandi said together.

Nichelle smiled, "His name is August…"

"August?" This time Nichelle rolled her eyes at the duet. "Yes, August. August First, like the day he was born. This is August the Second, his son."

"Where is he?" Charm asked looking past Nichelle. The trio agreed to meet at Nichelle's place to plan their trip to the Hoodie Awards and get their story straight about being in Wade Dennis' neighborhood especially since Heavenly was kicking it with an employee of the police department.

"He's on his way over here or it might be his baby mama, Miracle, picking him up."

Charm sucked her teeth, "Why are you babysitting for that Ho?"

"I'm not."

Charm looked at Brandi playing on the floor with the child, "Looks like it to me."

Nichelle sighed, "Well if you must know I'm watching the baby for August. There is nothing going on between August and Miracle anymore, and if she comes to pick the baby up, you can ask her ya damn self."

Brandi held her nose with one hand, "Oooo, he needs to be changed." She tried to hand the child back to Nichelle who held her hands up in surrender.

"You wanted him. You change him. The diaper bag is in the bathroom."

Brandi picked up August II and held the laughing boy at arms length in front of her until they disappeared down the hall toward the bathroom.

Nichelle fanned the air around her, "Did Brandi get the car painted?"

"Not yet. It might be a good thing to keep the car black since there's so many of that model in that color. It's a good alibi. Wasn't me." Charm snapped her fingers to the hook of Shaggy's song with the Caribbean beat. "Wasn't me." Then she was serious. "I almost had a heart attack when I saw the police surrounding Brandi's car that night. All I could think of was those vials of blood in our car that could link us back to the drive-by."

"How do you think I felt inside the car with all that crap? I shoulda tossed it out of the window."

"No. These things happen for a reason. God was looking out for us that night. No one got shot even though you guys were shot at. You didn't get caught even though the police was right there and you was as guilty as sin."

"What about you and Brandi. You two are guilty sinners too and ya'll left me there by myself."

"How was I to know the Man was coming to that spot? If I knew, I never would have stopped in that location. We all could have got busted."

"I was the one in the car though."

"I know. I saw the crowd and the helicopter. I felt so bad for you. I just knew my girl was caught, but if you got busted, I would have visited you."

"What?"

"Nichelle, you know I'm your girl and all that, but why should the three of us go to jail when only one of us was caught?"

"I knew it! Charm, that's messed up. When I was in the car, I knew you and Brandi were going to leave me hanging."

"But think about it. If you were me, wouldn't you have hung back to see what would happened. You wouldn't run up there while the police were questioning me saying, hey, Mr. Policeman, I was the one driving the car..."

"Just know this... I wasn't going down by myself."

"You cold Nichelle," Charm said, "I thought you had my back."

Nichelle folded her arms and the pair sat in silence until Brandi came back with August II and the diaper bag slung over her shoulder. There was no sense in being mad over what hadn't happened. Maybe Charm was right and God finally came through and made the police look the other way. "I got some snacks in the kitchen," Nichelle said. She knew Brandi would give in to the temptation and smiled when she handed August II to her. Brandi put the Gucci diaper bag next to Nichelle before disappearing inside the kitchen.

Miracle stood on the porch after ringing the doorbell at the address August gave her. She was angry that August left their son with Nichelle and knew it would be a long time before she allowed her son's father to even think about putting her in this position again. When Nichelle opened the door holding August II, Miracle reached for her son, turned and walked back to her car. She strapped the toddler into his car seat. Nichelle brought the diaper bag to the car hoping to see August First.

"Did he eat?" Miracle asked.

"An hour ago," Nichelle answered, and without a thank you, Miracle got inside the car, closed the door, started the engine and backed out of the driveway.

Charm and Brandi watched Nichelle and Miracle's interaction from the kitchen window. "I've seen that girl before..." Charm said. She tapped her fingernail on the table. "I want to say it was on TV. It was a while back, but I never forget a face."

Brandi filled her plate with cheese squares and put them in the microwave. She wanted nachos with warm melted cheese. When Nichelle sat at the table and started eating Brandi's nachos, Brandi sat back and watched her. She didn't like to share food. Brandi got another plate and melted more cheese, and she let Nichelle and Charm laugh. Sharing food was unsanitary.

"So, tell me, is August's last name, First?" Charm inquired.

"No. His first and middle name is August First because he was born on, wait for it, the first day of August."

"Was his son born on August second?" Brandi asked.

"No, dummy. August's son is named after him. He's August *the* second."

"What is their last name then?" Charm asked.

"Lord."

The silence was deafening. Even Brandi stopped eating. Charm spoke first, choosing her words carefully. "Are you saying August Lord as in the first family of the Storm Lords?"

Nichelle took her time chewing the nacho with cheese. "Yeah. The baby is August First Lord, the Second."

Charm's dealings were small potatoes compared to the organized crime of the Storm Lords. Maybe God wasn't looking out for them after all. What was the chance of meeting and hooking up with one of Storm Lord's sons in the street? Thank God she didn't touch August II because if something bad had happened to him, there would be no more Charm. "You're playing with fire."

"Yes, indeed," Nichelle agreed. "August Lord *is* hot."

Chapter 35

August could barely see more than twenty feet ahead as he navigated the dark streets, which were illuminated by overhead street lights. He walked alone, watching for any movement that would indicate another person or persons in his path, because it was more likely than not, since he was alone, he would be confronted. After a prosperous night of gambling, he was on his way to a friend's house to crash. Minutes ago, he walked away with two hundred dollars, which wasn't bad, considering his fifty dollar investment. When August arrived at 78th street, he looked down the ally that divided 78th and 79th Streets. A black Impala was parked between a group of overgrown trees, and a few large trash bins. It hadn't been moved in nearly a week. He figured the car was either stolen or about to be torched for the insurance money, as often happened in the southern part of the city. Abandoned cars like this one usually had mechanical issues or physical damage, but as August came closer, it appeared that the car was in very good condition. All it needed was a professional detail and some new rims to cherry it out.

Most law-abiding people working regular day jobs were nestled in their warm beds, but you never knew when someone would be watching, so August looked around for anyone looking back at him before attempting to open the driver side door. He mentally prepared for the unexpected and welcomed the adrenalin rush as his heart pounded in his chest. The door was unlocked and opened quietly. He smirked when the car alarm didn't sound. This made his job very easy. August slipped inside the car onto the firm leather of the driver's seat and closed the door. The Impala was nice inside too, practically new. After some manipulation of the electronics, in less than a minute, the car was his. August put the car in drive, glad to see the gas gauge indicated the tank was half-full, then backed slowly out of the ally. When he got to the corner, he took the time to change the radio station from an easy-listening station because the soothing sound of violins and an orchestra he found to be extremely irritating. August pushed the tuner until it stopped on *Power* 106 FM. He turned the volume up and bobbed his head, jamming to Jay-Z's latest cut and wondering how a fox like Beyoncé woke up to a mug like that? Thinking of Beyonce reminded him of Heavenly. That dime was one *fine* big-leg girl.

Now that he had a way over to her house, this was a good time to pay Heavenly a visit. It was still very early on a Saturday morning, so chances were that she'd be home alone. If her man *was* there, he would make up a story about looking for his lost his cell phone and ask if they'd seen it. The missing phone would also be a good reason he couldn't call before he stopped by. Perfect, but he really hoped Heavenly was alone. He had the munchies and longed for the feel of a woman's legs wrapped around his waist. He visualized Heavenly opening her front door and inviting him inside. Maybe she would offer to cook him breakfast. After he was full, he'd make it worth her while and leave her with a smile on her face.

About half way to Heavenly's downtown apartment, August slowed to a stop at a red light at the intersection of Western Avenue and Jefferson Boulevard. The morning traffic was light and the sun's rays were just visible over the horizon. He involuntarily jumped when someone tapped at his window. He scowled at the white lady, probably a crack-head. She looked bad. Her hair was plastered to one side of her face and sticking out all directions on the other. She obviously hadn't seen a comb in a while, but what surprised him most was she appeared to have all her teeth and they were white, not stained or rotted out from self abuse of meth or some other drug.

He turned down the volume of the music and lowered the window just enough to hear what she was saying.

"Please, sir. Help me."

The traffic light was about to turn green and August looked at her then back at the cars in his rear view mirror. This woman's problem wasn't his problem, but something about her plea kept him from ignoring her and driving away. Now that he was *on the outs* August tried to forget the lessons he learned in the prison chapel but something about the Good Samaritan dude crossed his mind. The world would be different if everyone had compassion for another person just because they were a person. This lady didn't belong out here. Then again, he heard first hand stories from his partners about being set up after trying to help a stranger. One time the person they tried to help pulled out a concealed weapon and jacked their car. At the same time, he could appreciate the irony in getting jacked in a stolen car.

Relying on instinct, August reached over and unlocked the passenger-side door. He rested his feet on both the brake and gas peddles, watching carefully to make sure no one else tried to get inside the car. Once the woman was seated, he pushed the automatic door lock button and re-locked all of the doors again. The woman wanted to thank him, but pleaded instead for him to go, to get away. She sunk down in the seat and glanced back at the motel building after August pulled back into the morning traffic. The lady didn't seem to care where he took her as long as it was away from where he picked her up.

It was then that he looked down and noticed her bare feet and the rope tied around her ankles. What kind of kinky-bull was this? In prison, he met a dude, Jake Burton, who claimed he was serving time for being a part of a white slavery ring. Jake was serving five to fifteen for his role in enslaving white females for sale on the international market. August thought the dude was making it all up. He'd never seen a white person abused outside of prison walls, but after today, he owed Burton an apology 'cause this female was 'tore up from the floor up.' Dark circles under her eyes, rope burns and bruises on her wrists and arms and wearing clothes that, by the smell of them, hadn't been washed in a while.

August couldn't show up at Heavenly's with a smelly white girl, so he pulled into a *McDonald's* drive-thru to order breakfast. Maybe he could give the girl some change and drop her off at a bus stop, so she could get back to wherever the hell she came from. At this point, the female was visibly shaking. August was no doctor, but he concluded she was either in shock and needing medical attention or going through detoxification or cold from walking bare foot on the concrete. Hoping it was the latter, August ordered two sausage biscuits with egg, a chicken biscuit, and two regular coffees with sugar and cream. After paying for the order, and driving through, August, as was his custom, backed into a vacant parking space.

The girl didn't say anything, but looked straight ahead while August prepared his coffee. "Yo. You hungry?"

Then she looked over at him with sad, vacant eyes, "Yes."

Damn. She just looked pitiful. August handed her his coffee and one of the sausage biscuits.

"Thank you," she tried to smile, but it was too much effort.

"I'm August."

"August," she said and opened the breakfast sandwich. She ate until it was gone before telling him her name was Patricia. Then slowly drank the coffee savoring every sip. When her cup was empty Trish let out a deep breath, closed her eyes and leaned her head back on the headrest. She still hadn't told him where she wanted to go and seemed fine with just sitting in the car.

August ate his food and thought about what to do with her. He didn't have to think long because a police car drove into the lot and looked right into his face. Ben Castro, the manager at *Mc Donald's*, was alarmed to see the condition of the female in the black Impala. There was a thug at the wheel he assumed was her pimp. Ben tried to play it off. He wanted to look the other way, but after noticing blood on the girl's feet and her ankles tied with a rope, he had to do something.

$\mathcal{C}$hapter 36

$\mathcal{D}$r. James and Sundae Glover were flying in their private plane from Victoria Canada to Los Angeles, California. Enough was enough. The Glover's were no longer going to wait around to find out what was being done to find their missing child. Dr. Glover contacted the Los Angeles Mayor Antonio Villaraigosa's office because he wasn't satisfied with the police department's handling of the case and why his daughter had not been found.

Dmitri Newhall, one of the Mayor's administrative assistants, informed Dr. Glover that the mayor was currently in Washington, D.C. Dmitri further assured the doctor (a generous benefactor during the last mayoral election fundraiser) he would personally, on behalf of the mayor, contact the chief of police to set up meetings to update the Glover's on the status of the case.

Patricia's grandmother, Martha Harrington, confined herself to bed, convinced her worse fears were realized and something terrible happened to her granddaughter. Martha was inconsolable and blamed her son-in-law, James, for encouraging Patricia to follow him into such a barbaric profession and attend school so far away from home. This is what happened to independent girls without chaperones, even in the twenty-first century.

James refused to believe he wouldn't see his daughter alive and whole again. He'd conquered every mountain in his life including a bout with prostate cancer, and he would conquer this one.

Sundae silently agreed with her mother, although she leaned on her husband for strength. As long as James stayed strong, she would as well. The alternative was to climb in bed next to her mother and never get out until Patricia was home and safe or succumb to the guilt and grief she would never get past, and let go of life.

Chapter 37

August set his coffee cup in the drink holder and in one smooth motion started the car and put the gear into drive. He quickly surveyed his surroundings and determined there was just enough space between the *Mc Donald's* drive-thru lane, the dark red Taurus entering the parking lot from the right and the police cruiser about to block him in on the left. If he made it between the two cars without 'trading paint,' he'd be back on Western Avenue traveling south and closer to those who would help him disappear.

He wasn't moved by the female's docile manner because he had witnessed many a delicate feline turn into a tigress under the right circumstances, so pushing her out of the car while he drove might not have the desired result especially if he didn't get away. There was probably a special place *under* the penitentiary for anyone caught in a stolen car with a battered white girl, which placed him instantly in survivor mode.

He pushed the accelerator to the floor and the Impala leaped forward. Police Officer Damon Richards was in the process of calling in the Impala's license plate and was startled by the sudden speed of what he thought was a parked car. He braced himself for the impact, but at the last moment the Impala swerved around him, barely missing his front fender. Officer Richards threw his car in reverse, preparing to give chase, when the driver of the burgundy Taurus slammed into the front half of his car.

Damon was dizzy from the impact, but his years of training kicked in and he quickly assessed the situation. Forget the Impala. It was gone and would probably be stopped for speeding or reckless driving. The immediate issue was that the driver of the Taurus was attempting to leave the scene of the accident. Only the damaged police car stopped the Taurus from exiting the lot. Officer Richards drew his weapon and stood behind his car using it as a shield. He made eye contact with the driver of the Taurus but she was still trying to turn the wheel and maneuver her vehicle up a small curb and around the police car. Fortunately, other vehicles were in the drive-thru and blocked any means of an escape.

"Turn off the car! Now!" Damon shouted.

When he heard the engine noise cease he called for back up. Damon approached the Taurus very cautiously and was surprised to see an older Caucasian female. She didn't seem to be injured and lowered her window.

"Officer, you don't understand. The man in that black car is a kidnapper!"

Damon's vision was blurred but he leaned one arm on the car for balance. "License and registration, ma'am." Thankfully, he heard sirens in the distance that were getting louder, so help was on the way.

The woman pulled a wallet out of her purse that rested on the empty seat next to her. "You're letting him get away." She handed the policeman her Oregon State driver's license and the rental receipt for the Taurus, then she gripped the steering wheel and tapped her right foot impatiently on the floor. If he wasn't holding her up, she would be right behind the Impala.

"Norma Lily, ma'am, are you aware that you hit my car?"

The police cruiser's front bumper was hanging down at an odd angle and the hood was bent upward from the impact.

"I would not have hit your car if it wasn't sitting in the middle of the lot. I don't see how I can be held responsible for damages to your car when you clearly were in the wrong."

I'm dealing with a nutcase, "Ma'am, have you been drinking?"

"Of course not, young man. It's almost seven o'clock in the morning." She craned her neck forward and squinted at his nametag. D. Richards; Badge number 717. He'd rue this day after she wrote a scathing letter to his superiors.

Two police cars entered the *McDonald's* lot from opposite directions. One of the officers directed the drive-thru traffic and kept spectators at a distance from the accident. The other one, after seeing the damage to the car, called for an ambulance and tow truck. Officer Richards was running on adrenaline and ignored the pounding in his head. "Please step out of the car."

Norma complied. This man was an idiot. She told him about a kidnapping and all he cared about was his stupid car and holding her up. She gladly submitted to a Breathalyzer to prove she wasn't driving under the influence but was shocked when the second officer handcuffed her while reciting the Miranda Rights.

"Yes. Yes. I understand them better than you think," Norma said. Her one phone call would be to the lawyer she had on retainer. No public defender for her. The officer helped Norma get inside the back of his car.

Officer Richards sat on the back of the ambulance bumper between the open doors. One paramedic took his vitals while the other one shared the information with a doctor on staff at Mercy Hospital. The police officer, who handcuffed Norma, walked over to the ambulance to check on his fellow officer.

"Do you think Norma Lily is running on all cylinders?" Officer Ahmad Patel asked.

Damon Richards watched his damaged vehicle while it was being hooked onto the police tow truck then glanced at Officer Patel. "No. I think she's a few bricks short of a load. But oddly enough, it was the *Mc Donald's* manager who made the original call. He reported seeing what he described as a black pimp come through the drive-thru with a white girl."

"And?" A pimp sighting in it self wasn't unusual in this neighborhood.

"He called it in because the female looked battered. She was barefoot and had rope tied around her ankles."

"Maybe that's what Norma Lily meant by kidnapped? What kind of car was it?"

"Late model black Impala. I was just about to call in the license plate when I was taken out by Grandma Flowers." Damon said, tipping his head toward the vehicle holding Norma Lily. Pain washed through him. His headache was getting worse.

"I remember an All Points Bulletin about a black Impala having to do with Police Officer Dennis, who was shot at work a few weeks ago. Did you notice if the plates were out of state?"

"I really don't recall." Damon said. The hammering in his head progressed to a mallet pounding at his temples. The paramedics were ready to transport Officer Richards and helped him get up and inside the back of the ambulance.

*B*ack at the Short Stop Motel, Shirley Abel walked the floors of the small room. How could she be so stupid? The one thing Miss Lily asked her to do was watch over Patricia. Shirley couldn't figure out how the girl managed to get free and slip out of the motel room. Patricia should have been too groggy to wake up this early…unless she didn't drink the juice. Shirley walked over to the bed Patricia slept in and ran her hand over the sheets. They were dry. How did she do it? The rope was gone so she must have taken it with her, but how did she walk?

Even prior to this past week, Shirley wanted Patricia to go away because Patricia was standing between Shirley and marital bliss with Douglas Brown. Douglas was so cute and clever, and he looked up to Miss Lily like she did. People made fun of Douglas because they didn't understand him. Miss Lily told Shirley she would be a good match for Douglas and Miss Lily was always right. Shirley was being groomed to be a wife; something she thought would never happen, then all the plans changed when stupid Patricia showed up.

Shirley was still sleeping when the shrill sound of Miss Lily's scream, after discovering Patricia was gone, shocked her awake. Shirley was knew Miss Lily was coming that day but thought it would be in the afternoon, giving plenty of time for Patricia to clean up, comb her hair, and change her clothes.

Norma rushed over to Shirley's bed and stood over her. "Which way did she go?"

Shirley wrung her hands, "I don't know."

"Just stay here in case she comes back."

Norma Lily left the motel in her rented car. She was very disappointed in Shirley and never should have left her by herself for this long, but it couldn't be helped. It took more time than originally planned for Norma to set up a house for the soon-to-be newlyweds. There were so many details to consider.

Norma was glad when the police officer got into the car and started it up. The sooner this ordeal was over the better. Her children needed her. Norma giggled causing Officer Patel to look at her in the rearview mirror. Norma smiled at him, overcome with joy because her daughter Patricia was getting married.

Chapter 38

The video from *Mc Donald's* security camera was grainy, but Dr. Glover and his wife Sundae studied the woman's profile and identified the female in the passenger seat as their daughter, Patricia Elizabeth Glover. Her parents were relived to know Patricia was still alive although most likely brain washed by the known felon driving the car. The man driving the stolen Impala was easier to identify and an APB went out over the airwaves for the apprehension of August First Lord.

A shell of the black Impala was found the next day under the bridge leading to the City of San Pedro. The car had been torched and the remains were left on the side of the road near the end of the Harbor freeway. There was no sign of Patricia Glover or August Lord. It was as if they vanished.

Dmitri Newhall from the Mayor's office assured Dr. and Mrs.

Glover that finding their daughter was the Mayor's top priority. Dmitri set up meetings with several people so the Glover's could hear first hand how the investigation was progressing. James and Sundae Glover sat in the Mayor's private office at an oblong table made from Birchwood, a gift to the city from a foreign diplomat. Across the hall, a group of individuals were crammed into a small waiting room with one sofa and several folding chairs.

Captain John Boswell's name was called first. It took him a couple of tries to stand up from the low chair but he was finally able to pull his massive body upright. Boswell stood for a moment while the circulation in his legs resumed and when he could feel them again, he walked, head high out of the room of the less important people and into the Office of the Mayor.

After three minutes, Dr. Glover ran his hand through his hair and turned to Dmitri. "The purpose of these meetings is to talk to those individuals who can tell us first hand what's been going on."

Dmitri understood, "Thank you Captain Boswell. I'll show you out."

Boswell had never been dismissed by anyone as important as the Mayor's administrative assistant, and since there would be no witnesses to dispute him, he was already framing his version of how the Mayor valued his help. Boswell shook hands with Dr. Glover before strolling out of the office.

Detective Tony Sloan entered the Mayor's office carrying his leather portfolio. He informed the Glovers of the assault suffered by police officer Wade Dennis at the police station. Sundae grabbed her husband's hand. What kind of city was this, that the police were attacked and couldn't protect themselves inside the police station?

Detective Phillip Covers spoke to the Glovers about the suspect seen on video who was seen fleeing the police station; this young Caucasian female was also seen by an eye witness. "We believe the black Impala that was parked on the east side of the police station the day of the shooting is the same car you saw on the *Mc Donald's* video being driven by a recent parolee, August Lord."

Dr. Glover sat still in his chair with his hands on the table in front of him, "What's the connection between the woman at the police station and this Lord character?"

"This is total speculation, but we believe this unidentified woman stole the car from Eugene, Oregon and drove it to Los Angeles. The owner of the car is a woman named Norma Lily. Does that name sound familiar?"

Sundae looked at her husband then back at Phillip. She spoke for the two of them, "No."

"I asked because Norma Lily was at the *Mc Donald's* location at the same time the vehicle, we believe that was her black Impala, which was driven from the parking lot. Norma Lily said she was trying to follow her car when she hit a police car, who was responding to a call that a woman, a passenger in the black Impala, had a rope tied around her ankles. Norma Lily claimed the woman in the car had been kidnapped."

Sundae and James Glovers' eyes were fixed on Phillip Covers' every move, "How could she know that?" Dr. Glover asked.

"She won't say. We suspect Ms. Lily is having trouble distinguishing fantasy from reality. She says Patricia is her daughter."

Sundae gasped and wanted to faint but she had to hear more. Dmitri involuntarily jumped when John Glover expressed his emotions by pounding his fist on the table.

Phillip continued, "Ms. Lily is still in custody. She took and passed a Breathalyzer test at *Mc Donald's*, so we know she wasn't driving under the influence, but she seems to be slipping in and out of reality. Do you know anyone by the name of Shirley? A friend of Patricia's, perhaps?"

James glanced at his wife who was dabbing her eyes with the corner of her lace-trimmed handkerchief. "No. The only friend Patricia talked about that we haven't met was a boy--a young man she was seeing named Keith. Oh my God. Is Keith Dennis related to the police officer who was shot?" Dr. Glover reached inside his jacket pocket and pulled out his wallet and a wallet size picture and pushed it across the table to Phillip.

Phillip looked at the picture of Keith Dennis and Patricia Glover that was taken the previous year. They were an attractive looking young couple dressed in formal attire. "Yes, sir. Keith Dennis is the son of Wade Dennis. May I keep this?"

Sundae wanted to say no. She wanted to keep every piece of her daughter in tact, but she looked away when James said Phillip could have the photograph. Sundae pulled at her handkerchief. *Who was this Shirley person? Did she steal Norma Lily's car? The same car Patricia was seen in with the criminal? And why was Norma calling Patricia her daughter? Was it some kind of cult? Was her daughter going to be carrying a rifle like Patty Hearst?* It was all so bizarre.

Officer Ahmad Patel was next and told the Glovers' what he saw after arriving on the scene of the accident. A few other people spoke with the Glovers', but there was no information as useful as what they already heard from Phillip Covers. Phillip was the only person who told them he was sorry for their suffering, and on behalf of the City of Los Angeles, he would find their daughter. It was a sliver of assurance that provided some comfort to the distraught parents.

After four hours of meeting various individuals, James and Sundae were exhausted. They thanked Dmitri for his help and were ushered to a waiting limousine with a police escort that took them to a suite at the *Four Seasons Hotel.* James was convinced the police were going to find Patricia soon, and if they had to de-program his daughter once they had her back, he would find the best facility in the world to do it while he stayed by her side. James thought that after medical school, Patricia would complete her internship and residency and help him in his private practice. He looked forward to sharing office space with her, Drs. Glover and Glover, M.D. In twenty more years, James would retire and leave the medical practice to Patricia.

Tomorrow, James wanted a face-to-face meeting with Keith Dennis, who he learned was still in Los Angeles. James needed to question Keith about his relationship with Patricia. Keith was the only young man that Patricia dated, that her parents didn't really know. He was always Patricia's date for school functions, but he didn't come home with her for Thanksgiving, Christmas or New Years Eve celebrations.

James had a gut feeling this Keith-boy was the key to finding Patricia. *Why else would his father, a police officer, be shot at work?* Then there was the August Lord connection. James had heard about the Storm Lords. There must be some gang or other organized crime involved. James couldn't share this with Sundae. She was holding on as it was, but James had his own way of handling trouble and would have answers. Or else.

hapter 39

Charm had to stand up when she saw who was on the television. She grabbed her cell phone and dialed. "Nichelle! Are you watching?"

Nichelle held the phone away from her ear because Charm was yelling, "I'm watching *So You Think You Can Dance…*"

"Turn to *America's Most Wanted*. Hurry up!" Charm said hoping the image would stay on the screen long enough for Nichelle to change channels.

When Nichelle screamed and dropped the phone, Charm hung up. Nichelle would call her back when she recovered. Charm had presence of mind to push the record button on her remote as soon as she saw a still photograph of August First Lord filling her screen.

August was on the run again, a suspect in the kidnapping of heiress Patricia Glover who was picked up at Los Angeles International Airport and not seen again until a few nights ago, a passenger in a black Impala, driven by none other than August Lord, a son of Storm Lord.

Charm was pretty sure August Lord was the father of both her daughters, seven-year-old May Alize and six year old Lexus June. Even her best girlfriends didn't know Charm was ever pregnant and thought she was sent to South Carolina for a couple of years to help out her aunt. Charm was almost five months pregnant with her first child when she left Los Angeles. Her baby daddy, August, promised to visit her, but he only showed up once in Florence, after May Alize was a month old.

Six weeks after he left, Charm discovered she was pregnant again, but she was messing around with a lot of guys back then. Lexus looked like her older sister and could have belonged to August, but he was serving time, and he wouldn't be around anyway so Charm never told him about her second child. Not that it would have mattered. When August left South Carolina, he never looked back. After Lexus June was weaned, Charm left both children with her aunt and left Florence too. She rarely looked back either.

$\mathscr{C}$hapter 40

$\mathscr{P}$astor McMillan answered the telephone on the second ring. His wife was on a shopping excursion leaving her husband at home to meditate on the message he was going to preach on Sunday. Tomorrow was Unity Day, and the Church of Christ was welcoming Ebenezer Missionary Baptist Church of Inglewood's members and their choir. The segregation of people by race during Sunday services had a lot to do with where people lived, but it still bothered Harvey McMillan. He stayed on his knees asking God for a solution to the issue and five years ago, during a conference of the Fellowship of International Word of Faith Ministries in Los Angeles, he met a kindred spirit in Pastor Jeremiah Stewart. Harvey was the only person Pastor Stewart allowed to call him Jimmy Stewart, and whenever Jeremiah had the microphone, he told everyone Harvey McMillan was his brother from another mother.

"Hello?"

"Pastor Mc, It's Keith."

The pastor took off his glasses and put them on his desk. "Hello, there Keith. How are you son?"

"I'm fine. My Dad is doing well, and yourself, and Mrs. McMillan?"

"We are very blessed. What can I do for you?"

"I need to ask a favor."

"Sure, what is it?"

"Trish's parents, Dr. and Mrs. Glover, want to meet with me, and I was hoping you would come with me."

"When is the meeting?"

"Tomorrow, but I told them it would have to be in the afternoon."

"No news on Trish's whereabouts?"

"Not since she was seen in that car with the black dude. I'm not convinced it's her on the video, but her parents are positive it is her."

"I'll be glad to go with you to meet with Trish's parents. I can't imagine what they're going through emotionally, but God is able to see them through. I'll let them know our congregation is praying for them, and I hope they allow me to pray with them as well."

Keith was grateful he wouldn't have to face the Glovers' alone.

Chapter 41

"You ready?" August asked. It was hard to believe he was talking to the same female he picked up off the street a few days ago especially since he discovered this shorty was rich, and not just rich, filthy rich. The story broke on all the news and entertainment news channels; Patricia Glover was the daughter of a famous Canadian doctor. The newscasters called her an heiress and showed pictures of the mansion where she grew up. It looked like a state park. On the other hand, August Lord's street cred doubled when he was put on blast during the crime/drama/reality program *America's Most Wanted*.

Trish took a deep breath and nodded. August turned to walk out of the room when Trish grabbed his arm to stop him from leaving, "August. I haven't had the chance to thank you. If you hadn't picked me up…I just don't know what would have become of me." She gave him a brief hug. August smiled down at her when she took a step back.

"Ah, Shorty, I knew you didn't belong in South Central. You as white as they come; whiter than white. You not even regular American white, you North American Canadian white." At first, Patricia looked at him with an odd expression, and then she bent over laughing. It had been a long time since she felt anything was funny and she welcomed the feeling. August was on a roll, "I *had* to pick you up, girl. You were making the crack heads look bad."

"Oh, no." Trish stopped laughing and turned to look at herself in the mirror. She did remember a couple of street people doing a double take when she passed by them. "Was I that bad?" She had lost a little weight, but the bag of makeup and clothes August gave her was a godsend.

August hid his amusement seeing Trish dressed in the urban designed FUBU outfit of jeans, hooded sweatshirt and running shoes mirroring the swag of a thousand black females in the hood. The only thing missing was a pair of big gold earrings and a head of cornrows. Patricia's straw-looking hair now a pretty auburn color fell in soft waves past her shoulders. The no-shine foundation on her face changed her complexion from looking blotchy to a healthy warm glow. Her charcoal gray eye shadow, dark brown eyeliner and mascara enhanced the color of her blue eyes. August stood behind her amazed at her transformation.

Trish didn't know how bad she looked when she approached the black Impala. Her parents warned her about the dangers of talking to strangers and being in rough neighborhoods, but none of that mattered when it came to life and death. Thank God she was in a neighborhood where a man who didn't know her picked her up; rescued her, fed her, saved her.

In the *Mc Donald's* parking lot after Trish closed her eyes for just a moment, then opened them again and saw Norma Lily, her nightmare came to life. Trish wanted to scream when she saw the driver of the burgundy Taurus, but before she could alert August to the danger, he started the car and took off. Once they made it out of the *Mc Donald's* parking lot, he commanded that she lean down in the seat and close her eyes. August made so many turns that there was no way for Trish to know the direction they were going, but she closed her eyes tightly and prayed they would get away. Far away.

After August stopped the car, but before they got out, he pulled a bandana out of his pocket and tied it over her eyes.

"This is for your protection and mine." He explained, so she could in no way identify their location. August cut the rope from around her ankles and led her inside some kind of safe house. The windows to the outside were covered, at least in the room Trish was taken to, but attached to the room was a private bathroom and she was able to take a shower. When she came out of the bathroom wrapped in only a towel there was an oversized t-shirt on the bed. Trish slipped it on very grateful that her hands and legs were free. She slept fitfully that first night, but whenever she woke up and could move her arms and legs, it meant everything was going to be okay.

When August hadn't said anything Trish glanced over her shoulder at him. "What made you pick me up? I'm sure I looked like, like… an escaped convict!"

Trish never knew that August wanted to laugh at her words because the worst thing she could think of to describe her appearance was that of a convict, but he hid his amusement because she was serious.

"I heard somewhere that you reap what you sow. I don't like people judging me cause of how I look and…see how wrong I would have been about you if I had. Remember this Trisha, always look forward and never look back at things you can't change." He slipped out of the room while Trish was still checking herself out in the mirror. It was almost time to go.

$\mathcal{C}$hapter 42

$\mathcal{H}$eavenly carried her lavender pumps to the side of the bed and dropped one on the floor, so she could step into it. Today was a special day. She was finally going to meet Phillip's grandparents. Samuel and Estella Covers were members of Ebenezer Missionary Baptist Church of Inglewood. This Sunday was Unity Day, the day the predominately African-American member, Ebenezer MBC, lead by pastor and Mrs. Jeremiah Stewart, united in worship with the host church, the predominately Caucasian member, Church of Christ, that was presided over by Rev. and Mrs. Harvey McMillan.

The highlight of the service would be the pastors' team teaching the message entitled, "One Blood, One Faith, One Baptism" and the battle of the choirs. Each choir sang a song of their choosing during the morning devotions and together they sang as a mass choir during the service, but the last item on the program was for each choir, in turn, singing the same hymn. The congregants loved it and looked forward to hearing the unique interpretation of the same song. This year the selection was "How Great Thou Art."

The Saturday after Unity Day, Ebenezer MBC hosted the annual picnic and softball game at Griffith Park. The churches worked together doing missionary and community work during the year, but when they worshiped together on Unity Day, it was always an extraordinary experience.

Heavenly was invited to Sunday dinner at the Covers' home after the church service. She offered to help cook, but Estella Covers sent word by Phillip that some of the church mothers, who weren't coming to the Unity Day Service, were going to prepare the meal.

It took a week to decide what to wear, but Heavenly finally chose a lavender sundress with a matching short sleeve jacket. She tied a purple ribbon around her braids and was getting ready to put her shoes on when the telephone rang.

"Hello."

"Yo. Is this Heavenly? I know it is. You got mad pipes just sayin' hello girl."

Heavenly dropped the shoe she was getting ready to put on. She couldn't quite place the voice. "Who is this?"

"It's August. Remember me? Your sister Nichelle invited me over to yo' crib a minute ago. You put yo' foot in them greens."

Oh my goodness. This man is a fugitive. "I remember you August. Why are you calling me?"

"Is your man there?"

"Phillip is on his way? Why?"

"Good. When he gets there tell him to go up on the roof. I left a package there for you."

"What is it?"

"Don't worry. It's not a bomb or anything."

Bomb? "What did you put on the roof?"

"It was cool talkin' to you Sweetness, but I gotta bounce but be sure to check out the roof."

"August?"

"Bye, Angel. Maybe we'll hook up in another life."

Heavenly stared at the phone. As soon as she hung it up, it rang again and she almost dropped the receiver. She slowly put the phone to her ear. "Hello?"

"Hey, Baby." Phillip said. "I'm almost around the corner but you stay inside. I'll come up and get you."

Heavenly sank down on her bed, "I'm so glad you're almost here."

Something was wrong. "Are you all right?"

"I will be when you get here."

The tension in her voice set off his internal alarm.

"Stay put. I'll be right there," Phillip drove faster than the speed limit to get to her side. When Heavenly opened the door she walked into his arms. Phillip made sure the front door was closed and locked. After a moment, he pulled Heavenly's arms back and held her at arms length so he could study her face, "What's wrong?"

Phillip got more and more heated as she told him about the call from August. He was pissed off that August Lord had Heavenly's telephone number and his on-the-run- America's-Most-Wanted-fugitive-behind had the nerve to call and upset his woman. Phillip began to pace in front of Heavenly while she repeated everything August had said to her. "You stay here," Phillip turned around and started toward the front door.

Heavenly grabbed his arm, "I don't want you to go up there by yourself."

"If I'm not back in five minutes do not follow me, call 9-1-1."

"Phillip!"

He drew Heavenly protectively in his arms and gave her a quick kiss on the lips. "Don't worry. This is what I do. I'll be right back. Lock the door behind me."

Phillip usually didn't wear his holstered gun when he was going to church, but an angel must have tapped him on the shoulder this morning. He stood in the hallway in front of Heavenly's door until he heard the deadbolt lock in place. Walking to the elevator, he thought about the multitude of things August could have left on the roof, and he hoped it was the man himself.

Phillip stepped inside the elevator and pushed the button labeled 'R'. He took his gun out of the holster to make sure it was loaded. Satisfied he was ready for anything; Phillip placed his gun in his jacket pocket and kept his hand wrapped around it. When the elevator doors opened he stood to one side and waited a few seconds before exiting the elevator. Phillip couldn't enjoy the crisp clean air or the beautiful view because he was on full alert, expecting the worse.

$\mathscr{C}$hapter 43

$\mathscr{T}$he excitement in the air was palatable as the congregants began filling the main sanctuary of the Church of Christ. The pastor's wives and significant others were seated in the front row on both sides of the main isle. The ministers and other men greeted each other with hugs and handshakes while the Ebenezer womenfolk were 'dressed to the nines' in colorful displays of pastel dresses, wide brim hats and matching gloves. The balcony was set aside for parents with infants and young children. Several of the more mature teenagers in the youth group were assigned to help with the children and were seated strategically throughout the balcony.

Kimberly was thrilled to be sitting in the second row next to Keith. They hadn't spent much time together since their self-imposed cooling off period, but the sparks between them were alive and well. She sat between him and their special guest, Wade Dennis.

Wade didn't plan to go on any outings like this. Since his wife died, he restricted his life to work and home. It was a giant step to be comfortable with Donna's visits. Wade told himself it was because she was bringing him food, but he was blindsided last Wednesday when Donna asked him to ride with her because she was tired of being a third wheel when Keith and Kimberly were together. Of course, Wade understood her not wanting to be alone with an engaged couple, but before realizing what he agreed to, Donna was telling him the time she would pick him up on Sunday morning for the Unity Day Service. Donna didn't play fair because Wade had just finished off another superbly prepared dinner; young tender turkey wings with wild mushroom dressing, sautéed spinach, candied yams, and iced tea.

His traitor doctor found no reason Wade couldn't attend a church service for a few hours, leaving Wade with no excuse not to attend. To make it through the week, Wade tried to focus less on being a pushover when it came to anything Donna would ask him and more on the fact that his brother Chris, who hadn't darkened the door of a church in years, would be attending the Unity Day Service too. It was the one good thing about having to go to this church service because Wade would be able to witness this miracle with his own eyes and meet Debby Curtin; the woman who had apparently pulled his brother's playboy card.

Estella and Samuel Covers rode the Ebenezer Church bus with the other seniors who didn't, or preferred not to drive. When the bus arrived, Estella went with the other choir members to prepare for the service. Her seat was in the alto section of choir stand; amidst a sea of dark blue choir robes with white collars. Estella had a good view of all the people coming and going and looked diligently for Phillip and his new lady friend Heavenly. What a nice name for a Christian girl. Her grandson seemed to think the world of her too.

Estella didn't want to get her hopes up too high, but she felt deep down in her heart this was the right time for Phillip to find a wife. The *Bible* said man should not be alone, and a man that finds a wife finds a good thing. It was clear that a man didn't need to be out in the world too long. She knew that men should sow a few oats, then pack it in, settle down and be the head of his family. It took their boy, DeSean, a lot of heartaches and headaches before he finally married a good girl and now he and his wife, Leslie, had four beautiful children. Good kids. Estella prayed it was Phillip's turn and he would follow her advice and do it the easy way.

She shook her head thinking about how she and Samuel would complete fifty-five years of marriage next July. In 1955, Estella was seventeen years old and a recent graduate from Millicent High School and Samuel was a handsome, twenty-year-old, U.S. Marine when they were joined in holy matrimony

Lively organ music filled the main sanctuary. Estella looked for her husband in what was becoming a full house. The Church of Christ could accommodate five hundred people and with folding chairs another fifty could be seated in the isles. After that it was standing room only. Samuel Covers walked carefully up the center isle of the Church of Christ. It was a shame to see Christian people practically running to get a so-called good seat. It reminded him of when Jesus was speaking and people were packed inside the building and climbed on the roof top when there was no room for them inside except these folk weren't interested in getting to hear from God, they wanted to be seen and see everything close up. Samuel chose an end seat half way down the isle and moved into the pew. Others behind him quickly hurried to the front of the sanctuary talking and laughing just like they were going to see a concert. Samuel closed his eyes, so he wouldn't have to see anymore of the lack of reverence for the House of the Lord.

He couldn't judge the younger people, because when he was young, he didn't always think about the importance of spiritual things; in fact, he liked to party on Friday and Saturday nights and thought the purpose of Sunday was to catch up on sleep, so he could work for another week. Samuel learned most of his good *and bad* habits during his active duty in the Marines, some fifty-eight years ago. He enlisted right after high school; six months shy of his eighteenth birthday. It wasn't hard to do because he was sporting a thick mustache that made him look like he could be years older than his actual age and records at that time weren't scrutinized in the same way as they are now.

It wasn't hard to leave home because from the time Samuel was eight years old, he worked many-a-day chopping cotton and helping plant the fields of the neighboring farms in the heat of the Mississippi sun. Samuel was the fourth of ten children and the third boy born to Belle and Taylor Covers.

Taylor was twenty years older than his wife. He was a carpenter by trade until he fell off a roof, injured his back and legs and was unable to work. This happened ten years and six children into the marriage, but that didn't stop Taylor and Belle from having four more children after the accident.

As was her custom, Belle was up before dawn preparing breakfast and seeing after her husband and children. She packed lunches for the day, got every one up and fed, then went out into the fields to help with the harvest. At lunchtime, Belle went back to the house to check on Taylor and the younger children, and then she started preparing dinner.

Two days a week, the oldest child, Marion, stayed at home to wash and iron for everyone. Marion used any spare time to study and keep up with her school assignments. The next two siblings were twin boys Herman and Truman. Even as children, they were big and strong for their age and liked working with their hands. Samuel, the fourth child, gained a love of learning from his big sister and learned to fix things from his older brothers. Herman and Truman, also taught him to smoke, gave him his first drink and snuck him into the Speakeasy Night Club when Samuel was fifteen.

Feather Talltree, a Native American woman, owned the club. She took a-liking to Samuel and hired him as a bus boy. Several customers paid Samuel tips for bussing their table and passing notes to one another.

At age sixteen, after getting his driver's license, Feather promoted Samuel to her personal driver. Samuel was paid very well to keep his ears open and his mouth shut. He and Feather got along well until she caught him in the backseat of the car with Giselle, Feather's sixteen-year old daughter.

For his protection, Samuel's brothers took him across the state line to Alabama to the first recruiter's office they could find. Samuel was almost seventeen, but he used his brother's identification and enlisted in the Marines as nineteen-year-old Truman S. Covers. Two years later, when Samuel was nineteen and on leave was the first time he saw Estella Sears. It wasn't the long cotton dress buttoned from her neck to her knees that got his attention, but the way she walked past a group of men looking straight ahead like she was a much older woman. Samuel followed the young lady down the street and ended up inside a church building.

Estella's normal life consisted of school, church, grocery shopping, tending the garden, cooking, washing and taking care of her Nana. She spent her spare time attending church and singing in the youth and adult choir. Samuel closed his eyes the first time he heard Estella sing. Her sweet voice told him the story of the love of God for his people. Samuel had to meet her and waited around until after choir rehearsal was over and the sanctuary was almost empty.

"Hello."

Estella was startled. "Oh. I thought everyone was gone." She couldn't help but notice the handsome young soldier sitting in the back while rehearsal was going on. Estella assumed he was someone's husband or beau. "Are you waiting for someone?"

"Yes. You."

Estella frowned, "Me? What can I do for you sir?"

"You have such a beautiful voice miss. I was wondering if you would like to go across the street to the coffee shop and have some pie."

Estella put the last of the sheet music in the cabinet, "I don't know you sir."

She picked up her purse and walked past Samuel. He watched her walk away and when she almost made it to the front door he rushed to catch up. Dressed in his uniform Samuel had become accustomed to admiring glances or outright flirting by young females. He was intrigued by Estella's dismissal and followed her outside the church.

"Can I offer you a ride?" Samuel asked gesturing toward a Ford parked down the street. It was a friend's car that he borrowed for the weekend.

Estella frowned and pulled the ends of her coat together. She didn't like how this stranger was looking at her. "Sir, I don't know you." She kept walking and stepped up her pace. The roof of her house was visible through the pine trees just down the road from St. Paul's Presbyterian Church. Estella always walked home from church and felt safe even when the path was only lightened by moonlight.

Samuel kept his eye on her while she walked away, her head high, her steps determined. She thought the cold shoulder she displayed would discourage him. On the contrary, it made him determined to get to know her better.

$\mathcal{C}$hapter 44

$\mathcal{T}$he next day, Samuel stopped at Miss Mae's flower stand and purchased an assorted bouquet of flowers, then drove to 37 Morningside Lane. An elderly woman was sitting on the porch of the house near the front door. As Samuel came closer, he saw she was seated in a wheelchair and her legs were wrapped in a thick quilt.

"Good morning." Samuel said.

"Mornin'," she replied.

"It's lovely weather for late June."

"It's alright. I expect it to be hot before long."

"Yes, ma'am. My name is Samuel Covers."

"I know. I had a dream about you."

Samuel tried to hide his surprise.

"You're here for Estella."

"Is that the young lady with the beautiful voice who sang at church last night?"

"Yes. That's my granddaughter Estella Sears. I'm Erma Sears."

"Pleased to meet you, Miss Erma." Samuel said. He held out the bouquet of spring flowers. "These are for you."

Erma chuckled. "Listen here youngin'. I know you come for Estella. You tryin' to butter me up, but I already told you, I knew you was comin'."

Samuel returned her smile.

"This is what you do. Leave the flowers, and I'll tell Estella you brought them, and you come back tonight and take her to dinner."

Samuel wanted to ask how Estella knew about him, but decided to follow her lead. The answers would come eventually. He dressed in one of his brother's suits and was more nervous on his way back over to pick up Estella than he could ever remember being on a date including his first one with Lorraine Jones.

Estella spent the morning cleaning her Nana's room. She changed the sheets, washed the curtains, swept the floors, aired out the bedspread and beat the dust out of the braided rug. Then she heated up some chicken and rice soup and went out on the front porch to bring her grandmother back inside to eat lunch.

"Who gave you the pretty flowers?" Estella asked while maneuvering the wheelchair back into the house.

"These flowers are for you honey."

"Me? From who?"

"His name is Samuel."

Estella pushed the wheelchair up to the table. She didn't remember any Samuel. "What did he look like?"

Erma bowed her head and said grace. She reached for her spoon and concentrated on holding it tight enough to get the soup to her mouth. Estella waited for her to eat a few spoonfuls and asked the question again. Erma closed her eyes. She was getting sleepy. "You'll see Samuel tonight. He's coming back to take you to dinner."

"Dinner? How do I know him?"

"He's one of Belle Covers' boys."

Estella wondered if her Nana's mind was drifting. Belle Covers' sons were kids and none of them were named Samuel. After lunch, she helped Nana get back into bed and finished cleaning the only bathroom of the two-bedroom cottage.

Estella plans for the rest of afternoon were to knit squares for a baby blanket she was making. After a while, she heard Nana's voice calling from her room.

"Are you getting ready?"

Estella put her knitting aside and went into Nana's room. "Are you ready to eat again?" Judging by the dimness of her room it was five o'clock. They usually ate dinner at sundown between six and seven o'clock.

"Why don't you try on that dark blue dress Sister Beckman gave you?"

Estella sighed. The dress was pretty, but it wasn't her style not that she had a style, but that dress was for a night on the town; but to humor her grandmother, Estella went to the closet. The silk dress was very pretty and felt good against her skin. The scalloped edges emphasized her bust line, which was okay for home, but Estella never could see herself being this exposed around others.

"That looks beautiful on you," Nana beamed. "Try on my silver jewelry."

Estella laughed and went right to the black box inside Nana's top drawer. She admired the sparkling silver necklace, earrings and bracelet set all her life. When she was a kid, Nana would let her wear it twice a year, on Estella's birthday and Christmas morning. Sometimes that was her only Christmas present along with an orange or an apple.

"Now put your hair up and get my wrap out of the back of the closet."

Estella decided it was fun playing dress up. She combed her hair into a French twist and pinned it in place and she paraded around in the cashmere stole while her Nana clapped her hands.

The baby blanket Estella was making was for Ruby Lee Irving. Ruby Lee paid Estella a little on it every week. The blanket was for Ruby Lee's sister who was expecting to deliver a baby in a few months. When Estella heard a knock on the front door, she figured it was Ruby Lee. As a joke, Estella planned to model her look for her friend, but when she opened the door, Samuel Covers stood there looking more handsome than she remembered. Estella forgot how she was dressed until he spoke, but not until after he looked her up and down, hardly believing this was the button down songbird from yesterday.

"Wow, you look amazing."

Forgetting her manners, Estella replied, "You're a Covers?"

"I'm Samuel Covers. Thank you for coming to dinner with me."

"Dinner? I can't leave my grandmother alone."

"Yes, you can!" Erma shouted from the bedroom.

Just then, Ruby Lee Irving knocked on the open door. "Hello."

"Come on in, Ruby Lee."

"Wow, Stella, you look beautiful. I didn't know you had company," Ruby Lee said.

Samuel introduced himself to Ruby Lee, while Estella went into the front bedroom to reason with her Nana. Ruby Lee overheard the discussion because Erma was not about to be whispering in her own house. Ruby Lee joined the women while Samuel stood near the fireplace and waited for the outcome.

"I can stay Estella," Ruby Lee said. "I don't have anything to do tonight. I'll stay with Miss Erma until you get back."

Estella sighed. Any other time Ruby Lee would be in a hurry. Out numbered, Estella left with Samuel, determined to try and enjoy eating out for a change.

"Have you heard of Starr's Restaurant?" Samuel asked once they were inside the car.

"Yes."

"Have you ever eaten there?"

"Once or twice." Actually it was one time, two years ago after the youth choir won a competition at the Presbyterian Church Convention.

"What do you recommend?"

Estella felt bamboozled, but she was trying to be mature about the whole thing. It wasn't Samuel's fault her Nana sold her up the river. She should have fun tonight just to spite everyone who thought they knew so much about poor pitiful Estella—the church singer. She was never the popular girl in school and her only worldly possessions were a few cotton dresses purchased from the Salvation Army that she washed out every night. She wanted to be a normal teenager, but she was her Nana's caretaker and that meant being on-call day and night. Some of the church members stopped by the house to look in on Erma when Estella had to go to school during the day, but she never told Nana about the parties and the school dances she missed. Estella never kept up with the latest styles and fashion, and she usually felt like an ugly duckling, until tonight. Pastor Beckman's wife Claire sorted through clothes donated to the church and thought the navy colored, silk spun dress would fit Estella. It did but where would she wear it? So the dress stayed in the closet for the last six months.

The evening was pleasant. Samuel was charming, and Estella became more and more excited to be on an actual date on a Saturday night. A few of her classmates saw her out with the dashing young man with the mustache. Samuel was a bronzed-honey color with wavy black hair and bright brown eyes. He was tall with a trim waist. Oh, there would be talk in their town on Monday. Even the fact that buttoned up Estella who only opened up when she was singing in church was looking good. Who knew that under all those clothes was a shapely body now revealed in the navy blue dress?

As Estella relaxed, Samuel discovered her wry sense of humor. She kept him chuckling most of the night. Estella knew Samuel was going back to the base in a few days. At the end of the night, she agreed to write him and thanked him for taking her to dinner. Samuel walked her to the front door and placed a gentle kiss on the back of her hand. Estella didn't see him again for a year. They kept in touch by writing letters. Estella kept all of them in a shoebox under her bed, tied together with a strip of silk fabric.

It was all so innocent until Samuel came back to attend Estella's graduation from high school. In a year, she'd blossomed like a flower and now dressed like a young woman, not an old maid with many of the male bees buzzing around her. Samuel couldn't keep his eyes off her either. He was quick to ask her to marry him, and after a short engagement, they became husband and wife.

The new Mr. and Mrs. Covers honeymooned in New York City where Samuel took his bride to all of the tourist sites. Estella especially enjoyed shopping and was amazed that so much merchandise was in one place. The only sadness during that time was that Nana passed away one week after they returned. The doctor told them Nana said she was ready to go now because Estella had a husband to take care of her and wouldn't be alone.

Estella mourned for her grandmother but having Samuel made everything bearable. They sold Nana's little house and moved across town to a four-bedroom, two-bathroom ranch style house that Estella hoped to fill with children. She enjoyed fixing up each room in the house and always had dinner ready when Samuel came home. Estella listened attentively as her husband talked about his work as a salesman for *Atlantis Auto Parts*. After six months, Samuel was promoted and given a larger sales area requiring him to travel throughout the county taking orders. This new job prevented the newlywed from being at home by six o'clock, and sometimes, he didn't arrive until ten.

Estella was home day after day, and when her husband came home, he just wanted to sleep. When the loneliness became unbearable, she had to get out of the house. Estella started attending Wednesday night bible study, Thursday night choir rehearsal and helping during Friday Night Teen Night. Even with all this activity, she usually made it home before Samuel. He didn't seem to care about fulfilling his wife's emotional needs, and Estella didn't know what to do except pray.

Steven Noble was a deacon at St. Paul for the last ten years. He was widowed a few years ago and took notice of the nice young woman who always was helping out. He and Stella struck up an easy friendship based on church activities, and because they were together so much, they were sometimes mistaken for husband and wife.

Steven would laugh and say, "I'd be robbing the cradle," even though he was flattered anyone thought a young lady like Estella would be interested in him. Everything changed when Samuel came home early a few times and found a note from his wife rather than a hot meal. He was ready to talk and now she was gone. Samuel decided to go to the Wednesday Bible Study and could hardly believe his eyes. His wife was sitting next to another man and sharing a *Bible* with him. The two of them laughed and whispered like a couple, who was all too familiar with each other.

Samuel left *Atlantis Auto Parts* and took a job in purchasing with *Sears & Roebuck*. Now that he was working a forty-hour week, with a thirty-minute commute Estella could count on her husband being home every night on time. Samuel got up early on Sunday to drive them to church and made sure everyone knew Estella was his wife. He took her out to dinner at least once a week and brought her a small gift every month …just because.

It wasn't long before Samuel looked forward to Sunday service and learning the *Bible*. It brought him comfort especially when Estella never got pregnant. After five years of no babies, when she was just about to give up on being a mother, Samuel laid his hand on her stomach and prayed for a child, and wouldn't you know, she conceived and nine months, later bore their son. They named him Samuel DeSean Covers. DeSean was a cute, chubby baby with curly black hair that grew into a headstrong toddler. Estella jokingly asked her husband not to pray for anymore kids because having DeSean was like having a house full of children, and she was more than satisfied with just the one.

Estella finally spotted her husband sitting near the middle of the sanctuary on the inside isle. When they made eye contact, her heart fluttered and she smiled at him still seeing the tall, light brown, handsome solider she met and fell in love with more than a half century ago. His hair was gray and thinning, and he didn't walk so tall and straight anymore, but fanning herself, Estella looked away to keep her thoughts pure in the house of God. She greeted some of the choir members she hadn't yet spoke to and then turned back around to survey the crowd. Where was Phillip? If he didn't come soon he was going to have to stand up during the whole service.

*P*hillip Covers wasn't thinking about being at church at that moment. He was on the roof of a downtown apartment building, gun drawn, walking slowly around corners and looking for anything suspicious. When he didn't see anything unusual, he wondered if the telephone call was a decoy to get him away from Heavenly? Phillip was just about to get back on the elevator when out of the corner of his eye something moved. He crouched and pointed his gun toward the movement.

A young woman was standing almost behind a door near the elevator. She lifted her hands. "Oh." She stood there looking back at him and hoped he wasn't trigger-happy.

Was she alone? Phillip stood straight and lowered his weapon but held his finger on the trigger. "Do you live here?"

"No, sir. I'm Patricia Glover."

Of course. He recognized her from the photograph Dr. Glover gave him. She looked very different from the Patricia Glover he expected to see. "Patricia. We've been looking for you. Are you alone?"

"Yes. I'm all alone. I was dropped off this morning and told to wait here."

"Are you alright? The last time you were seen it was reported, you may have had some injuries."

"I still have a few bruises, but I'm feeling pretty good." Trish said.

"Who dropped you off?"

"Can we go inside? It's kind of windy up here." Trish asked. She wanted to put off having to talk about August Lord, hoping to give him extra time to get further underground.

"Of course, we can. I'm Detective Phillip Covers of the LAPD. I'm so glad you're okay. My girlfriend lives in this building." Phillip said and pushed the down button of the elevator. "Your parents are in town. I can't wait to let them know you've been found safe and sound."

Trish was overcome with emotion at the mention of her parents and the thought of being able to see them this very day. She covered her face in her hands and wept. When the elevator doors opened Phillip guided her inside. Heavenly looked through the peephole after hearing the knock and quickly opened her front door.

"Oh my goodness! Come in." She stepped back so Trish and Phillip could enter. Heavenly recognized Patricia from the multiple reports about her on television.

After the introductions were made Phillip took a card out of his wallet and dialed a number.

"Dr. Glover."

"Yes?" James Glover had been awake for hours and was thinking about his meeting with Keith Dennis. Before answering this call he planned to get dressed, go down to the gym and walk a few miles on the treadmill, then shower and get a massage before returning to his suite, waking up his wife and ordering breakfast.

"This is Detective Phillip Covers. I have some good news for you, sir."

James Glover gripped the telephone receiver tightly, "Yes?"

"Your daughter is with me. She is fine. I'm going to put her on the phone."

Trish's hand shook when she took the cordless phone from Phillip. "Daddy? Yes. Yes. I'm okay. I'm… well, I don't know where I am but I'm safe. Oh, Daddy. Mum? Oh Mum, stop crying. I'm okay."

She spoke to both parents, and then Phillip took over the conversation with James Glover. Heavenly let Trish cry on her shoulder as she released the joy and pain previously bottled up inside. In less than thirty minutes, the Glovers' and it seemed like half of the Los Angeles police department, as well as the media, descended on Heavenly's building.

Captain John Boswell, Phillip's supervisor was present as well. He didn't approve that Phil called the girl's family first. That was not protocol. A wonderful photo-op was missed and there was no way the captain could claim credit for the discovery other than being Phil Cover's direct supervisor. Dr. and Mrs. Glover couldn't say enough wonderful things about the man who returned their daughter to them safe and sound just like he promised. Eventually, Boswell jumped on the bandwagon and started praising Phil Covers too.

Across town at the Church of Christ during Ebenezer's individual choral selection, Keith Dennis received a text from the Mayor's administrative assistant, Dmitri Newhall. Trish was found and was safe. The scheduled meeting with the Glovers' was cancelled. Several members of Ebenezer MBC thought Keith 'caught the Holy Ghost' because he was so exuberant in his praise.

It was really something to see when white folks got excited about praising God. First Lady Gwendolyn McMillan was the exception to the rule. She was one anointed Christian woman, who didn't care who was watching, and always let the Spirit use her. Several Ebenezer members gave the young man in the second row, understanding smiles because he stood with them and clapped his hands (*on beat*), while the Ebenezer choir was raising the roof with their rendition of "How Great Thou Art."

When the song ended, Pastor McMillan shared the news with the congregation about the lost girl, Patricia Glover (who they all had been praying for) had been found. She was alive and was being reunited with her parents at this very moment. The congregation shouted for joy and continued praising God. The congregants hugged each other like their very own lost relative had been found. Pastor Jeremiah Stewart felt the strong anointing of the Holy Spirit and knew it was harvest time. He delivered a mini-sermon about the lost being found and issued an invitation for whosoever will to come and receive Jesus Christ as their personal Lord and Savior. Seven people responded to the call and came forward to be prayed for and were ministered to in an adjoining room.

When the service ended, all agreed that Unity Day was very special and members of both congregations were looking forward to next year's program at Ebenezer. Something good always happened on Unity Day.

Chapter 45

The Monday morning press conference was moved outside to the city hall plaza because a multitude of news crews wanted to see and show the heiress, alive and well. The weather cooperated and the outside temperature was seventy-three degrees, bringing another opportunity for the city to brag about Southern California weather while most of the nation was suffering the effects of a heat wave.

Patricia 'Trish' Glover and her parents were seated at a long skirted table that was on top of a raised platform. Next to the family was Los Angeles Mayor Antonio Villaraigosa. On the other side of the podium were two of city councilpersons and the Chief of Police. Other dignitaries sat in padded white folding chairs that faced the raised platform. The press was delegated to two areas on either side of the area reserved for dignitaries. They were close enough to be able to ask questions, take unobstructed pictures and block the view of the less important people who were standing behind them.

After the Mayor greeted everyone, the Chief of Police gave a general overview of the kidnapping, but he explained how the case was on-going; therefore, some questions may have to wait for answers. The question and answer segment began and representatives from the press directed most of their questions to Patricia Glover.

"Miss Glover. Pete Minor, *Starlight News*. August Lord is a known felon, just out of prison, a member of the notorious black gang, the L.A. Storm Lords...

"Do you have a question, Mr. Minor?" Patricia asked.

"Weren't you just scared? This guy picks you up, keeps you hidden away for days then leaves you on the roof of a high rise..."

Patricia interrupted. "As far as I'm concerned, August Lord rescued me. I was a stranger to him, but that didn't stop him from helping me. He bought me food, gave me clean clothes to wear and never asked for anything in return."

"But Miss Glover, you are a white female in a gang-infested neighborhood, South Los Angeles, where crimes are being committed as we speak. You had to be afraid..."

Patricia spoke over him. "August's car wasn't the first car I approached. Other people, white people, ignored my cries for help, but it was the kindness and compassion of a man who happens to be black, who you call a felon and a gang banger that is responsible for me being here today. Mr. Minor, two white women kidnapped me at gunpoint, kept me drugged, starved, and tied me up. So I ask you sir, who would you, be afraid of?"

The *Star News* reporter sat down while his colleagues typed furiously on their portable electronic devises in an attempt to capture the moment in words. Patricia was providing them with great sound bites. More questions were asked concerning Norma Lily and her connection, if any, to the shooting of policeman Wade Dennis; and the identity of the mysterious woman seen leaving the police station parking lot after the shooting. Phillip Covers' name came up on several occasions and his grandparents along with Heavenly, who were sitting with Phillip on the front row, beamed with pride. When the questions started being repeated the Mayor ended the Q&A session by moving on to the next item on the program, the awarding of recognition to those who reunited Patricia Glover, safe and sound, with her parents.

*N*ichelle was in a foul mood. Her so-called friends Charm and Brandi went to Las Vegas last Friday and enjoyed a weekend of partying including the Hoodie Awards with radio personality Steve Harvey. Brandi's brother Kyle and his girlfriend Bettina decided to drive to Las Vegas. Kyle drove a really nice Yukon SUV. Bettina's cousin lived in a five-bedroom house in North Las Vegas, so the group only had the expense of buying gasoline and individual tickets to the awards show. There would have been plenty of room for Nichelle too, but o' selfish Glenda Carlson decided to come home on Friday. If Nichelle wanted to be paid and keep her job, she actually had to work. It wasn't right when everybody else was away having fun. She needed a break too.

But no, Nichelle had to run an errand for Glenda. This meant being downtown early Monday morning to pick up a document Glenda needed, having to do with her disability. Nichelle couldn't get over how all of a sudden 'Ms. Vegas' had to come home the weekend of the Hoodies. Nichelle stomped down the stairs of the Hall of Records. Her life sucked! Now Brandi was going to come back and brag about all the fun they had without her.

Then on top of being stuck in L.A., the person Nichelle referred to as her man, (which always got an eye-roll from Charm, but too bad, so sad) August Lord, was wanted for kidnapping which turned out not to be a kidnapping, he just gave a ride to a rich girl. August needed a woman like Nichelle in his life. She would have told him to ask for a reward even if the girl's family wasn't loaded. As it was, the girl's parents would have been glad to give them a few dollars or maybe a house for the return of their princess. Life wasn't fair. Her man disappeared and she was cheated out of the fun she missed and would have to forever hear about it from Charm and Brandi.

Nothing was working right in her life. Nichelle hadn't even won five dollars on her weekly lottery scratcher in months, and she faithfully bought her tickets from Dom's Liquor store. She wouldn't be surprised if Dom was keeping her paying ticket and telling her she hadn't won. Maybe that was the problem. She should try buying her lottery tickets other places. Nichelle crossed the street toward the city bus stop that would take her back to her residence when she noticed the crowd at the city hall plaza.

A closer inspection revealed Philly shaking hands with the mayor, who looked to be frozen in place, while the multitude of photographers took their picture. Tyra would have been proud. In Philly's left hand, he was holding up a brown plaque with what looked like gold writing. All of the people on the stage were standing and smiling and clapping for him. What did Philly do but bring the girl down from the roof in the elevator? It wasn't like he carried her down the outside of the building on a rope? Her slow sister, Heavenly, should have asked for a reward for letting the girl stay in her apartment. Everybody was missing the point of doing good deeds.

Nichelle came closer and stood among the crowd of people. Most of them had been standing for an hour already having claimed their physical and personal spot. Nichelle used her advantage of being very thin to move through the crowd until she was in the front, just behind the section reserved for the press.

If Heavenly was there, Nichelle could bum a ride. While she looked for her sister, someone trying to get past her bumped her hard. It was so rude and today was not the day to be rude to Nichelle, especially to crash into her and not apologize. Her nerves were bad. Her life was in the pits and this female who didn't know how to dress in the summer, wearing a long brown coat, was trying to push her out of the way. Oh, hell no. Nichelle grabbed the woman's shoulder and pulled back hard. "Can't you say excuse me?" After Nichelle saw the weapon in the woman's hand and the wild crazy look in her eyes, everything seemed to move in slow motion. Nichelle shouted as loud as she could. "GUN!" But to herself, she apologized to Philly for stealing his fifteen minutes of fame.

Several uniformed and plain clothed police officers in the audience felt for their weapons and looked toward the noise. They saw a woman standing behind the press section with her gun pointed in the direction of the raised platform. She might have gotten a shot off and hit her intended target, but by taking the time to shout, "This is for you Miss Lily!" it allowed just enough time for Nichelle to jump on her back. Nichelle and the woman fell forward into the back of the folding chairs, then to the ground. Although the gun discharged, no one was hit. The city's security team surrounded Nichelle, who, with both hands, was holding down Shirley's hand, that was still gripping the pistol.

The people on the podium were ushered to safety and the crowd, for the most part, ran away from the sound of the discharged weapon. Gunfire also ended the press conference except for the video cameras capturing the scene as it unfolded. The woman on the ground stopped moving when a uniformed police officer jammed one of his size thirteen shoes on her wrist and she was forced to let go of the gun. The same officer picked Nichelle up with one arm and held her back while Nichelle cursed out the woman for causing her to break several of her acrylic finger nails. Nichelle got her nails done at *Perfect Nail Salon* less than a week ago in preparation for partying in Las Vegas. It cost her an extra five dollars for the design.

Nichelle was glad to see the woman arrested and placed in handcuffs because Nichelle was definitely going to press charges against her and get reimbursed for the twenty-five dollar full-set plus design. She would add another seventy-five hundred dollars to her claim for pain and suffering.

"I'm Officer Jonah Johnson. I'll take care of you Little-bit," the policeman with the big shoes said. He escorted Nichelle to an unmarked state-issued car, ignoring the cries from reporters for her name and requests for a statement. Nichelle would have talked with them, but Jonah shielded her from the reporters by standing in front of the open car door until she got inside.

Nichelle checked out Officer Johnson during the brief ride to the police station downtown. He was definitely macho; tall with big muscles and a take-charge attitude and knew how to handle himself under pressure. Maybe Heavenly was on to something by dating a cop. Jonah was much more hip than Philly and it didn't hurt that he had big feet.

Chapter 46

At the police station, the City Hall shooter was identified as Shirley Abel.

"When can I see her?" Shirley asked. She and two men were sitting in a small windowless room. One of the men was Nathan Stevens; her court appointed attorney, and the other was his supervisor, William Burns. A mini-recorder was the only item on the table. Shirley repeated her request to speak to Norma Lily and seemed surprised when she noticed that one of her wrists was still handcuffed and shackled to the metal table.

"I need you to answer some questions. Please state your full name," Nathan said.

"Sheryl Lynn Abel, but everyone calls me Shirley."

"I am Nathan Stevens and also present is…"

"William Burns," the more senior attorney said on cue.

Nathan continued. "It's Monday, the twenty-third of August, twenty-ten at eighteen hundred hours." He looked directly at Shirley. She calmly watched the attorney and kept her free hand in her lap.

"What is your address Ms. Abel?" Nathan asked.

"5445 Sutter Lane, Eugene, Oregon."

"Why were you at the Los Angeles City Hall today?"

"I was there because Patricia Glover was there and I wanted to shoot her… between the eyes."

Nathan Stevens' eyes glazed over. William Burns was also stunned by her bluntness, but he managed to keep his emotions from showing on his face.

"Ms. Abel, why did you want to shoot Patricia Glover?" Nathan asked.

Shirley scowled, "I can't stand her. She ruined everything."

"What did Patricia Glover ruin?"

"My life…"

Nathan Stevens was a patient man, "What specifically did Patricia Glover do to ruin your life?"

"Let me start at the beginning, okay?"

"Please do."

"I was hired by the United States Postal service in 2007 the same year as Douglas Brown. That's B-R-O-W-N. Got it?"

"Yes, continue."

"Norma Lily is our supervisor and an excellent instructor. She was the best and because she taught us, Douglas and I were the best clerks in the department, even better than the people who transferred in with more experience, but anyway, Norma and Douglas had a special relationship. I wasn't jealous because I understood Norma was trying to help him. It was the other staff who made fun of Douglas. It wasn't right how they talked about him behind his back, but when they did, I would find out which car that person drove and slash one of their tires;

Like the *Bible* says 'An eye for an eye'." Shirley covered her mouth with her free hand when she laughed. "They never knew how or why their car tires always went flat. They couldn't understand how it could happen in the employee lot with all the security around."

Shirley chuckled and looked over at William Burns. He didn't look too happy. No wonder. Who would want to be a lawyer? "Anyway, one day Norma asked me what I thought of Douglas and I told her I thought he was a wonderful man. That's when Norma told me that I was a good match for him. Me. Not that Trish." Shirley scowled again when she said her name. "What kind of a name is that anyway? It should be Trash! Anyway, I was so hurt the day Norma told me Trish was going to be married to Douglas, but Ms. Lily, that's what I called her around the others; Ms. Lily was always right and so precise. She told me there was another man for me, but I was very disappointed to lose Douglas. We were so right for each other, but when Norma told me she needed a special person to get rid of Trish's boyfriend, Mr. Keith Dennis, I told her I would help her. I would shoot him between the eyes." Shirley pointed her index finger at William Burns, paused then bent her finger to show them how she would pull the trigger.

William Burns popped an antacid into his mouth, closed his eyes and chewed; trying to ease the pain his client was causing him.

Nathan Stevens had a feeling another bomb was about to be dropped. "What happened next?"

"Norma told me not to shoot Keith."

William Burns opened his eyes

"*Not* to shoot him?" Nathan repeated.

Shirley nodded. "She said we needed a plan to get him to go away, but she meant move away. So, Norma looked up Keith father's address in L.A. then told me to drive her car to Los Angeles…"

"Can you tell me the year, make and model of the car?"

"It is a black 2004 Chevy Impala. Anyway, Norma told me to check into a motel and find out what I could about Wade Dennis, and that's what I did. I followed him from home to work and back for a few days. Then, Norma told me to handle it."

"What did she mean by handle it?" Nathan asked.

Shirley smiled at him. She mimicked picking up a gun and pointed her finger again at William Burns, "Pow! Right between the eyes."

Attorney Burris felt the pain of his ulcer slice through his side. He was too close to retirement to deal with this woman, who gave him the creeps. Burns was determined to find a way to dump this case on another supervisor.

"Did Norma Lily tell you to shoot Wade Dennis?

"Do you want to hear what happened or not?" Shirley asked.

"Please, continue." Nathan said.

"Anyway, I parked on the side street at his job and ducked down next to his car in the employee parking lot. I was only supposed to shoot him, you know, injure him, while he was getting into his car. I just like saying, right between the eyes. It's more poetic don't you think? Anyway, we knew once Keith got the news about his father being shot, he would leave Oregon. But for some reason that night, Keith's father didn't come out to his car at 5:30, like all the other nights. I got nervous because many of the other employees were leaving the lot and it was getting harder to hide between the cars and not be seen. Finally, I saw a janitor prop the back door open, so I slipped inside. I walked up the stairs and through the offices until I found Wade Dennis' name. Most of the other offices were empty, but there he was sitting in his chair, yakking on the telephone. I aimed, shot two times, heard him fall, and I got out of there. Even though I used a silencer on the gun, the police were everywhere. I barely made my get-away before the streets were blocked off and helicopters were flying overhead. I decided to abandon the car in an alley in a seedy part of town. I caught the city bus back to the motel and called Norma. Did I tell you she entered my name for employee of the month? We have a special bond."

Yeah, both of you are Looney Tunes. "Where is Douglas Brown?"

"My Douglas? He moved; took a temporary leave from work. Norma has an old family home in Washington. I think he's there."

Nathan asked a few more questions but the confession was more than enough for Shirley to be charged with first-degree, attempted murder of Wade Dennis and probably Patricia Glover as well. "Why did Norma Lily come to Los Angeles?"

"Miss Lily was upset that Trish made plans to follow Keith to Los Angeles because that would ruin everything. I rented a car and picked Miss Lily up at the airport."

"How did Norma Lily know when Trish was leaving?"

Shirley covered her mouth again to hide her amusement. "Douglas bugged her apartment. He heard mostly everything going on over there. After work, he would come home and listen. He figured out a way to tap into her e-mail too. He was so clever."

More like crazy. Another one to add to the crazy-bin.

"Anyway, I picked up Miss Lily at the airport. She told me to get into the backseat and Miss Lilly drove up to the curb and asked Trish to help her find her hotel. Once Trish was in the car, we took her to the motel. Miss Lily told me to watch her. She left me money to buy food and gave me a suitcase full of clothes and toiletries. Miss Lily always thought ahead."

"What was the name of the motel?"

"The *Short Stop Motel*; kind of catchy, huh? That's why I picked it."

"Miss Lily left you at the *Short Stop Motel* with Patricia Glover?"

"Yup. Trish tried to befriend me. She thought I was too stupid to know what she was trying to do. She wasn't my friend. That floozy stole my husband-to-be. I wanted to shoot her between the eyes, but Miss Lily wouldn't have liked it, so instead, I made Trish wear the same clothes every day. I let her shower, but she had to put on the same smelly clothes. I wouldn't let her comb her hair. I wanted everyone to see she wasn't so cute. She didn't fool me. I saw her for who she was."

"How did she get away?"

"How should I know? I was asleep. I hog-tied her wrists and ankles like I did every night. I gave her the crushed up sleeping pill in the juice like Miss Lily told me to do. You tell me how she got away?"

William Burns was only half-listening. His mind was focused on which supervisor would want to deal with the publicity garnered by this trial.

Shirley told them of their surprise when Norma came back and Patricia was gone. Norma Lily left the motel to look for Patricia and never came back. That night, Shirley saw the breaking news story that heiress Patricia Glover was believed to be kidnapped by gang member, August Lord, because Patricia was seen in a car driven by the recently paroled felon.

"I couldn't believe that August-person was driving Miss Lily's Impala. I hid that car in a bad part of town and like a Phoenix-rising, it returned," Shirley said.

Nathan had heard enough. "Thank you Miss Abel. You've been very cooperative."

William Burns and Nathan Stevens took a break and stood outside of the interview room. Nathan shared his conclusions that August Lord found the 'stolen' Impala and picked up Patricia Glover who must have just escaped from the motel. Norma Lily was in the area looking for them and noticed a car like hers in the parking lot of *Mc Donald's*. When she saw Patricia in the car, Norma tried to pull in front of the Impala, but the police car was already coming in the opposite direction. August was able to get passed both cars and left the parking lot while the accident Norma Lily caused totaled the police car. Once Shirley was cut off from her mentor, she took it upon herself to take out Patricia, hoping to be reinstated as the potential wife of Douglas Brown. Attorney William Burns nodded while Nathan was speaking, but he had already mentally checked out and couldn't leave the building fast enough once they concluded the debriefing.

When Nathan Stevens returned to the interview room with a police officer, Shirley Abel smiled at the man in uniform, "Now, can you take me to Ms. Lily? I need to know what to do next."

Chapter 47

"We're ready to board, dear," Sundae said to Patricia. Mother and daughter had been inseparable since their reunion.

"Okay, Mum. Let me say good-bye to Keith."

Sundae nodded and let go of her daughter's hand. She didn't want to let Patricia out of her sight, but she understood her daughter needed some privacy. Thank heavens in a few minutes Patricia would be in the air, on her way back home. Victoria, Canada never sounded better.

After Sundae called her mother with the news that Patricia had been found, Martha got up out of her bed although Martha wouldn't be completely convinced until she saw Patricia with her own two eyes. On Monday morning, Martha sat in the sunroom, a room that faced the roadway to her home and watched the press conference. She was going to wait up for them to come home, even though her family wasn't due to return to Victoria until late that evening.

*H*arvey McMillan drove Keith to the airport, especially wanting to personally meet and pray with James and Sundae Glover and tell them how the members of two churches had interceded for them. Keith watched from the passenger seat of Rev. Mc Millan's car as Patricia's parents exited the limousine and boarded their private plane. Harvey Mc Millan got out and boarded the Glovers' plane after them. Keith went directly to the limo where he knew Trish was waiting for him. It was wonderful to see her. It was their first time alone in weeks and now they sat only inches apart. For several seconds, no words were necessary as they looked into each other's eyes. Finally, Keith rested his hands on her shoulders then leaned forward until his forehead rested on hers. "I'm so glad you're alright Trish."

"Me, too." Patricia whispered.

Keith leaned back and took one of her hands in his, "Are you going to medical school like you planned?"

"No. Not for a while. I'm taking some time off. I want to spend it with my family. How about you? Are you going to Stanford in the fall?"

"I don't think so. I still want to get my J.D., but I want to be closer to my Dad, and oh, by the way, I've been wanting to break up with you. I just couldn't find you to do it."

Trish pulled her hand out of his and socked Keith in the arm, "You trader."

He worried she was serious, but when she smiled, they both laughed.

"Keith, I can't deal with a relationship right now, and if I hadn't gone through what I just did, I would have been hurt and not understood why you want to change courses. But now, I totally understand. I want to break up with you too."

Keith put his hands on his knees. "I'm sorry you had to go through the whole ordeal. I never knew you had it in you to handle yourself with that tough guy."

Trish looked up at him. "People label August Lord as a gang banger, a felon, a tough guy, but to me, he was a friend. God knows where I would be if it hadn't been for him."

"You're right. We owe August and the Storm Lords props."

"Oh my gosh, stop." Trish said laughing at his attempt at slang.

"Maybe, I should say August Lord rocks!"

Trish shook her head, "Bye, Keith."

He leaned over and gave her a brotherly good-bye kiss on her cheek, "Bye Trish. Look for my e-mail. I have a lot of stuff to tell you, but before you go back home, I want you to know that I'll be praying for you everyday."

Trish wondered what prompted him to say that as she gathered her purse and jacket. They would always be connected. F4L's: Friends for life. She turned to open the car door, but just before she pushed it open, her father was on the other side, having come back to get her. Rev. McMillan stood behind him. Trish grinned up at her father. "You told me you would travel the world to find me if I ever got lost."

James Glover hugged his only child and tried to hold back the tears. He was touched that she remembered the promise he made to her when she was only four-years old. Thank God he was able to keep it. Patricia wiped her eyes as she made her way to board the plane.

"Good-bye, son," Dr. Glover shook hands with Keith. He actually liked the young man and could admit it now that Patricia was safe and he knew Keith had nothing to do with her disappearance.

Keith and Rev. McMillan watched the runway until their airplane took off. They walked together in silence to the pastor's car, each lost in his own thoughts. Sundae asked Rev. McMillan to e-mail her the dates of the next Unity Day so she could thank everyone in person for each of their prayers.

Keith felt an overwhelming freedom because now he could court Kimberly with a clear conscience. He pulled a business card out of his wallet and punched a series of numbers into his cell phone. It was time to make an appointment for the next premarital class with Pastor Josiah Edmondson.

Rev. McMillan couldn't help overhearing the conversation. He privately gave God thanks in his head, but in his heart, he was dancing a holy dance that would make his wife proud.

The End

Epilogue

Phillip Covers accepted an administrative position created for him in the mayor's office. His salary doubled. Phillip plans to ask Heavenly to marry him in the near future.

Keith Dennis attends Stanford School of Law. At least once a month, he returns to Los Angeles to visit his father and his fiancée, Kimberly.

Kimberly McMillan and her mother are glad to have a few years to plan her dream wedding. Kimberly is still working at First and Ten but was promoted to hostess. She will complete her bachelor of arts degree in education before the wedding.

Wade Dennis is back to work. He has dinner, most evenings, with Donna at *First and Ten Restaurant*. Wade likes this arrangement, but lately, Donna has been talking about wanting to settle down. Knowing his track record, Wade has already picked out an engagement ring and plans to surprise Donna with it on her next birthday.

Chris Dennis and *Debby Curtain* decided to take a year off, pool their money, and see the world. Chris is particularly glad to be in locations where the *Cheaters* program is not on television. The pair keeps a blog, and their last entry indicated they just arrived on the island of Fiji in the South Pacific.

The warrant for the arrest of *August Lord* is still active. He has not been seen in Los Angeles since the incident at McDonald's; however, Charm's aunt in Florence, South Carolina, needed assistance and hired a young man fitting August's description. The live-in helper goes by the name Frankie B. Maze. He takes care of the yard, shops for groceries, and drives the girls, May Alize and Lexus June, to and from school.

Norma Lily is in a state mental facility. She will stand trial when she is deemed fit to do so.

Shirley Abel is still incarcerated. She asks about Norma every day and hopes to get in contact with her soon.

Douglas Brown denied having anything to do with the kidnapping of his former neighbor Patricia Glover. He agreed to testify on behalf of the State. Douglas admitted to renting the house in Washington from Norma Lily, but told the police that his supervisor was sexually harassing him at work. Meanwhile, Douglas has been surfing the Internet and collecting any and all information on the whereabouts of Patricia Glover.

Nichelle Evers enjoyed the attention of the press, which, for a short time, wanted to know about the woman who tackled the shooter at the press conference. The news story was pulled to make room for a bigger story about Norma Lily being sent to a mental hospital. Nichelle was released from the employment of Glenda Carlson and got a new job checking coats at Hollywood Park Casino. She was fired after being seen partying at the Real Player's Ball when she should have been working. Nichelle is currently collecting unemployment benefits and continues to faithfully play the weekly lottery.

www.ingramcontent.com/pod-product-compliance
Lightning Source LLC
Chambersburg PA
CBHW032033240626
47154CB00003B/892